"Grant's brain i
Kane said.

"More like his consciousness is spread over two levels. Like a shadow cast on an uneven surface," Brigid told him. "Here, he's a ghost. Pure ego."

"And in the past, his body is running around with… what?" Kane asked.

"A good vocabulary, but not much memory, going by our encounters with him," Brigid explained.

"So Grant's not operating at his best," Kane said.

He could read his own face reflected in Brigid's concerned features.

"We'll find him. We'll bring him home and make him whole again," Brigid told him.

Kane squeezed his eyes shut, then looked down at the darkened pit, where weak, helpless moans rose. He didn't want to think of what horrors Grant had to face five millennia in the past.

Other titles in this series:

James Axler
Outlanders®

CRADLE OF DESTINY

A GOLD EAGLE BOOK FROM
W❂RLDWIDE®

TORONTO • NEW YORK • LONDON
AMSTERDAM • PARIS • SYDNEY • HAMBURG
STOCKHOLM • ATHENS • TOKYO • MILAN
MADRID • WARSAW • BUDAPEST • AUCKLAND

Recycling programs
for this product may
not exist in your area.

First edition February 2011

ISBN-13: 978-0-373-63869-7

CRADLE OF DESTINY

Copyright © 2011 by Worldwide Library

Special thanks to Doug Wojtowicz for his contribution to this work.

Printed in U.S.A.

The present life of men on earth, O king, as compared with the whole length of time which is unknowable to us, seems to me to be like this: as if, when you are sitting at dinner with your chiefs and ministers in wintertime... one of the sparrows from outside flew very quickly through the hall; as if it came in one door and soon went out through another. In that actual time it is indoors it is not touched by the winter's storm; but yet the tiny period of calm is over in a moment, and having come out of the winter it soon returns to the winter and slips out of your sight. Man's life appears to be more or less like this; and of what may follow it, or what preceded it, we are absolutely ignorant.

—The Venerable Bede
c. 673–735

The Road to Outlands—
From Secret Government Files to the Future

Almost two hundred years after the global holocaust, Kane, a former Magistrate of Cobaltville, often thought the world had been lucky to survive at all after a nuclear device detonated in the Russian embassy in Washington, D.C. The aftermath—forever known as skydark—reshaped continents and turned civilization into ashes.

Nearly depopulated, America became the Deathlands—poisoned by radiation, home to chaos and mutated life forms. Feudal rule reappeared in the form of baronies, while remote outposts clung to a brutish existence.

What eventually helped shape this wasteland were the redoubts, the secret preholocaust military installations with stores of weapons, and the home of gateways, the locational matter-transfer facilities. Some of the redoubts hid clues that had once fed wild theories of government cover-ups and alien visitations.

Rearmed from redoubt stockpiles, the barons consolidated their power and reclaimed technology for the villes. Their power, supported by some invisible authority, extended beyond their fortified walls to what was now called the Outlands. It was here that the rootstock of humanity survived, living with hellzones and chemical storms, hounded by Magistrates.

In the villes, rigid laws were enforced—to atone for the sins of the past and prepare the way for a better future. That was the barons' public credo and their right-to-rule.

Kane, along with friend and fellow Magistrate Grant, had upheld that claim until a fateful Outlands expedition. A displaced piece of technology…a question to a keeper of the archives…a vague clue about alien masters—and their world shifted radically. Suddenly, Brigid Baptiste, the archivist, faced summary execution, and Grant a quick termination. For

Kane there was forgiveness if he pledged his unquestioning allegiance to Baron Cobalt and his unknown masters and abandoned his friends.

But that allegiance would make him support a mysterious and alien power and deny loyalty and friends. Then what else was there?

Kane had been brought up solely to serve the ville. Brigid's only link with her family was her mother's red-gold hair, green eyes and supple form. Grant's clues to his lineage were his ebony skin and powerful physique. But Domi, she of the white hair, was an Outlander pressed into sexual servitude in Cobaltville. She at least knew her roots and was a reminder to the exiles that the outcasts belonged in the human family.

Parents, friends, community—the very rootedness of humanity was denied. With no continuity, there was no forward momentum to the future. And that was the crux— when Kane began to wonder if there was a future.

For Kane, it wouldn't do. So the only way was out— way, way out.

After their escape, they found shelter at the forgotten Cerberus redoubt headed by Lakesh, a scientist, Cobaltville's head archivist, and secret opponent of the barons.

With their past turned into a lie, their future threatened, only one thing was left to give meaning to the outcasts. The hunger for freedom, the will to resist the hostile influences. And perhaps, by opposing, end them.

Prologue

Were his face capable of showing more than just the crudest replication of human expression, Ullikummis's features would have been cast in a brooding, troubled scowl. He had come to Earth in an effort to usurp this fragile blue globe from the talons of Enlil and his brethren, only to find himself dealing with humanity itself. What had most troubled the godling was a face that he had encountered millennia ago, before his banishment.

The one whom he knew by the name of Enkidu, the warrior who had pummeled one of his thralls into unconsciousness, lived in this time as a man called Grant. The last time Ullikummis had seen him was when he was still a child, in the court of his half brother, Humbaba....

As a boy of eight, Ullikummis was already different from his fellow Annunaki. He was larger and stronger than those his age, and the early buds of stone that would form his famous invulnerable hide were mottled discolorations on his scales. As he walked with his mother in his half brother's court, the beautiful alien rulers of Earth cringed at the sight of him.

Ullikummis knew he was a freak, but his mother told him of the glories that would be bestowed upon him at the hand of Enlil. As it was, the young Annunaki covered his distortions beneath his cloak, glaring from the shadows of a hood at those who knew not the beauty of raw power that had been cooed in his ear by Ninlil, his mother.

"Your half brother, Ullikummis, and his mother, Ninlil," spoke one of Humbaba's reptilian Igigi slaves, introducing the pair.

The master of the court of Urudug cast his cold amber eyes to his kin, taking in his height, taller than many of the reptilian slave folk who worked in Humbaba's court, whose flesh resembled a dried clay tablet, stony with a cracked and pocked surface. Humbaba's mouth, catlike in nature with a deep cleft, the upper lip dimpled with the bases of several undulating, tentaclelike whiskers underneath a black triangular nose, turned up in a semblance of a smirk, or as close as the feline giant could manage. It was an ironic grin as he recognized his father's tinkering with the Annunaki perfection.

Humbaba himself was a cast of the die thrown by Enlil. Where the child before him, growing plates of granitelike skin, was obviously an effort at recasting Annunaki genes in a silicon-based life form, Humbaba was combined with one of the races discovered in northern Africa, the Anhur. Conquered by Enlil's armies, the lion folk had impressed their mutual father enough to warrant experimentation. Though Anhur had been all but scourged from Earth, Enlil had saved a bride from the feline colonists as an experiment to relieve his boredom, curiosity and lust.

The result was nine feet and four hundred pounds of rippling, coiled muscle sheathed in a blend of golden fur and glimmering scales along his chest, belly, arms and legs. Humbaba had proved his might in single and multiple combat with Nephilim and Igigi, showing his might as a match for any five of those servitor beings. Humbaba mused over Ullikummis and what kind of beast he would be in adulthood.

He was tempted to throw the brat before his new prize, but Humbaba didn't want to waste his slave or incur the ire of his father, depending on who won their conflict. Even under Shamhat's influence, Humbaba was not certain the man-beast would accept orders. Enkidu had arrived, unable to speak the language of the apekin the Annunaki ruled over, not a problem with the mental abilities of the overlords. Telepathic communication enabled Enkidu to understand their words, even though the wild man's brain was a scramble of disjointed information, making it nearly impossible to know his origin. All they could tell was that he was human, and he bore technology far beyond the simple tools that the apekin had developed.

The cloak he wore, the weapon strapped to his arm, even the small implant put subcutaneously on his mandible, were materials either thousands of years distant for humankind, or inspired by the technological genius of the Annunaki and their slaves. The cloak and weapon hung on a pillar, not far from the bound giant. His skin was shades lighter than the ebony of the natives of the continent of Africa, indicating that somewhere along the course of his family, the blood of Europeans and Asians had mixed into his genes. He was a melting pot of all manner of humanity's strengths—that much was apparent from Humbaba's gene crafters. They had even seen some of the hand of such gene tampering in the protein strings that decided his form.

His musculature had only improved in the time since he had first appeared, and his will was still strong, despite the brainwashing techniques of Shamhat, the finest of Humbaba's scientists. That iron determination not to be dominated and the odd scrambling that had stripped Enkidu of his identity had stopped them cold.

"Do you like my man-bull?" Humbaba asked his half brother.

"He's…impressive," Ullikummis replied. As tall as the young Annunaki was, this was the first human who towered over him. Dark eyes blazed with rage and defiance, a fire inside that was not quenched. "How long have you had him?"

Humbaba frowned. "Not long enough."

"He hasn't been broken," the son of Enlil said. "I repeat…how long have you had him?"

"Four months." Humbaba sighed with resignation.

Ullikummis looked at the chains wound around Enkidu's wrists. Shoulders swelled like melons, his forearms corded so tightly that the veins stood out on them. He was straining against secondary orichalcum, one of the strongest alloys developed by the Annunaki. "He's that strong?"

"He could not burst the links on the steel chain we put him in," Humbaba said. "But he used those bonds to crush the throats and break the necks of four Nephilim."

Ullikummis tilted his head.

"He's just a human," Humbaba said.

Ullikummis narrowed his eyes.

Humbaba didn't sound quite so convinced of his superiority as the chained apekin stood. This was not a beast who railed savagely against his captivity. This one quietly flexed, his muscles struggling to find a single weakness in his bonds, all the while watching for the opportunity to get the upper hand.

Either Humbaba and Shamhat would break him, or this giant among humans would see their downfall.

It would be worse should Enkidu remember his true name.

The man who would be known as Grant five thousand years from now bided his time, waiting for his chance to break free, to find out who he truly was, and return to where he knew the language and the people.

Chapter 1

When Grant's eyes fluttered open, consciousness seizing him once more, the first thing he saw was the tanned, soft shoulder of Shizuka. The beautiful, black-haired woman breathed deeply in the peace of sleeping bliss. The jet-black silk of her hair poured over his right biceps and her back pressed against his barrel-like chest, while his left forearm rested in the saddle formed by the curve of her waist between her rib cage and one sleek, muscular hip. Nothing separated their bodies save for a thin sheen of perspiration. The only other things that touched them were the cool predawn air, the futon mat they lay upon and a thin sheet of slick gossamer cloth.

Shizuka was entwined with him, her supple form spooned against his, and Grant let the heaviness of his eyelids drag themselves closed. He didn't want to disentangle himself from the Japanese goddess, her cheek lying on his muscle, using it as a pillow. He allowed himself a small smile, enjoying the scent of her hair, the warmth of her skin.

For all intents and purposes, Grant and Shizuka were man and wife, one heart that had been repaired when the warriors of Cerberus redoubt had encountered the Tigers of Heaven from New Edo. It had been hard weeks since he had last seen her, his time claimed by the arrival of a grim godling from the stars. At the memory of Ullikummis, Grant's joy at his reunion with Shizuka was plucked out like a worm in soft, moist soil.

"Grant?" Shizuka asked sleepily, roused from her slumber by the deep, guttural rumble that rolled through his chest, riding the crest of disappointment washing over his heart.

"Sleep," Grant whispered, kissing the back of her head, but Shizuka was a leader, not a follower. Her strength of will and her warrior spirit were strong enough to dispel centuries of tradition to make her the commander of the fabled samurai of the Tigers of Heaven.

She turned with effortless grace, and her dark, almond-shaped eyes stood out in the premorning gray that crept through the rice-paper wall panels of Shizuka's Spartan abode. Concern had creased her brow and Grant's frown followed the downward curve of his gunfighter's mustache.

"I didn't want to wake you," he said.

"I felt your turmoil when you first stepped from the mat-trans," Shizuka answered. Her slender but rope-muscled arm reached up, looping around his neck, and Grant winced as he realized that his deltoids were drawn taut with tension. "We managed to put it away for a while, but it's returned strong enough to wake me."

"Can't even take a full night's sleep." Grant folded his arm, putting his hand under his head as a pillow between his head and the futon, fighting down the regret that weighed heavily on his broad, powerful shoulders. His eyes met Shizuka's, drawn into the dark pools, succumbing to the depths as he peered through the windows of her soul.

Grant had loved Shizuka almost from first sight, and while the attraction to an athletic, confident and beautiful woman was hardly a mystery, there was something in her that seemed a sort of anchor, a bond that immediately formed between the two warriors. He cupped his free hand at the nape of her neck, black silk cascading over his fingers like cool water, and pulled her gently to him, meeting her halfway in a kiss. It was a cleansing of his mind, driving away his doubts, regrets and worries as he sheltered himself in her loving embrace.

Shizuka's delicate fingers caressed his cheek as the kiss broke. "It's time for me to wake up anyway."

Grant sighed. Shizuka was disciplined, and as much as he would have enjoyed having her in his arms again, she would do her exercises, the regimented katas that honed her into one of the finest samurai warriors on the planet. For his sake, however, Shizuka forwent putting on her robe. Her muscles glided under her tanned skin like sinuous serpents writhing beneath a blanket as she moved. Each motion was precise, intended to insure limberness, not an actual movement to counter an enemy's attack. Her daily training was designed to keep her muscles supple and joints flexible, able to respond to any threat.

Grant looked down at his own body. There was no doubt that he was a powerful man, his lifestyle keeping the tone of his arms and shoulders prominent as he was active, often serving as pack mule for the Cerberus explorers as he was reluctant to go anywhere underprepared. Still, his frame was not lean and taut. He was too old for his waist to slim down to hard-packed abdominal muscles, his torso becoming a sculpted V. While everyone else who knew him saw a slight thickening of his waist since his years as a Cobaltville Magistrate, he hadn't tried to fit into the perfectly tailored polycarbonate armor that served as the uniform of the Magistrates, or enforcers of the villes. No longer young, Grant was indisputably powerful and menacing, and he could arm wrestle any two of his fellow Cerberus allies with one arm, except for Edwards. But even then his strength was an edge higher.

Grant had even been powerful enough to go hand to hand with Maccan and Marduk. The former was the last of the pure-blooded Tuatha de Danaan princes on Earth, while the latter was an Annunaki lord standing a full seven feet of perfectly sculpted muscle and other-worldly strength. The battles had been inconclusive, to be honest, but they had been tests of might that showed Grant's guile and his brawn. He was capable of holding his own with nearly any opponent on the planet. That was before the arrival of the stone-bodied son of Enlil, a towering eight-foot creature with limbs as thick as small trees and eyes that glowed like magma.

Ullikummis was nominally an Annunaki, but the son of their mortal enemy had been genetically modified, his body augmented with materials that had allowed him to survive the cold vacuum of deep space for four-and-a-half millennia and repair bodily damage, even after being dropped in a furnace after being pelted by volleys of hand grenades.

Such a monster gave even Grant pause. Grant knew that he wasn't the most physically powerful being on Earth. However, among the triad of heroes who had formed the core of the Cerberus resistance, he was the man who provided the muscle. Since few weapons could harm Ullikummis, it would take either the scientific genius of Brigid Baptiste or the skill and determination of Kane to bring down the mountain that walked as a man.

Grant let his head drop back down to the futon, rolled onto his back, and looked at the plain wooden boards of the ceiling. Their dark stain provided a sharp contrast to the white rice-paper windows that made it seem inky-black, even on the most moonlit of nights, giving him a focus on which to meditate. With the growing light of dawn, he wouldn't be able to concentrate on the empty space to clear his mind of his doubts.

His clothes lay folded in the corner, the external component of his Commtact placed with them. Normally, the device was unobtrusive as it adhered to the pintels subcutaneously installed along his mastoid bone, but Grant was loath to have it on during his quiet intimacy with Shizuka. There were multiple threats in the world, and Cerberus would not hesitate to summon him in the event of an emergency. It was his first night here in New Edo, and he thought that he could get at least one evening of peace.

Reluctantly, he rose from the futon, folded their light blanket and went to get dressed. He held up the Commtact as if it were a dead rat, looking at it for a moment, hesitant to put it back on. Grant slipped it into place, and keyed it to call the redoubt. Given the time difference between Montana and New Edo, in the island chain of the remains of California, there was a good chance that he'd get in touch with Bry on his morning duty.

"Reporting in," Grant said. "Everything quiet on the home front?"

"Boring as any other day." Bry's voice reverberated through his skull. "Well, most other days. Why? Afraid we'd call you back home?"

"Yeah," Grant answered.

"Both Lakesh and Kane have threatened me in their usual manners if I pull you from home too soon," Bry answered.

Home, Grant thought. That's what this tiny island remnant of the sunken West Coast of the United States had become to him. New Edo and its neighbor, Thunder Isle, were among the new archipelago that had formed in the wake of the nuclear holocaust that nearly drove humankind into extinction on January 21, 2001. Powerful earthshaker bombs had shattered California, dumping entire cities into the Pacific Ocean, utilizing the instability of the San Andreas Fault to wreak havoc. While the nuclear war was primarily between the United States and the Soviet Union, the conflict had been touched off by an incarnation of the Annunaki god king Enlil, then disguised as Colonel Thrush.

How many billions had been scoured from the face of the Earth, literally by the hand of their greatest enemy? With the arming of a bomb placed in the basement of the Soviet Embassy in Washington, D.C., Thrush/Enlil had ushered in an age where the hidden and sleeping Annunaki overlords could awaken and recast the planet as their renewed jewel, as it had been millennia past.

This was history that had been drummed into Grant, so much that it came unbidden just as he thought of the island where his true love resided. A turmoil of those memories could flood unbidden if he couldn't preoccupy himself. Right now, though, even the splendor of his unclad lover, flexing her taut, beautiful body in the near-poetic dance of martial arts katas, wasn't enough of a distraction.

"Grant?" Bry asked. "You all right?"

"Yeah," Grant answered. He regretted using Shizuka as an excuse, but there was no other way to explain his inattention. "Just admiring the view this morning...."

"Say hi to Shizuka for me," Bry said. "I'd say give her a kiss…"

"But I already got to that," Grant concluded, trying to inject some lightness into his tone. He wished he could feel that bit of joy he'd fabricated.

"Kane says get to it some more," Bry added. "His orders."

"Since when is Kane my boss?" Grant asked.

"He figures that this will be his only chance to order you to do something and have you do it gladly," Bry answered. "Forget the world for a while, okay?"

Grant nodded, then winced as he realized the motion was useless over the Commtact. "I'll try."

Shizuka appeared at his shoulder, and she put her head against Grant's, skull-to-skull contact allowing her words to be heard, as well. "Grant will have some help."

Bry laughed.

It was something that Grant hoped that he would remember how to do.

THE FERAL ALBINO outlander known as Domi swept her ruby-red eyes across the empty, desolate shores of the Euphrates River. They were dozens of miles from the nearest large settlement, and on this part of the mighty thoroughfare, there was no gradual drop-off to the water, no beaches. There was a six-foot miniature cliff on either side of the flowing river.

It was a lonely, desolate place where there was no irrigation, so vegetation was sparse, no different from the desert wilderness back in America. It was at once familiar visually, but alien in terms of scents, the feel of the sun's heat beating down on her shadow suit's shoulders. Domi was a small woman, just under five feet in height, but her body was athletically sculpted, muscles coiled like cables around her lean limbs. The black sheen of the high-tech shadow suit poking out from under her cargo shorts and multipocketed vest made her arms and legs seem sticklike where they poked out.

Given that she had accompanied Kane, Grant and Brigid Baptiste from the depths of Africa to the Moon itself, Domi knew the likelihood of running into an environment that would require the suit's protective qualities. Also, even after two centuries, radioactive wastelands were not uncommon. Radiation poisoning was something that Domi had been lucky enough to avoid during her brief, hard-fought life. She wasn't about to endanger that successful run by not taking the proper precautions.

Those precautions included a foot-long fighting knife worn in a cross-draw scabbard that hung off the belt of her cargo shorts, and the small but powerful Detonics .45-caliber automatic in a holster on her opposite hip. Backing it up was a steel-tube-framed crossbow that hung, folded on a sling, from her shoulder. Raised in the Outlands, Domi didn't need much more than a knife to sustain herself, but the crossbow was good for hunting and the little handgun had evened the odds in countless battles.

More equalization came in the form of Edwards, a tall and broad-shouldered former Magistrate who had been recruited to the Cerberus cause with the fall of the nine baronies. The blunt-headed man stood at the other end of the small expedition. Edwards was a beast of a man, nearly as tall as Grant, but stocky and bulky, not long limbed and well proportioned by the man who often served as her surrogate father.

Edwards, like all Magistrates, had been given only one name by the hybrid barons, who once ruled the baronies before their evolution into overlords. Their singular appellations combined with the grim, black carapace-like armor to separate them from the rest of the barons' subjects, all the better for brainwashing them and transforming them into the dreaded judges and juries who ruled as the ultimate enforcers. Domi and Edwards had tangled once when they were assigning the leadership of the Cerberus Away Team they shared. Edwards had been a difficult opponent, but Domi had put him in his place. Like most of the Magistrates, he was an alpha male, someone who felt that his brawn made him the most appropriate leader. But like all good wolves, Edwards had conceded when he was shown that he could be physically bested by the slender little albino wraith.

Since then, he and Domi were amicable allies and trusted teammates.

Edwards glanced over one thick, bulky shoulder, then shrugged his head back toward the two women who dug in the dirt around a small ring of stones with worn but barely readable inscriptions carved into them. Domi smirked. She knew that Brigid Baptiste was someone who could lose herself in scientific investigation easily, in the most unusual of climes. Though the sun beat down relentlessly on their uncovered heads, the environmental adaptations of the shadow suits kept their body temperatures low thanks to cooling systems woven into their high-tech fabric. Even sweating under a tied-off bandanna, Brigid was unwavering in her attention to the ancient scratches in the rock.

Brigid was a foot taller than Domi, and where the feral girl was cast in pale porcelain, the archivist was an explosion of color. Brigid was adorned with hair that looked like red silk interspersed with golden threads, sun-beaten skin that managed to tan despite her ginger tresses and emerald eyes that glimmered like precious gems. Right now she hid her orbs behind a pair of wire-rimmed glasses that allowed her to better inspect the stones around the small, nearly unnoticeable circle of rocks where the interphaser had deposited them.

The interphaser ferried the Cerberus explorers along a web of energy trails that connected at parallax points. So powerful were the currents rolling through these threads that when they intersected, humans felt the urge to build monuments to the power that coursed in the very ground. The Cerberus personnel had mapped many of the parallax points, both around the world and beyond, and built a device that exploited these naturally occurring focal points as a means of transferring people and goods.

Bored beyond the end of his usual impatience, Edwards resorted to sarcasm. "So, what are we looking for again? Humma Humma and the Cedar Chest and the city of Airy Do?"

"Humbaba and the Cedar Forest, and the city state of Eridu," Brigid corrected. "Though I suspect that you, like Kane and Grant, have a better memory and comprehension than what you're displaying."

"Let me get this straight. We have an eight-foot stone monster running around, and you're taking time out of dealing with this crisis to look for trees in the middle of a desert?" Edwards asked.

"Ullikummis is old," Domi told Edwards. "Myth is old, and might have some truth. Maybe we can find weakness for Stoneface by looking in his old stomping grounds."

"That freak was here?" Edwards asked.

Domi noted that the big ex-Mag was rubbing his forehead, brows furrowed in the unmistakable sign of a splitting headache. After Ullikummis's first appearance, Edwards had been taking more aspirin of late, and his Commtact was no longer able to transmit; hence the bulky transmitter unit he wore on his hip.

Domi and the others could hardly blame the big man. Ullikummis had made Edwards one of his pawns by planting one of his seeds in his head. That kind of intrusion by a small pellet of intelligent stone must have been only slightly more comfortable than Domi's own major headache after the mad god Maccan pumped unholy amounts of sonic energy straight into her skull. Domi had been on wobbly knees for a while after that, so she could empathize with her fellow CAT member. Such a violation would have been enough cause for a few weeks of rest and recreation, but Cerberus couldn't spare the manpower.

At least Edwards retained his mobility and reflexes. Domi needed time to get back onto her feet after her brief coma.

"That freak," Maria Falk spoke up. "Or one much like him, if Brigid's reading is right."

Falk was an older woman, her brown hair showing glimmers of silvering gray here and there. Domi loved the lunar scientist's smile. She found more than a little kinship in the way that Falk always perked up but quietly chose to observe without drawing attention to herself. They shared a curiosity, but Domi felt for Falk. If the geologist was a house cat with just a little too much inquisitiveness, she wouldn't be as adept at fighting her way out of trouble as the wildcat albino.

Falk was used to studying rocks, but she had complained before they made the interphaser jump. She wasn't an archaeologist, but Brigid wanted a set of eyes that knew about terrain and natural earth formations. Tomb raiders were in short supply among the redoubt's newly expanded staff.

Edwards tilted his head. "Okay, now I really am playing dumb. One like him?"

"Humbaba, or Humwawa, was appointed by Enlil himself as the guardian of the Cedar Forest. He was a giant with the face of a lion in some sources, and in others, his features resemble coiled entrails of men and beasts," Brigid said.

"Maybe he's a sloppy eater, or saving leftovers for later." Edwards chuckled nervously.

Brigid raised an eyebrow at the thought. "That is a possibility."

Edwards rested his face in his palm. "Great. A man-eating giant kitty cat."

"He couldn't be that big," Domi said. "If he can wear the guts of his meal as a face mask."

"Well, the legends said that Ullikummis was a giant who was so large his shoulders scraped the skies," Brigid said. "The real one was nowhere that huge."

"Small favors," Edwards grumbled. "Humbaba's alive, or dead?"

"Allegedly, Gilgamesh and Enkidu slew the beast," Brigid answered.

"Who and what?" Edwards asked.

"King Gilgamesh, one of the original human heroes of mythology. His ally was a bull-man, sent by the gods to slay Gilgamesh—Enkidu," Brigid said.

Edwards looked a little unfocused for a moment. "Why does *that* name sound familiar?"

"Which? Gilgamesh is a rather—"

"The other one," Edwards cut Brigid off.

Brigid stepped closer to the large man. "Perhaps it's a residual memory?"

"From when Ugly Commish took me over?" Edwards asked.

Brigid nodded.

Edwards closed his eyes, as if looking inside of himself for answers. "I don't know why I'd remember anything."

With that, he opened a small pill bottle and downed a couple of pills without benefit of a splash of water from his canteen. "Not everyone can remember everything like you, Brigid."

Brigid smirked at the subtle jab, then turned back to see Falk dig a little more furiously at the ground. The geologist's spade hacked at rocklike sand that disintegrated as the steel of Falk's tool smashed into it. Nervousness set in on the older woman's features. "What's wrong?"

Falk tugged on a length of stretchy fabric. Brigid knelt next to the woman, tugging it from deep, hard-packed sand. As soon as she touched the leatherlike material, Brigid knew what it was. She had never worn it, but Kane and Grant had donned the long, armored dusters, one sleeve outsized to accommodate the folding Sin Eater blaster. Domi recognized the jacket sleeve, as well, and her stomach twisted. Edwards had not brought his duster.

"This is a Magistrate jacket," she pronounced. "How long has it been here?"

"Given the density of the sand, it's hard to say," Falk hedged.

"That's a lie," Brigid answered. "How long has this been trapped here?"

Falk looked at Brigid, swallowing before she dared to answer.

"It's been here for nearly five thousand years," Falk answered.

Brigid looked down at the uniform embedded in the stone. "We need to dig deeper. See what else is in there."

"I haven't found any skeletal remains," Falk replied.

"They might not have been buried here with the clothing," Brigid answered.

Domi could tell from the stress and urgency in her friend's voice that one of the Cerberus people was going to be lost in the depths of time.

The question was, who would go missing?

Chapter 2

Gongs reverberated throughout the Tigers of Heaven dojo in the heart of New Edo. Though the transplanted Japanese had access to technology such as radios, they were also traditionalists. Alarm Klaxons produced by loudspeakers were not an improvement over the classic padded hammer striking a gigantic dish of bronze. The loud, air-shaking noise drew attention and focused it like few other sounds could.

Instinct pushed Grant and Shizuka to grab their weapons, the big ex-Magistrate sliding the Sin Eater holster over his thick right forearm. Shizuka slid her *katana* through a single loop of the sash around her waist, slung a quiver of *ya* arrows over her shoulder, and scooped up her *kumi* samurai bow. Every member of the Tigers of Heaven was trained in the arts of the samurai, so that even with a wild supply of automatic rifles and handguns, they were still deadly with their "primitive" weaponry. The penetration ability of a *ya* launched was insufficient to spear through the polycarbonate plates of full Magistrate assault armor, but Shizuka's aim was quick and accurate enough to slip her deadly arrowheads in the gaps between those panels and through the Kevlar and Nomex underneath.

Still, the exchange of technologies and ideas between New Edo and the Cerberus redoubt had been enough for the Japanese archers to utilize shafts and bows of carbon fiber over a laminated wood core, and stiff nylon supplemented turkey and swan feathers to make the *ya* fly true. While Grant himself was a man who appreciated powerful firearms like the Sin Eater or his Copperhead, Shizuka had been teaching him *kyudo*, the samurai's "way of the bow." His upper-body strength was more than sufficient to handle a *kumi* with an eighty-eight-pound draw and keep the bowstring nocked and on target with very little vibration. It was a slow process, however. Grant was familiar with the basics of marksmanship, but it was akin to the early six months of training that he had been given on the dangerous, lightning-fast Sin Eater machine pistol. He could hit a bull's-eye given a few moments, but he was not adept at utilizing the bow in combat. Shizuka, on the other hand, could nock, draw and launch a *ya* shaft in the space of a second.

A 20-round, full-auto machine pistol firing armor-crushing 240-grain 9 mm slugs would have to do for now, Grant mused. He paused and looked at his folded Magistrate trench coat. Shizuka had already slithered into the bamboo-and-polymer-plate armor, and Grant was loath to go into action without some protection. He had left behind the shadow suit at Cerberus redoubt, but the protective long coat was sufficient armor, its leather-like material interwoven with polycarbonate strips and ballistic-resistant cloth, and extremely comfortable. The duster fluttered as he picked it up, whirling it like a cape around his shoulders as he shrugged into the roomy but supple garment.

"You really need to wear that with your shadow suit," Shizuka spoke up. "You look magnificent with your coattails flapping."

Grant managed a smile. "I sometimes worry about snagging this thing."

"Have you ever?" Shizuka asked.

Grant thought about it for a moment as he and the samurai commander prepared to rush to the Tigers of Heaven's small fleet of motorized launches. "Nope, but I don't wear this much."

The two lovers exited Shizuka's Spartan dwelling and at the railing saw the gong ringer, his brawny arms and shoulders glistening with sweat as he swung the hammer to alert the city. As the gong was centrally placed, everyone could quickly get their bearings by the row of lanterns mounted on the support beam that the great bronzed dish hung from. Grant could see that the lantern indicating trouble on Thunder Isle had been ignited.

"Shit," Grant muttered.

"We'll get to the boats," Shizuka said. She pulled her radio from its place on her sash. Now that the Tigers of Heaven had been alerted, they would be waiting for indications of who should respond and where they should go. "Nagumi, harden the perimeter in case this is a diversion. Ichira, Honda, bring your squads with me to the island. Full force."

Grant knew that "full force" was not inconsiderable. Twelve samurai warriors with composite armor, high-tech bows and arrows and thousand-folded pure steel blades with nearly monomolecular edges were easily a match for Magistrates with submachine guns, grenades and bulletproof armor.

Grant and Shizuka took their places aboard the *Gamera-maru*, the same vessel that the two of them and their samurai allies had been on when they'd prevented an assault by the barons on New Edo when the island colony was first discovered by the Cerberus explorers. It was unofficially the flagship of the New Edo fleet, and as such, it had been upgraded with new motors on the aft. While the engines had been designed for twentieth-century inflatable rafts called Zodiacs, they had easily been adapted to the rattan-hulled craft. The increase in speed from traditional outboard motors had been dramatic, enabling a quicker response to a crisis on Thunder Isle.

Grant perched on the bow of the *Gamera-maru* as the twin Mercedes engines pumped out hundreds of horsepower, producing rooster tails of white, frothy spray, writing the massive energy impulse in twelve-foot-high jets as the craft accelerated from its berth. Two other craft, each laden with a quartet of Samurai, as well as their crews, had started only moments apart, but that was sufficient for Grant and Shizuka to achieve a twenty-foot lead on the other boats.

The two archers assigned to the *Gamera-maru* strung their bows, the composite nature of their laminated-wood-and-carbon-fiber cores building enormous potential energy. The mist of seawater coming over the rail of the speeding sea craft wouldn't affect either the resin-lacquered bows or the inelastic cord, which couldn't be warped by absorption. A bowstring that stretched under any conditions lost efficiency in transferring the potential energy of the bow to the arrow. Pig tendons and horsehair were two of the materials that the Tigers of Heaven had used, and even late twentieth-century polymers provided by Cerberus hadn't improved on the archers' capabilities.

The boat archers used larger bows than Shizuka wore, as they were not expected to wade in close. The Japanese warriors had called them "two-man bows," as they were the height of one man riding on the shoulders of his friend—about eight feet tall, given the average diminutive stature of the Asians.

"Grant," Kane's voice crackled over his Commtact from a thousand miles away. "Bry told me you were on the way to Thunder Isle. Don't go ashore."

"Too late. We're on our way to a four-gong emergency," Grant answered. "Why?"

"Baptiste just called me to say she found one of our off-duty Mag coats buried under around five thousand years of sand in some sort of tomb," Kane told him. "Thunder Isle's one place we know of that has an operating time-travel machine…."

"Mag coats?" Grant asked. He looked at the armor-laced duster, its tails flapping from his hips. "I'm wearing mine right now."

"Damn it, Grant," Kane growled. "Baptiste thinks one of us—"

"Well, if she found the damn duster buried for a few thousand years, then we've already fallen down the rabbit hole," Grant answered, cutting him off. "Nothing's going to change that. Did she find any bones sticking out of the sleeves?"

"No, but she only found a piece of it sticking out," Kane replied. "That doesn't mean our carcass isn't nearby."

"Let me know if she finds any bones. Otherwise, what's happened has happened," Grant said. "We'll be jumping at shadows every time we get called here."

"Grant…" Kane's voice was laced with frustration, but Grant knew that there were people in danger; otherwise the alert wouldn't have sounded on New Edo.

"Kane, we can discuss this all you want later, right now, people who are our friends may be dying," Grant grumbled. "Or am I worth more than them?"

Grant knew that Kane's answer would be a hard choice. The two former Magistrates were closer than brothers, bound by blood, sweat and tears, but Kane was driven by the same selfless urge to protect innocents that had made them the finest enforcement team in Cobaltville.

"You don't have permission to die," Kane said. "If you do, I'll drag you back to life and beat you to death again."

"It'll take a lot to get me out of your life. If I don't see you for five thousand years, you'd better behave. Remember, the more you complain, the longer you live, and five millennia ain't going to be shit off the bitching I've done," Grant answered.

There was a soft chuckle on the other end of the Commtact. "I'll hold you to that."

Grant managed a smirk, seeing the shore of Thunder Isle. "Grant out."

THOUGH HER HEADBAND was meant to keep the sweat and her flowing red-gold hair out of Brigid Baptiste's eyes, she still needed to mop her eyes as she paused. Her hands had been callused from her years of adventure, but the effort of prying apart the sunbaked sandstone with a foot-long utility knife was raising new blisters on her fingers. The pebbling on the Micarta Fiberglas handle had worn a red patch between the base and knuckle of her index finger.

So far, she'd gotten the sleeve out to the shoulder, and from the tailored length of what she'd freed, there was no doubt as to the owner of the duster. She sat back, a wave of nausea rumbling in her stomach.

Brigid raised Kane on her Commtact. "Did you warn Grant?"

"Yes," Kane answered. "His response was that you've found the coat, so he's already destined to go on a trip to the ancient past. You're sure it's his coat?"

"By now, absolutely," Brigid answered. "No one else in Cerberus has arms as long as he does."

Brigid glanced to one side, and saw Domi's ruby-red eyes locked on the armored leather spilling out of the crack in the temple remnant.

"You heard what Kane said?" Brigid asked.

"Was on party line," Domi answered, her diction returning to the abbreviated Outland form of speech. It was a sign of nervousness or heightened stress, and Brigid could feel sympathy for the young albino. Usually, when her words became terse and tense, she at least could engage in combat to deal with what had gotten under her skin. When Domi couldn't utilize the energy pumped into her bloodstream by the fight-or-flight reflex, Brigid could see her grow morose and withdrawn.

Domi was walking an emotional edge, especially considering how close she had grown to Grant since he had first saved her life back in the Tartarus slums under Cobaltville. Grant had been the first person in a long time to show the wild woman kindness. Domi had gone from fighting, literally tooth and claw, for survival to being one of pit-boss Guana Teague's prostitutes. Gentleness and humanity had been a rarity in her life, and Grant's act of protection had earned her undying loyalty, first demonstrated when she stopped Teague from strangling Grant to death.

There'd been a brief period when Domi had thought their relationship was sexual in nature, but it eventually settled down that she had found a father figure. When Cerberus was a much smaller staff, before the influx of lunar staff, she had finally found her family. The added freezies from the Manitius Base had made her uncomfortable, intruding on her sense of community, which only drew her closer to Grant, Kane, Brigid and Lakesh.

Brigid didn't want to think of the pain Domi would be in if Grant was gone forever.

"We know roughly when he was transported," Brigid said. "And this place has none of the traditional indications of a Sumerian crypt."

"So not cemetery," Domi muttered, looking around. "Not much temple."

"Not now, but we have millennia of erosion and deterioration that's removed most of what this place used to be," Brigid answered.

"Erosion?" Domi asked. Her face screwed into a mask of skepticism. "Or bombed."

Brigid frowned as she looked around. "We've only been digging for a few minutes—we can't tell."

"Snake-faces ruled here," Domi mentioned.

"Don't think I've forgotten that," Brigid answered.

"Never forget anything," Domi agreed. "But didn't say so."

"You're trying to say that I'm keeping information from you?" Brigid asked.

Domi looked away from the sleeve, the first time in the several minutes since they'd discovered the armored garment. "No. Softening news. Maybe. Not say lying."

Brigid rested her hand on the diminutive albino's shoulder. "We would have found skeletal remains if he was killed here. This was just a memento…buried and lost in time."

"Too hot for long coat here, even then?" Domi asked.

"Absolutely," Brigid answered.

"News is getting better," Domi said, recovering some of her language skills, stress lessening.

"Plus we're not even sure he's going to be tossed through time just this minute," Brigid said. "It could be some time in the next thirty years, for all we know. Or even Grant's son, if he has one."

Domi snickered. Brigid tilted her head.

"Remembered line about assumptions," Domi said. "You make an ass out of you and umption."

Brigid nodded.

"Because, you know, I'm pretty big, too," Edwards interjected from his overwatch of the temple dig. "Grant could have lent me his coat."

"Too fat," Domi replied.

Edwards grimaced. "That's muscle."

"You want to get punier?" Domi asked.

Mariah Falk let out a sigh. "Brigid, I thought that you wanted to see the chamber that this coat seems to be walled into."

Domi tilted her head.

Brigid explained for her friend. "That device she has is a sonar locater. It registers echoes off loud noises returned from objects of heavier density."

Domi smiled with comprehension. "So when Mariah set off the boom stick on the ground, she was looking through the sand."

"When did you start getting so smart?" Edwards asked.

"Boyfriend cuts holes in universes as shortcuts," Domi noted. "Brigid friend is living encyclopedia. Six years hanging around with them, knowledge rubs off, newbie."

Edwards smirked. "Attitude rubs off, too."

"It's not attitude if you can back it up," Brigid countered. The archivist walked over to Falk, who had put another image on her portable tablet computer. "You've double-checked this?"

"I don't know what kind of scientists you've worked with in this time, but I didn't get assigned to Manitius by being sloppy and second-rate," Falk answered.

"Point taken," Brigid said. "My apologies."

"None necessary," Falk replied. "I just wanted you to know who you were working with."

"How deep is that pit supposed to be?" Edwards asked.

"From ceiling to floor, we're looking at thirty feet," Falk explained. "The overall floor space looks to be the size of four football fields blocked together, with pillars that could easily be five feet in diameter."

"Football fields?" Edwards asked. "Say it in postapocalyptic terms for those of us without a frame of reference."

"Two hundred yards long, and we're looking at about fifty yards wide," Falk translated. She snorted with amusement.

"What's so funny?" Edwards asked.

"First time I knew more about football than someone who is so stereotypically a jock," Falk said. "Football was a game full of men who wished they were as big as you or Grant."

Edwards smirked at the obvious compliment. "You know, instead of fucking around with knives and shovels, why don't we blow a hole in the side of this thing?"

"We want to see what's inside, not collapse the whole damn place," Brigid explained.

"The roof's thick, easily two yards," Falk said. "And the support pillars are thick and intact according to the sonar."

Brigid frowned as she thought about it.

"I'm not talking about a nuclear blast," Edwards said. "A controlled, focused explosion. Back when the Magistrates had to get into a place without bringing down the whole shantytown, we used loops of detonation cord that cut through walls without a blast wave that would level huts around our target."

"Kane generally just throws grenades," Brigid mused.

"He also was a pilot on a Deathbird gunship," Edwards told her. "Firepower is its own solution for those guys."

"I guess the old saying is correct," Brigid said.

"There's no problem that can't be solved with the application of high explosives?" Edwards asked.

Brigid nodded. "And not to judge a book by its cover."

Edwards shrugged his huge shoulders. "Don't attribute it too much to brains. Just a good memory and some damned impatience."

"Do you have that kind of explosive power?" Brigid asked.

Edwards scooped up his war bag. "I can roll my quarter kilogram blocks of plastique into det cord."

"Why do you have them separated into quarter kilogram blocks?" Brigid asked.

Edwards smiled. "Sela told me about her time with Special Forces who made these things called 'eight balls.' A wad of C-4 with a detonator made a big stunning sound without throwing shrapnel all over the place. You could deafen a room full of bad guys with one of these, maybe even knock them cold, but they're still useful enough for ripping shit apart when packed properly."

"Then set it up and let's see what this place really is," Brigid said.

The explorers worked together to open the ancient underground temple, hoping to learn when and where their friend Grant lost his coat in this foreboding tomb.

BRONDA STRODE along the perimeter that the Millennial Consortium had placed around the Thunder Isle facility. The barrel of his 9 mm Calico submachine gun rested on his left forearm, and his finger lay on the frame above the weapon's trigger in an effort to keep the weapon safe but ready to go. One twitch of his finger, and he could start spitting out bullets from the Calico's 100-round helical magazine, sawing an opponent in half.

He reached the end of his patrol circuit and saw Lonmar. Where Bronda had been a grim, brutal raider who had attacked caravans that crossed the Outlands, Lonmar was a tall, powerful giant who was once been a Magistrate from Beausoleilville, a violent enforcer who obeyed the whims of the bitch-goddess who had evolved into the merciless Annunaki overlord Lilitu. These were the raw-muscled head breakers who the millennialists had known were the backbone of their effort to set up a technocracy over the shattered Earth. Both men were given power and the freedom to utilize it in service to that scientific cabal.

That Lonmar and Bronda got to engage in their heartless excess of cruelty was icing atop a cake whose ingredients were pay, logistical support and the backing of an army of like-minded brutes.

The guards and scientists who were manning the Operation Chronos time trawl facility had given a modicum of a fight—they had even brought down a couple of millennial mercenaries—but it hadn't been enough to slake the two sentries' blood thirst. There was a little hope, though. A radio message had gotten out to New Edo.

The Tigers of Heaven had received that call.

Bronda took a deep breath, and nodded to Lonmar. "Any sign of those primates?"

"The samurai are going to be sneaky," Lonmar answered. "I heard from Snakefishville about a raid their Mags went on. They had their asses handed to them."

Bronda's crooked scar of a mouth turned up at one end. The other side had been immobilized by scar tissue and nerve paralysis when he'd been slashed across the face on one of his first caravan raids. "Scared?"

Lonmar's bushy eyebrows wrinkled, inching together like hairy caterpillars over his black, soulless eyes. "Snakefishville is full of pussies. If I'd been there, I'd have broken off their own damn swords up their asses."

Bronda chuckled. "Keep your eyes open."

"You, too," Lonmar replied.

Bronda turned and went back along his section of perimeter. With the consortium, the former raider had found the closest thing he could call kinship and family. Maybe it had been a design by one of the technocrats, some form of social engineering that turned the mercenary thugs under their sway into a more cohesive fighting unit. Bronda liked people like Lonmar and the rest of the hired guns working with him. It might have been a form of manipulation, but Bronda didn't mind. The group he fought alongside worked. Let the Tigers of

Heaven come get them. When the Calico drained empty, the Outlands pirate would draw the wicked foot-and-a-half-long sword and show the primitive Japanese how to really carve up flesh.

There was the smack of fist on flesh from behind, and Bronda whirled. Lonmar staggered backward, recoiling from a punch hurled by a tall monster of a man dressed in a long black coat. Lonmar had been a physical giant, but the titan in the leather duster threw a follow-up punch that felled the ex-Magistrate like a rotted tree. Bronda didn't think that anyone could have laid out the man, but the stranger whirled to look at the raider.

Seeing the skin of dark mahogany, the drooping gunfighter's mustache and the swelling musculature shifting under the coat, Bronda had a moment of recognition.

It was Grant, one of the three who had escaped from Cobaltville, turning their backs upon the barons of the monolithic city-states. A jolt of panic passed and Bronda swung up his Calico to rip the bald, black giant in half.

The machine pistol stuttered out a short burst, and Bronda knew that he'd hit Grant, but the outlander ignored the impacts of his bullets. If Bronda hadn't been distracted by a goose-feather shaft jutting from his rib cage, he'd have had the time to realize that Grant's coat had been armored. Bronda looked at the end of the arrow that had transected his torso, then into the woods. The arrow had flown scant moments before Bronda had opened fire, his ability to recover from surprise only a moment quicker than the archer's estimate.

For a brief moment, he saw a beautiful woman in samurai armor nock another arrow onto her bowstring, her hands moving swiftly. It had felt like minutes to the dying, shocked Bronda, but Shizuka had gotten off her second deadly missile in under a second, this razor-sharp point slicing through Bronda's left eye, pinioning his brain.

Shizuka heard the ugly crunch of neck bones disintegrating, and she turned to see Grant rise from Lonmar's corpse. The samurai wondered why Grant would have killed an unconscious man, but her eyes fell to the bloody scalps hanging off the millennialist's belt. The broken neck was swift, painless justice, sparing the murderer potential reprisals in the form of torture.

Grant's eyes met hers, and he jerked his head toward the entrance that the two millennialists had been guarding. Other cold-blooded killers were crawling the halls of the Operation Chronos laboratory. If there had been hostages, their captors would have been alerted by the brief stutter of automatic fire. Grant was spurred on by the impetus of imperiled lives.

With the silence and grace of a jet-black tiger, the big Cerberus warrior slipped through the side access.

Chapter 3

With Cerberus Away Teams Alpha and Beta broken up, Kane pulled in the remaining third of Domi's team, Sela Sinclair, to join him on an emergency jump to Thunder Isle. Right now, in the mat-trans chamber, Donald Bry and Daryl Morganstern were busy trying to override the lockout placed by the Millennial Consortium hijackers at the Operation Chronos facility. Kane didn't doubt Sinclair's ability. The woman had fought for Cerberus redoubt for a year, proving herself as brave and skillful a warrior as any he had met. Sinclair had been born in a different time, an air force security officer whose training had been geared toward protecting United States military bases from terrorism. She was a freezie, a cryogenically preserved relic from centuries in the past, and upon awakening, she had sided with Kane, Brigid and Grant in battling another temporally displaced set of opponents.

Kane was in his shadow suit, the high-tech polymers conforming to his lean, wolflike musculature like a second skin, except this skin would protect him from hard vacuum decompression and intense heat or cold, though it could not redistribute kinetic shock from small-arms fire. Due to its high-tech composition, the shadow suit did protect its wearer from hard impacts such as falls and even punches from foes of great size and strength.

Kane preferred the shadow suit over his old Magistrate armor. It provided him better mobility and superior comfort. It also hid easily under other clothing, being low profile and formfitting. He didn't mind being able to ignore the biting, frostbite-inducing chill of arctic winds or the blazing, mercilessly hot suns of deserts in nothing more than the shadow suit and its hood. Other features, such as camouflage and protection from radiation, were simply icing on the cake.

Sinclair wore another shadow suit, identical to Kane's, but her forearm was not adorned with the Magistrates' weapon and badge of office, the folding Sin Eater machine pistol. Rather, Sinclair had her Beretta M-9 pistol hanging on a pistol belt, along with a collapsible combat baton, a fighting knife and various bits of security kit that gave her a continuity of force from mild restraint to lethal response that compensated for the relative lack of size compared to big, muscular men like Kane, Grant or Edwards. There was no doubt, thanks to the curve-hugging properties of the shadow suit, that Sinclair was athletic and strong, but without the feral ferocity of someone like Domi, she had to supplement her strength and skill with an assortment of equipment that would give her an edge against the rare opponent whose greater might was matched with fighting ability.

Kane, after years of adventuring with some of the most dynamic women on the planet, had no doubt that a woman with training and experience could handle herself quite well in almost as many situations as he could. But he also appreciated Sinclair knowing her limitations and adapting strategy and preparations for them. Kane himself knew that he was not the strongest or the most skilled warrior on the planet, nor was he the smartest. That was one of his strengths.

Grant had relayed some wisdom from the Tigers of Heaven from a swordsman named Musashi, one of the most celebrated samurai warriors in the history of Japan. Musashi had said that "to know one's limitations is to be limitless." Kane had innately understood that, and it was what had carried him and his allies to victory over gods, armies of cultists and other threats to humanity's tenuous existence in the dangerous world that existed in this postapocalyptic time. That bit of philosophy passed on from a swordsman hundreds of years ago was simply a confirmation for what Kane didn't have the words. Right now, however, he was more interested in the limitations of technology.

Because the mat-trans unit on Thunder Isle was part of the Totality Concept, a Continuity of Government program in the event of an apocalyptic event, it would have been easy to pop into the Operation Chronos facility if it weren't for the fact that the mat-trans was on total lockdown because of the millennialist's attack. Kane had suggested using the interphaser, a unit that acted in concert with natural vortices of magnetic energy.

The Thunder Isle facility was constructed around such an intersection of magnetic force lines, often called Ley Lines by western alchemists or Dragon Roads by Asian geomancers. The interphaser would drop them somewhere in the control room. While the sudden appearance of Kane and Sinclair would give them some advantage, there was no way to know if they would emerge in a murderous crossfire.

"You will end up in their mat-trans, which could easily be put under guard. You'd be gunned down—" Lakesh said.

A glare from Kane cut him off.

Right now, Donald Bry, Lakesh's right-hand man for running the functions of the Cerberus redoubt, was working code and math together with Clem Bryant and Daryl Morganstern. Bryant wasn't a computer expert or a mathematician like Bry or Morganstern, but he had rapidly become one of the premier scientific problem solvers. His field of expertise had been oceanography, something that was not immediately necessary in the struggle against the Annunaki and other forces threatening the freedom of humanity. He'd originally become the chef for the redoubt, but his ability to think outside of the box had granted Lakesh and the others the spark to reach conclusions.

The three men were an odd amalgamation, from the slender, rust-haired Bry to squat, pudgy-faced Morganstern to tall, goateed Bryant.

Kane looked to Sinclair. "We could just take a Manta…"

"No good," Bry said. "Grant's already in motion, from what I heard over his Commtact."

"Lakesh, we don't have time to dick around," Kane said. "Just jump us in. No one has a gun that can punch through the armaglass chamber doors."

Sinclair managed a smile. "I do have something that could help us with that."

With that announcement, she drew a flashlight from her well-stocked utility belt.

"Flashlight," Kane noted.

"I'd show you what it does, but it'd take you a few seconds to get over the strobe setting," Sinclair answered.

"What kind of candlepower does it put out?" Kane asked.

"Ten thousand," Sinclair said. "It'll still be sharp enough to leave a millennialist seeing spots for about fifteen seconds."

"That should buy us enough time to get out into the open," Kane returned. "Lakesh?"

The chief scientist of Cerberus frowned, but his decision process was quickened simply because of the swiftness of Kane's decision. The former Magistrate was a man of action, but also one with an uncanny danger sense that had kept him alive in conflicts against menaces powerful enough to erase the solar system. "Bry, can we send them?"

Bry nodded and he and Morganstern exited the mattrans unit. Kane and Sinclair entered the armaglass chamber with swiftness and purpose.

Kane wasn't going to let Grant, his partner and best friend in the world, disappear into history without a fight.

GRANT AND SHIZUKA STALKED through the entrance into a well-lit corridor. The millennialists were too savvy to allow stretches of shadows to obscure the approach of enemies. It didn't matter, since the hallway was empty of sentries, which made this approach all the more suspicious. For a brief instant, Grant wished Kane, with his uncanny point man's sense, was by his side instead of the beautiful samurai Shizuka. She was highly skilled, but Grant had yet to encounter another with Kane's instincts and reflexes.

The former Magistrate pushed the thought from his mind. Instead of occupying his thoughts with what could have been, he needed to concentrate on the here and now. His eyes and ears couldn't pick up on minuscule details with the same razor-sharp precision that Kane could, but he hadn't survived years as a Mag without relying on his own well-honed awareness. That's when he saw the smears of mud tracking along the otherwise mirror-polished floors.

Grant slowed and Shizuka, shadowing close to him, did likewise, her attention falling to the mess on the tiles. Neither of them spoke, but they both realized that something else was waiting down the hall, out of sight. The smell of the mud was the same primal stench of jungle that they had passed through. The Tigers of Heaven had done their best to clear the road between the beach and the installation of the dangerous feral predators trawled from the Jurassic and Cretaceous periods, then utilized speakers producing uncomfortable infrasonic pulses to keep them away.

The speakers had made manning Thunder Isle much safer, but nothing was perfect, necessitating sidearms and a contingent of sentries on the island at all times, just in case a predator's taste for human flesh was stronger than the discomfort that pumped through his eardrums every time he neared their world.

Those speakers, unfortunately, had a limited range. Behind the walls of the facility, anything carted past them would be unhindered, save by locked bulkhead doors, just like the one that sat at the end of this corridor. As Grant and Shizuka kept to the cover of a wall outcropping, minimizing their exposure to security cameras, they realized that something else could have been curled up in nooks down the way.

"Judging by the size of the mud smears, trailing off into man-size footprints, we're looking at deinonychus," Shizuka said.

Grant, who had grown familiar with the time-displaced dragons of Thunder Isle, nodded in agreement. "More than one, too. And check it out, feathers. Definitely those little 'terrible claws.'"

The predators that they'd referred to were the height and weight of German shepherds, but were infinitely more dangerous, possessing intelligence and teamwork in addition to flesh-rending killing claws on their hind legs and mouths filled with razor-sharp teeth. The deinonychus were masses of muscle that could sprint at upward of thirty miles per hour, as well. All of that combined into an opponent that was a lightning-quick slashing wind that could bring down elephantine sauropods outweighing an individual raptor tenfold. The Tigers of Heaven had suffered losses because of these cunning, dangerous creatures, and Grant and his other Cerberus companions had nearly succumbed to their threat, as well.

"Damn consortium must have drugged them and brought them here to be guard dogs," Grant grumbled.

As if on cue, a feather-crowned head poked out, cat-slitted eyes staring manically over a grin full of daggers. Though the deinonychus had existed millions of years before humans had even developed consciousness, there was something primevally terrifying about that wild, un-hindered smile that reached down into the mammalian DNA and still resonated in modern humans. This was the cackling wyvern, a fanged cockatrice that was the horror of mankind's nightmares, the source of myths and horror tales.

Another head, then a third, all looked down the hall, nostrils flaring, heads tilting and twitching inhumanly to locate the source of any sound.

Grant grimaced, realizing that even hushed, his voice carried to the sharp ears of the deadly predators. Shizuka tensed, knowing that they didn't see all of their dinosaur opponents. A sudden movement would be the trigger to the raptors' charge. The three hunters, given the height of their heads around the outcroppings they'd nested at, were crouched on haunches of coil-wound muscle that could launch them as swiftly as even Shizuka's arrows.

One of the raptors padded warily into the open, body and head held low and parallel to the floor tiles. Grant could see the predator's killing claws, three-inch-long hooks of gleaming black talon, cocked perpendicular to the ground, its other nails providing it traction in the polished corridor. The raptor's thigh muscles flexed and swelled, the promise of blinding speed stored in the tightly clenched limbs.

Grant sneered. The dinosaurs were simple animals, no matter how dangerous they could be. They were pawns of the millennialists, who simply saw every living thing as their subjects. That these creatures, magnificent examples of an evolutionary line ended sixty-five million years prior, would either kill or die was of no matter to the conspirators. At the same time, Grant was not a man who relished killing animals unnecessarily and hated it even more when those creatures were used as fodder for cowards too lazy to fight their own battles. As much as the initial sight of the deadly predators had awakened instinctual horror in the pit of his stomach, these dinosaurs were not malicious or gleefully violent. The only adversaries whom Grant had ever encountered who had taken joy or pride in their violence were humans. The deinonychus hadn't made a choice to be here and be killers.

Still, Grant wasn't going to stay his hand, not with Shizuka's life at stake. The Tigers of Heaven commander had similar feelings. While one of them could have possibly retreated back out of this corridor, the two of them would not be able to dive through the door without entangling each other. They had to stand and fight, especially since there were citizens of New Edo and Cerberus on the other side of the door the raptors protected.

Grant would make note to provide a little extra pain to the sociopaths who threw away lives like table scraps as he extended his fingers for a countdown. Shizuka nodded, understanding his intent. From the behavior they observed, there was a path that didn't involve violence and would result in their betrayed presence and injuries inflicted at the talons and fangs of the deinonychus. As Grant's index finger folded down into his fist, the two warriors stepped into the open swiftly and suddenly, so much so that the lone predator crouched in the center of the hall stepped back, startled into recoil.

Grant's step was punctuated by the sharp clack of his Sin Eater extending into his hand. The only sound that Shizuka had made was the creak of her bow flexing under the force of her strong arms. Both people were ready to let their weapons speak, and they stood with confidence and strength. Of course, this was surrendering any attempt at stealth on their parts, thanks to the noise the Sin Eater would make.

There was a method of dealing with animals, and predators were not too interested in engaging in combat with prey that could injure them. Successful hunters sought out targets that would provide them minimum risk, or stack the odds in their favor due to surprise and terrain. Here, in an open corridor, with foes who were armed and obviously capable of fighting back, the deinonychus would pause before a foolish head-on rush.

Those yellow-black slitted eyes locked on to Grant, which meant that Shizuka could slip back behind his bulk and head toward the bulkhead access to the outside. If they were to have a chance to advance farther without gunshots warning the millennialists on the other side of their blast shield, Grant and Shizuka would need a path for the deinonychus to run away.

It helped that the two adventurers could tell the difference between territorial challenge and hunting mode. From what they knew, no raptor would expose itself if there was no net of fellow predators to catch fleeing prey. This was the deinonychus pack standing their ground against a threat, the pack leader taking point and presenting the knowledge that the humans were approaching a very defensive, confused and frightened group.

Grant didn't flinch, keeping eye contact with the pack leader, but other than showing off his size and weapon, he made no menacing actions toward the raptor. This was a fine line, a balance between a show of strength and passive standing. Too strong, and the deinonychus would take Grant as a threat. Too passive, and the prehistoric killing machine would advance, perhaps even attack.

Grant heard the door behind him—they hadn't come that far down the corridor—and the smell of the jungle beyond the sonic fence rushed him. The pack leader's nostrils flared at the familiar scent of home. The predator's sensitive ears, or rather the feathers around their ear holes that funneled sound akin to mammalian ears, turned to the doorway, and they recoiled momentarily. He spoke in low, calm tones. "Don't forget…"

"I haven't. Just locating the speaker," Shizuka replied just as softly.

Grant didn't need any verification that his love had disconnected the infrasound generator. The sudden decrease in uncomfortable sonics was flagged by the reaction of the deinonychus pack leader and its kin.

The pack leader's yellow eyes flicked from Grant to the jungle behind him. The human stepped aside, allowing the confused, uprooted predators a way back to where they were comfortable. Slowly, cautiously, the dinosaurs walked out into the open, the pack leader padding up to Grant. Their eyes were still locked, the raptor's signal was clear.

To harm my family, you must go through me.

The deinonychus, five of them, zipped past their pack leader, darting through the doorway and beyond, disappearing into the jungle. Once its family was safely away from this place of humans, the leader backed away from Grant, showing its strength while giving itself distance from a potential opponent and the freedom of the forest. Grant hoped that Shizuka hadn't reset the infrasound projector, but once the lead raptor's feet felt soil, not tile, it whirled and exploded away into the wilds of Thunder Isle.

Though he had not incurred the wrath of the dinosaur's claws and fangs, Grant had to lean against the wall. He'd flexed his muscles, making himself appear larger and more menacing. That and the concentration needed to keep the animals at bay had taken its toll. Shizuka appeared in the doorway, closing it behind her before tending to him.

"You all right?" she asked.

Grant nodded, taking a few deep breaths. "Staring down a killer dinosaur is hard damned work."

Shizuka brushed her hand across his broad chest, sparing a slight, tight-lipped smile. "So taking on some hired guns should be a snap, right?"

Grant chuckled and kissed Shizuka's forehead, or rather the helmet chevron over her eyes. "Yeah. Can't go taking a nap now."

The two warriors headed down the hallway.

BRIGID BAPTISTE WAS impressed with the precision of Edwards's breaching charge. The reshaped plastic explosives had cut a perfect hole large enough for Brigid, Domi and Maria Falk to slither through. Edwards had no intention of climbing into an ancient underground temple, and a hole large enough to fit his muscular, massive form would risk a weakness in the wall that might cause the improvised entrance to collapse.

Domi took point, putting her head and shoulders through the opening. Though not much sunlight got past even her slender frame, the albino's ruby-red eyes were attuned to even the deepest of shadows, and could pick up details as necessary. She came out of the hole and reached into a gear bag, pulling a length of rope adorned with knots every two feet.

"Anchor," she ordered.

Edwards nodded and secured the end of the cord and the grapnel hook to which it was attached in some rocks. When the steel tines of the grapnel were anchored, Edwards gave the hook a tug with all of his strength. If the former Magistrate couldn't unseat the grapnel, then the combined weight of Falk and Brigid wouldn't be too much for it.

"Shall we?"

"Maria last. You second," Domi said to Brigid, slithering through the hole. A slender arm snaked out, snatched up her gear bag and yanked it into the shadows. Brigid waited a moment, wondering what would be the feral girl's signal to follow her. The hiss of a flare, followed by a reddish glow in the darkened hole was a good preamble.

"Come on," Domi called.

Brigid slipped through the hole, holding on to the rope. The drop to the ground was only twenty-five feet, but it was certainly nothing that she'd have wanted to attempt in the dark. Chunks of broken stone on the floor provided an uneven surface to simply hop on to, promising a broken ankle if she'd made the attempt. The knotted rope also provided an easy, low-profile ladder with which they could leave the temple. Thanks to Falk's ground sonar, the hole itself was braced by sufficient struts to be fairly stable, if too small for Edwards to want to go through.

Even if he wasn't wary of crawling into a claustrophobic space, Brigid, Domi and Edwards all agreed that someone standing guard at their entrance would be vital. There was no telling who was here on the Euphrates. The explorers had arrived in via parallax point, so knowledge of local bandits, pirates or tyrants was slim. If it weren't for a heretofore unknown threat from the time of the Annunakis' rule, and now new hints of another monstrosity from past millennia, Brigid wouldn't have come here, making a wild stab for historical data that could be an edge in their next conflict with the Annunaki overlords.

Blindsided by Marduk's horde alongside New Olympus, then the blade of Ullikummis and later Ullikummis himself, Brigid was getting tired of being caught behind the curve.

The vaulted underground chamber was large enough to be an aircraft hangar. Knowing the ships of the Annunaki, Brigid wouldn't have been surprised to discover that this been a parking garage for ancient astronauts. She didn't see any form of doors through which skimmers could flit in and out, but she wasn't able to perceive the wall opposite the one they'd entered through, thanks to the gloomy shadows and the interruption of support studs. She remembered Falk's original measurements as the geologist finally made her way down the rope.

Two football fields in area.

"Anything, Domi?" Brigid asked.

"Stale air," she answered. "Scurrying vermin. Not much."

Outside of Kane, Domi had some of the sharpest senses of any human that Brigid had ever known. Part of it was due to the sensitivity inherent in an albino's eyes, the rest coming from growing up in the wilderness. Though her skin was alabaster in color, and her closely shorn hair was the hue of aged bone, the feral woman was hardly the fragile creature that albinos of previous centuries had been. She was strong and tough, having survived trauma that would have killed a less resilient human.

Brigid couldn't have asked for a better companion to slink through the darkness of a temple that might also be an Annunaki tomb. She glanced over to Falk, who checked the Glock in her belt holster. Brigid saw a mirror of herself in the older woman, a scientist who was willing to journey into the unknown but who hadn't been tested or tried in conflict. There was a difference between the two scientists, though. Falk was beginning her adventuring in her later years, while Brigid was still young and fit. The former archivist was also tall and heavy enough to make her gender less important should she ever get into conflict with a man. Falk was more petite, larger than Domi was but with none of the animalistic fury and wilderness instincts of the albino warrior.

The Glock was the simplest and easiest firearm to operate in the Cerberus armory, so Falk wouldn't be completely inept if it came to gunplay. Without spending time on learning the operation of the mechanism, Falk and the other Manitius Base scientists could be grilled on marksmanship. The archivist knew the scores from their training, and Falk was above the median in skill, able to tear the heart out of a paper target. Still, Brigid knew that she'd have to watch out for the geologist, because a printed silhouette was very different from a menacing opponent.

Domi had stopped, looking at the other part of Grant's trench coat. It hung like a flag, and from this side, there was no doubt that it had been crafted for a giant of a man. Below the empty coat was a pile of rodent-chewed bones. Brigid swallowed hard, but the feral girl knelt and picked up one of the bones.

"Too big," she announced.

"How do you know?" Brigid asked.

Domi stood up the bone she was examining. It was a femur that was nearly as long as Domi's entire leg. "Grant's tall, but his thigh don't reach to my waist. Someone else was wearing his coat."

Brigid looked at the sunken, buckled ceiling, wondering how the skeleton had gotten nearly through the roof of the temple. She could only hope that it was a victorious situation for Grant.

She didn't want to think of how someone else had gained possession of her friend's coat.

Chapter 4

Merkel's head shot up as two simultaneous events were announced by the consortium mercenaries under his command. One of the mercenaries was not so much a hired gun but a computer technician named Milo Donaldson, the key tapper who was given charge of the mattrans and the time trawl. He was, to Merkel's mind, the perfect example of a computer nerd, slender and full of himself because he had abilities that were as vital to the scientists as those of a dozen gunslingers. He got on Merkel's nerves simply because of his perceived sense of power, which was only as good as his fingertips dancing across a keyboard.

The other was Kovak, who was a former Magistrate like Merkel. However, Kovak was not a war leader like Merkel was. Kovak was just another minion, someone who cleaned up. Merkel would be the one through the door first, while Kovak would hang back, fire a few shots into a twitching corpse and scoop up any dropped magazines. He was simply a cleaner, someone who took care of any messes that Merkel made while he was actively *doing*.

Not that Merkel himself was in any good mood. Ever since the fall of the baronies, he'd been in business for himself, a walking trigger finger for hire, living hand to mouth in the basest of mercenary lifestyles. He'd long ago sold off any pretense of ethics when he'd learned that he didn't have a retirement plan. He had felt that his work as a drone under another baron was ignored and degrading. His desire for recognition and glory, despite only excelling at the lowest of achievements, was what finally got him to go from picking up profit in the baronial system to going all out to become his own man.

Of course, that manhood was predicated on being a brute, stripping his office of lawman down to its lowest common denominator. He was a thug, alone in the wilderness. He'd momentarily thought of throwing in his lot with Kane and the people of Cerberus, like a few other Magistrates had done, but Merkel knew he could do better than Kane. Kane had thrown away his life of power and prestige for a half-assed idea of freedom and equality.

Merkel saw a world that he could take on, provided he could scrounge the right people. He'd regarded Donaldson and Kovak as necessary pains, and maybe at some time in the future, he could pick someone better or use them as faceless drones of his own.

Merkel knew that if he told the right lies, he could get his followers. He knew that the consortium had lied about Kane, but most of the soldiers hired by them didn't care, or had their own vendettas, just like Merkel did.

Men like Allen, another Magistrate who'd been through the same disillusionment. Allen had served under the barons' whims. He'd upheld baronial law, and when the barons said to kill without mercy, Allen had no compunction about putting a bullet into the head of every single person he was told to. It was his job; it was his life. When the barons abandoned the Magistrates, there were all manner of options that the lawmen could have gone with. They could have gone to Cerberus or continued their career of upholding law and protecting the citizens of the few bastions of civilization in post-apocalyptic America, but Allen and Merkel knew that they could do so much better.

The two former law keepers knew better. Serving the unwashed masses without profit didn't fit their mercenary feelings. The Magistrates had been raised in law, but as Kane and Grant had proved, such rearing was not infallible. Dozens had strayed from the course. Merkel and Allen figured they could convert their strength and training into sustenance of a life they preferred, one where they were in control, and to hell with anyone else's concepts of what mattered and what was important. Having that power was everything to Merkel, so anything that got in his way was more than an annoyance: it was a declaration of war.

Kovak and Donaldson were simply the messengers of bad news, but Merkel was willing to shoot them.

"Sir! Movement in corridor Alpha!" Kovak announced. "The dinosaurs are leaving."

"We've got an incoming matter transmission," Donaldson said.

"Shut the door! Lock down the chamber!" Merkel shouted, responding immediately. "Allen! Don't let the hostages be recovered alive!"

"You've got it," Allen said. "If those Goody Two-shoes bastards want to save something, they'll be returning corpses to be buried."

Merkel sneered. "If we can't have Thunder Isle, they'll have a tomb. No one takes what I own," Merkel growled. "Not without great price. Not even Kane and Grant, damn their very existence!"

AS SHE MATERIALIZED the mat-trans chamber, Sela Sinclair felt as if her stomach was a few hundred feet behind her, in the void they'd just crossed. Bry and Morganstern had cracked the lockout codes put in by the millennialist raiders, but since it was a standard jump, there was residual jump sickness. It was nothing that she hadn't hardened herself against, but it was still disorienting. Her knees went rubbery for a moment, but Sinclair was a strong woman. She hadn't fought her way into the traditionally male-dominated world of the United States Air Force without having guts.

"Sinclair," Kane called out, getting her thoughts refocused.

As if it were a code word, a post-hypnotic suggestion trigger, Sinclair reached down to her security torch and swept it out of its spot on her utility belt. Kane saw consortium mercenaries rush down the corridor to hem them in, Calico machine guns held in firing position for the moment that the chamber door hissed aside.

Sinclair focused the lens of her flashlight on the hallway, then thumbed the panic button on the side. Kane ducked his face behind his shoulder, and the normally nonreflective shadowsuit was painted with a brilliant blue-white glow.

The trio of consortium gunmen in the hall let out grunts of pain as their eyeballs were seared by the brilliant burst of light pulsing from the torch. Sinclair had been on the other end of the lens, so she knew that the only thing residing in their optic nerves was an orange halo around a void of nothingness. The effect would last for as long as ten seconds, an eternity when it came to close-quarters combat, but they wouldn't feel long-term effects, depending on how mercifully Kane and Sinclair treated them.

She turned off the light and was hot on Kane's heels as the two Cerberus warriors charged the gun-wielding blinded men. The former Magistrate skipped the first of the millennialists, leaving him for Sinclair to deal with as he fell upon the two at the rear. It wasn't a case of macho posturing on Kane's part; it was simply the fact that he had the arm reach to engage the gunmen quickly, simultaneously if he moved correctly.

Sinclair drew her collapsible ASP baton, snapping it open with a flick of the wrist. The harsh snap of the telescoping steel tubing caused her target to "look" in the direction of the sound, despite the fact that all he could see was an all-consuming fireball. She whipped the tip of the baton around like a scythe, lashing it across the millennialist's knees. The sudden impact knocked his feet from beneath him, and Sinclair pivoted the top section up and chopped it hard on his neck, just over his jugular.

That particular shot was a stunner. The blood vessel transmitted hydrostatic force back into his brain, not enough to rupture anything vital, but the sudden rush of fluid was overwhelming enough to interrupt the raider's consciousness.

Sinclair looked up in time to see Kane using the toppling form of one of the consortium mercenaries as a brace to swing both feet up, one boot cracking the man's jaw, the other spearing his breastbone. The millennial gunman's head rebounded off the wall, and then he crashed face-first into the floor, a numb, groaning sack of insensate thug. Kane landed on the balls of his feet as his "support" folded to the ground, landing on his knees and vomiting. Kane turned and jammed a knife-hard hand into the stunned gunman's neck, ending his suffering for the time being.

"Sinclair, make sure he doesn't choke," Kane ordered, gathering up the unconscious men's firearms.

Sinclair knelt next to the man, dragging his head from the puddle he'd made after Kane struck him hard in the sternum and groin. She left him lying on his side, then took a rag from one of his pockets to clear the remaining bile from his mouth. He wouldn't choke. It might be a waste of time, especially since these three hired guns may have been responsible for the deaths of a Tiger of Heaven sentry on the island. If they were murderers, their heads would roll.

Still, the Tigers of Heaven had a stringent code of justice, and the samurai were loath to kill incapacitated opponents, just like the Cerberus warriors. There was time for ruthless slaying ability, but cold-blooded murder didn't live in the hearts of the two societies.

"He'll live," Sinclair announced.

"If he deserves to," Kane replied, voice low and grim. The Sin Eater hissed into his hand, lightning swift. "These three are our last free lunch for a while."

"I didn't sign on for an easy time," Sinclair answered, drawing the Beretta from her hip holster. She took a moment to affix a suppressor to the extended barrel. Kane latched a stealth module, a squared, vented device as opposed to the round pipe on her Beretta, onto the nose of his Sin Eater, as well. Neither gun would be whisper quiet—the enemy would definitely know that firearms went off—but they wouldn't give away their positions so easily due to the alteration of the weapons' acoustics.

"Bry, tell me you've cracked the security cameras," Kane said into his Commtact.

"I have, but the millennialists are staying out of sight," Bry answered. "These guys aren't stupid…oh, my God… Grant!"

Sinclair could see Kane stiffen at the alarm in Bry's voice. Then the Cerberus warrior exploded into motion, and she had to push herself to keep up with Kane.

GRANT AND SHIZUKA MOVED like shadowy wraiths among the corridors of the Operation Chronos laboratories. They had barely ducked out of sight when a group of millennialist gunmen hurried to the hall where they'd entered the base. They avoided notice, and as soon as they were out of earshot, Shizuka got on the radio to her Tigers of Heaven allies. The samurai would deal with the millennialists, bringing them down swiftly and silently.

The two people had the option of going right at the commander who had taken control of the installation, but the fear for the safety of the hostages, if there were any, kept them moving with silence and speed. They had to verify any captives the millennialists had taken and insure their safety. Grant thought of the difference between the consortium and Cerberus. The consortium would sacrifice their hired guns, cutting and running or blasting the facility to oblivion in a scorched-earth campaign. Grant, however, couldn't write off an ally. These were friends, and if there was one thing that the ex-Magistrate had developed, it was loyalty to the people of New Edo, enough that he'd risk his life for them as readily as he did for his family at the Cerberus redoubt.

Grant frowned, deepening the angle of his gunslinger's mustache as he mentally reviewed the map of the Operation Chronos labs. When he spoke to Shizuka, it was softer than a whisper. "Two places where they could be holding people."

Shizuka nodded. "Specimen storage and the temporal dilator itself."

"They save ammo by tossing the hostages… where?"

"When," Shizuka corrected. "Prehuman times. The nuclear winter after skydark. Lots of eras would be fatal to modern humans."

Grant sneered. "It's scary that we can imagine the actions of sociopaths."

"We've encountered enough to expect the worst," Shizuka answered.

"I'll scout specimen storage," Grant said. "Call me and wait if you see anyone."

Shizuka nodded and disappeared. Grant didn't worry about her. If the Japanese woman didn't want to be noticed, she wouldn't be. And he had stressed that they were only doing a reconnaissance, not taking action. That didn't mean either of them would sit still if a hostage was threatened with death, but the two of them were in contact with each other. One call for help, and the other would be with them in a heartbeat.

Grant slunk down the hall to specimen storage, where the scientists who ran Operation Chronos had deposited time-trawled people and animals, like the raptors that they had just encountered, and even larger creatures like the carnotaurus they had met on one of their first visits to Thunder Isle. The trawl could easily accommodate the one-ton, fifteen-foot-long predator with the unusual, almost demonic horns adorning its broad, powerful skull. Temporal disorientation made it easier for the Chronos whitecoats to control even the strongest of beasts.

The population of prehistoric animals on the island indicated that the scientists were prolific in their efforts. The breadth of specimen containment's cells was another clue, a dozen cages of various sizes. On quiet feet, Grant looked into the darkened prison, listening for signs of habitation.

The hostage takers might have cast the area into shadows, but there was no way that they could muffle the nervous shifting and breathing of captives. Grant tossed a pocketed pebble into the hallway to make certain, but no reaction left him with the impression that this place had been cordoned off and abandoned. He turned away to rendezvous with Shizuka and spotted a half-dozen consortium soldiers moving with purpose toward the Chronos trawl.

"Shizuka, you've got company on your six," Grant warned over the radio.

"Busy," came the hissed reply.

From the grunts transmitted over her hands-free microphone, Grant knew that he was going to have to hustle. From stealth to explosive acceleration, the big man charged down the hall, his long strides ending in loud thumps on the tile floor of the laboratory, each footfall loud enough to be a gunshot. If things were going to hell, Grant wanted to draw attention away from Shizuka.

"Hey!" shouted one of the group of soldiers who'd passed only moments before, hearing the ex-Magistrate run.

As Grant rounded the corner, he saw that three of the millennialists were in midturn, the front half of the group continuing on its path. Three Calico submachine guns would still have the potential of causing Grant injury through his armored coat, so there was no pause on the brawny titan's part. Leg muscles surged, and he sprinted forward like a human bull, his arms swept out like the horns of a steer. Instead of making himself a smaller target, Grant gambled on causing as much disruption as possible. His wide, sweeping limbs struck each of the three gunmen, bowling them over.

Grant could feel the jaw of one mercenary dislocate as his melon-sized shoulder slammed up against it. His fingers disappeared into the wet mushy holes in another's face as he sunk them into eye sockets. The last of the trio's throat thudded hard against his right forearm, wrapped in the hydraulic forearm holster, and there was a dull pop as the gunman's larynx collapsed and his neck bones separated. It was a brutal assault, and there was at least one fatality in the attack. It was necessary; if any of the three had managed to get their fingers on the triggers of their machine pistols, the resultant gunfire would have alerted all of the hostaged Chronos facility.

Things were already going downhill, and there were three more hired soldiers to deal with. The crash of Grant against their compatriots was now enough to draw the lead group's attention. Two stunned men and a corpse fell to the tile floor as they turned. Grant snapped off a hard punch with his left fist, the blow crushing the cheekbones of a millennialist, the impact enough to toss the man insensate to the ground. The second of the gunmen swung his Calico up, but Grant launched the Sin Eater into his grasp by flexing his wrist tendons. A heavyweight 9 mm slug exploded through the stealth module on the machine pistol's muzzle, making a throaty pop that was matched by the bursting of ribs and lung tissue. The mercenary jerked violently backward as 240 grains of high-density bullet turned his internal organs to froth and shattered his spine.

The last of the consortium thugs managed to aim at the center of Grant's chest, the Calico only the blink of an eye away from opening up. Grant took another gamble, shoving his torso hard against the submachine gun's muzzle. The contact range blast against his armored coat muffled the noise that the weapon would have made. The impact of the rounds hurt like a hammer to the ribs, but the gunshots were far quieter than even a silenced pistol. The thrust of Grant's chest against the barrel had the added bonus of jamming the enemy's weapon.

The gunman cranked the trigger again in vain as Grant leveled his Sin Eater at his enemy's face. The Magistrate weapon chugged once, very effectively, exploding the mercenary's skull in a brutal spray of a stringy, sticky mess. Grant looked at his Sin Eater in dismay. The gun had fired once, but he'd flicked the selector to burst-mode.

This is why we never use the stealth modules on these things, Grant thought bitterly. The suppressor for the Sin Eater was notorious for robbing energy from the weapon's cycles and trapping gunpowder in the action, keeping casings from ejecting from the breech and jamming them up. It had always been kept concealed in a pocket of Magistrate armor, and only the stickiness of a hostage situation made the silencers a necessity.

Grant retracted the weapon back into its forearm holster and scooped up a Calico. It was going to be noisy, and not quite as intricately balanced as the Sin Eater, but it would have to do.

SHIZUKA HAD the advantage of leverage over Allen, but only momentarily. The millennialist commander had Magistrate training, and as such, he knew many of the same tricks that Grant had used against her. She'd held him at bay for this long, keeping the consortium's lackey from hitting the control panel for the temporal dilator. On the transmitter plates below them, a dozen bound men and women, bloody and helpless, were on the verge of being disassembled on a molecular scale and squirted through a wormhole to some other point in the cosmos and the history of humanity.

There was no way that she could rescue the captives before the dilator engaged, and she knew that despite her strength and skill, she couldn't hold off Allen forever. He had easily one hundred pounds on her lithe frame, and he knew enough martial arts to begin to counter her grappling against him. Sweat drenched her forehead, sticking her silky black hair to her face. If she could see herself, her pale skin against the midnight void color of her tresses, and the strain on her features, she would have thought herself a porcelain doll in the process of shattering and cracking.

Only for the speed and skill of her bow did she manage to bring down the three other sentries with Allen. Three corpses sported *ya* shafts from their upper chests and throats, the deadly potential energy stored in her *kumi* spearing them through Kevlar body armor and bone to sever major arteries within moments.

One of the three dead consortium mercenaries was folded over the railing next to the wrestling pair. Allen had appointed this particular gunman to work the controls in case a rescue attempt had been made. He had been Shizuka's first target, her *ya* piercing his windpipe and spine in one shot. Paralyzed and unable to breathe, all that the millennialist lackey could do was collapse and sputter as he hung half over a steel pipe. No nerve impulses could impel his unplugged limbs to hit the transmit button.

Shizuka had perforated the other two gunmen, but Allen moved with the speed of a panther, his Sin Eater having shattered the top bow of her *kumi,* rendering the weapon useless. Shizuka discarded the broken tool, the need to save lives overriding her sentiment for the crafted bow. They had met in the middle, and Shizuka hit Allen with a nerve punch and proceeded to restrain him in an armlock.

At first, it had been brute muscle against biomechanically balanced strength, but Allen was not an idiot. Even as Grant's voice came over her radio, Shizuka knew that Allen was struggling to twist his way out of her grasp. He was an eighth of a ton of honed, sculpted sinew and might. Though the physics of leverage were on Shizuka's side, he was working his way to loosen her balance and apply gravity's pull on him to escape what would have been an unbreakable grapple.

Shizuka could feel the veins stand out on her neck, her locked talons of fingers bursting at the knuckles. Blood from her partially uprooted fingernails was mixing with that which seeped from Allen's torn skin. He was growing more slippery, though he was taking a toll on his own muscles as the iron-claw technique refused to yield to Allen's struggle against it. The man's fingers stretched, yearning to tap the transmit button.

"Gonna break soon, bitch," Allen growled.

"Break this, fucker!" a stentorian roar split the air.

Both combatants froze at Grant's challenge, giving the Cerberus warrior the pause he required to hurl himself through the air like a human missile. Shizuka, Allen, Grant and the dead mercenary all sailed through the air, landing in a tangle of arms and legs on the floor only a few feet below them.

"Get the hostages," Grant ordered. His instruction to Shizuka was long enough for Allen to recover his wits and punch the big man across the jaw.

Shizuka knew better than to remain where she'd be a concern for Grant. She drew her *tanto* knife and raced forward, slashing through ropes with the precision of a surgeon. She tried to block out the sound of hammer impacts on meat and bone, but the rapid thuds and crunches were too quick and furious to ignore. All she could do was ensure the lives of the surviving Thunder Isle staff, hemp slicing apart against the finely honed edge of her forged steel.

"Shizuka!" Grant bellowed, a desperate warning that anchored her attention.

The console that Grant and Allen had been warring over was a spray of sparks, peppering them with burning embers of white-hot wiring and circuit board fragments. Shizuka glanced down to the alloy floor plates she and the last of the hostages were atop. The horns atop the central pylon glowed, and Shizuka saw fountains of odd light vomiting from their tips like volcanic kaleidoscopes.

"Move now!" Grant yelled, punctuating his cry by plunging Allen's head into the gaping wreckage of the command console. The millennialist began a macabre dance as high voltage ripped through his nervous system.

Shizuka had shoved the last of the freed captives off the alloy floor plate when something gripped her. It wasn't physical; it felt more like she was immersed in water, tiny pricklings running along the surface of her skin. The world outside of the odd glow and sensation fit her mind, but the people were rippling. Instead of moving, their limbs seemed to flow like quicksilver. She wanted to move, to speak, when she saw her hand above the surface of the event she was in.

Shizuka had experienced the mat-trans before, so she had a frame of reference for her body's responses, but right now, the hand sticking out of the field seemed unseemly and alien. Fingers melted together, turning into a webbed fan or a smooth, featureless ball. It seemed like an eternity of watching her digits mutate crazily before she realized that she wasn't watching her hand destroying and remolding itself but was instead experiencing her hand's movement from an angle only available across a dimensional fold.

A strong arm gripped her hand. Shizuka wanted to cry out to the person coming to her rescue, but she saw the thick trunk of Grant's thigh and lower leg press against the temporal dilator's platform. If she could have made a sound—her lungs felt as if they were immovable despite the fact that she hadn't needed a breath in what felt like hours—she doubted he could have heard her.

Shizuka grimaced as she was stretched across the event plane of the time field. When her head went through, it was as if she was being born again, parts of her brain exploding to life and normal status even as the rest of her mind reeled at its now disjointed nature. As soon as Shizuka's head was in "real" time, she sucked in a ragged breath, trying to speak even though her larynx was seeming miles away.

Grant was half-submerged into the shimmering temporal disruption. His face was a grim mask as he struggled to push her to safety. She wanted to speak to him, but as she regained the ability to speak, his head subsided to the other side.

"Grant!" Shizuka cried.

Other hands grasped her free arm. She turned to see Kane and Sinclair hauling with all their might as Grant's wall of muscle seethed from the other side of the time barrier. "Hold on to him!"

"We're trying!" Kane snapped back. The muscles on his wolf-lean arms were swollen with effort. She noticed that Kane and Sinclair had anchored themselves by heavy electrical cable to the wall of the chamber. Grant had secured himself, as well, but the only thing left on this side of the malfunctioning platform was the cable and Grant's right foot.

"No!" Shizuka yelled. Some instinct told her that if that last bit of Grant disappeared behind the wall, he would be gone, for no tether could resist the pull of currents across a dimension she couldn't comprehend.

Suddenly, as if hurled by a tornado, Shizuka was free from the vortex. She collapsed to the floor of the chamber. She'd been birthed from seeming nothingness, her molecules yanked apart like taffy as she was drawn through a hole. If she hadn't been one of the most physically fit people in New Edo, she'd be suffering a heart attack.

Instead, her heart broke as she knew that she was safe in the time she belonged, while Grant was gone, on the other side of the temporal event horizon. She looked and saw only an empty floor as the plates powered down, the shorn electrical cable that was Grant's tether lying mockingly beside her.

"Damn it, Grant…"

Chapter 5

Never before had Shamhat been struck so soundly, even by Humbaba, his half-Annunaki master. The Igigi staggered back to his feet, wiping the ichor from the corner of his mouth, smearing it across his reptilian scales. Four mindless Nephilim drones struggled against the human who had appeared in their midst in the court of Urudug.

"He is human, is he not?" Humbaba asked. "He's large, even for the Africans we know as the Watusi."

"Nearly the size of an Annunaki," Shamhat said. "Much larger than we, your servants."

Humbaba's leonine head rose and fell in a slow acknowledging nod. "Human, yet he wears garments not of the people we idle among."

Shamhat's yellow eyes narrowed to slits. "Chemically processed polymers blended beneath a biologically refined shell for his cloak. Interwoven plant-based fabrics with metal and synthetic additions for the vestments on his trunk and limbs. His footwear—"

"I noticed their uniqueness, Shamhat. Do not bore me with the fashion critique," Humbaba's lion voice grumbled. "If I'm not mistaken, the creature also possesses two chemical-powered, repeating projectile weapons. Such technology shouldn't exist on this backwater world for millennia, should Father have his way."

Shamhat nodded. "Perhaps a slave or a descendant of a slave sent off world?"

Humbaba's eyes narrowed. "No. The language he spoke…it was gibberish. Even telepathic contact is elusive. A slave would be far more communicative."

Shamhat watched the long-coated newcomer avoid a punch from one of the Nephilim drones with practiced speed, deftly catching the extended limb and bending it using a knowledge of body mechanics that was rare among the peoples of this world. Certainly, the humans calling themselves the Greeks had a similar hand-to-hand maneuver in their wrestling art of *pankraton,* and those in the Orient were only now developing a fighting craft they called *hwarong do.* Whoever this man was, he combined strength with skill in such a way that his enemies appeared to be moving at half of his speed.

Shamhat cast out his thoughts in an attempt to reach into the man's mind, and was repulsed by a torrent of confusion and disjointedness. Tears welled in his yellow orbs in an attempt to salve the sudden, piercing ache behind his brow.

"Ah, you've tried your mind against his, as well?" Humbaba asked. "And what say you?"

"That is no man. His brain seems as if it's at right angles to this universe. What surface memories I could grasp are incomplete and scrambled," Shamhat replied. "Is he perhaps a shadow from another dimension?"

"A higher plane of existence, perhaps the echoes that a three-dimensional intellect could comprehend only in the shape of a human?" Humbaba asked.

"Theoretically such a creature would exist, but to carry such mundane equipment and garments when his very body would be superhumanly charged in our almost ethereal plane?" Shamhat asked. "He'd also be much faster in reaction to my Nephilim. I've honed their reflexes to an edge few have ever known before. This creature seems to be operating at a different time scale, but it's nothing unique."

A Nephilim grew tired of the conflict and employed his ASP blaster, twin strings of yellow lightning twisting from the snakelike projectors wound about his wrist. The powerful bolts struck Grant solidly, and he collapsed to his hands and knees.

The other Nephilim fell upon him as one, fists raining down on him.

"Enough!" Humbaba bellowed, his roar causing every creature in the court of Urudug to freeze, even the battered Grant. "He is to be taken alive!"

Strong arms wrapped around Grant's limbs, the effects of the ASP energy discharge scrambling his thoughts even more. He didn't know his own name, and he didn't know why the world seemed to be moving in slow motion around him, but the reptilian creatures who restrained his powerful arms were eerily familiar, though other beings were strange. Some part of him wanted to work his lips, to communicate, but what would fall from them, even if he could form the odd barking sounds shared by these inhuman strangers around him?

He was tired, and he ached from injuries old and new. Phantasms of memories, things that felt familiar and friendly, hovered just out of reach of his consciousness. While he could put terms to things like *floor, wall, arm, Nephilim,* he had nothing for the faces, the entities attached to the ghostly images in his mind. They should have names, but like Grant's own name, they eluded him like frightened cockroaches before a sudden light.

I know how insects react to a man's approach, yet I don't know the men and women who are a part of my life, Grant thought grimly. Not even my name.

"You may tame this one," Humbaba said. "Teach him some language if his consciousness will abide it."

Shamhat nodded, glaring at Grant. "Come, giant. We have much to discuss."

The Nephilim pushed Grant toward the doorway that Shamhat had indicated. Grant stomped the ground with all his strength, anchoring himself against their efforts. There were four of the reptilian guards, applying their incredible physiques against his own, and yet he was stalling them. This wasn't right to the lost and confused Grant. He had no right to be this strong, as if he had traded his mental clarity for muscle. Though he felt no heavier, he was indeed even swifter.

Shamhat nodded to the Nephilim who had shot Grant. "Give him another taste of discipline. It will do him good to realize who his masters are."

The searing energy of the ASP charge struck Grant in the kidneys, his legs buckling. Pain blinded him, and he thrashed, hurling his captors away from him out of agonized reflex. Despite the display of strength, he sank to the floor, unable to breathe.

Shamhat, having recovered from Grant's first blow against him, reached down and pulled on the human. Grant's coat sloughed off his shoulders as the man struggled to escape his captivity. "Hit him again!"

More ASP lightning burned through Grant's nerves, an onslaught of punishment that would have left him a smoldering briquette of charred flesh.

Who am I? Grant thought, staggering back to his feet.

Grant looked up in time to see nearly ten feet of leonine godling, all sculpted muscle and long limbs, standing over him.

"I said enough! I am tired of this foolish game!" Humbaba roared. Grant felt all the solid power of the giant's crashing fist on his jaw, as if the half-Annunaki lord of this time-lost court were the only other real thing in this turgid dream.

Blessed unconsciousness descended upon Grant.

SILENCE REIGNED in the Operation Chronos laboratories. Kane had watched his best friend in this or any world disappear into the ether in an effort to save Shizuka. The warrior woman trembled, her body trying to reacclimate itself to the reality outside of the strange energies she had been bathed in.

When Kane and Sinclair had burst into the temporal-dilation chamber, they had seen Grant anchored by a heavy cable, tugging on an arm attached to something that Kane was still trying to describe mentally. The limb was pulled thin, like putty that was extruded through a pinhole. The person it had been attached to was a featureless blue ghost shimmering as if underwater. Though his eyes weren't transmitting the ghost's identity to Kane's brain, some instinct told him that it was Shizuka, even before Grant had bellowed her name as he grasped her hand.

Kane had experienced much in his young life. He'd even traveled in time and to other universes, though those journeys either required his consciousness anchored to the body of his counterpart in that casement, or his existence as an ethereal phantom, incapable of interaction with the universe. He'd also encountered others who had been dragged through time and space to this planet—dinosaurs, black magicians from other eras, even alien energy beings seeking to tap the life force of humans.

However, after witnessing his partner's disappearance into a stream of temporal disruption, Kane had called to Cerberus. Brigid Baptiste was good at explaining things like this to him. Kane wasn't stupid, but the kind of science at work here was well outside his realm of knowledge. He had no mental touchstone through which to make the necessary connections for comprehension.

"Brigid's still exploring the city of Eridu," Lakesh said over the Commtact link they shared. "But I'll be out with some scientific help."

Kane frowned deeply, waiting for Lakesh to arrive. The India-born scientist was one of the few people on the planet who could comprehend the mechanics of space folding, wormholes and matter transmission to the point that he could design the interphaser, a portable unit capable of sending Kane and his allies to naturally occurring energy vortices along the Earth's magnetic lines. Superseding the necessity for local redoubts and their mat-trans chambers had made searching the world for allies against the Annunaki and chasing threats to humanity so much easier.

Lakesh had explained that he didn't have a complete mastery of Operation Chronos technologies, but the temporal dilator and the mat-trans units shared principles.

Kane knelt next to Shizuka, who was still shaken by her ordeal. A blanket had been cast about her shoulders to prevent shock, though her body temperature was normal. There wasn't a mark on her, not even on her wrist where Grant's massive hand had clutched her against a tide that swept her out of step with reality. The woman's dark, almond-shaped eyes scanned Kane's features, and the kinship of their shared loss weighed heavily on Kane, so much so that it felt like a struggle just to breathe in.

"He said that he could be lost on this trip," Shizuka said. Kane had to admire the strength of will that kept tremors from her voice. "You discovered his clothes… where?"

"In an area once called Iraq," Kane answered. "An ancient city called Eridu."

"Did you find his body?" Shizuka asked.

"No remains. Just his coat," Kane told her. "Brigid and Domi are looking now. We can find him and bring him back."

"That's why he used his mass to push me back here. That was the decision he would have made in order to abandon this time," Shizuka said. "Saving another's life."

Kane nodded. "Just don't talk about him as if he's dead, okay?"

Shizuka managed a weak smile.

"How are you feeling now?" Kane asked, to take her mind off Grant's fate.

"I feel like I was yanked through the eye of a needle by a team of oxen," Shizuka replied. "Stretched out, stressed out and fighting off nervous tics."

"The aperture you were drawn through is much like the eye of a needle, friend Shizuka," a familiar voice explained. Kane didn't have to look up to recognize Lakesh.

"Moe," Shizuka said in terms of greeting.

Kane kept the smile off his face in response to Lakesh's sigh. Domi had taken to calling the centuries-old scientist "Moe" as a term of endearment, and as a playful means of getting under Lakesh's skin. It hadn't hurt that she'd named a wild raccoon she'd adopted "Moe" as a sign of affection, much to the old man's chagrin. Shizuka had enjoyed the man's squirming, and her gentle ribbing was enough to tell Kane that she was getting her strength and spirit back. It was simply a matter of Lakesh figuring out what had gone wrong with the console and time platform, and Grant would return.

Lakesh was a swarthy subcontinent native with blue eyes, thanks to an anonymous body-bank, and silver-gray hair courtesy of a life extended by cybernetic surgery and cryogenic stasis. That he walked with pep and vigor despite being well over 250 years old was a gift from Sam the Imperator, who had also adopted many other identities, most notably Colonel Thrush and Enlil, leader of the Annunaki overlords. Lakesh's cybernetic implants had been broken down on an atomic scale by a swarm of Sam's nanites, the artificial and synthetic materials recombined as organic molecules, temporarily restoring his youth. *Youth* was a relative term, as physically the scientist was now in his late forties.

"You've done a number on this place," Lakesh said with disapproval in his tone.

"Not me. Grant busted the joint up," Kane replied, looking over the founder of Cerberus and the two young men with him.

Lakesh pursed his lips. "I'll have to ask him when we bring him back."

Kane nodded. "That's the idea, Lakesh. Getting my friend back is just a side effect of clearing my name."

"See, you can tell he's the hero. He's got a witty bon mot for every situation," a slender, bespectacled black man said to Morganstern, the Moon Base mathematician. The thin scientist was carrying a large duffel bag with him, as well as a laptop computer satchel over one shoulder.

"Waylon, this is real life. Not a TV show," Morganstern admonished.

Kane looked over the numbers genius's skinny friend. "Is this the Waylon who wanted to power the soda dispensers with plutonium?"

The scientist pushed his glasses up his nose, lips turning up in a chagrin-laden smirk. "That's me. Stephen Waylon, at your service."

"Good. We'll need that kind of brainpower to put the Chronos machinery back together," Kane said, resting his hand on the engineer's shoulder.

"Thanks, sir," Waylon replied. "I'll get right to it."

"You're here to work out whatever math is needed to pinpoint Grant?" Kane asked Morganstern.

"We have the approximate coordinates where Mr. Grant had been sent, and the general era, too," Morganstern said. "I'm more for computer support since Bry is sitting in as commander of Cerberus."

"Plus, young Daryl and friend Clem had been brainstorming as to what Grant's physical condition is on the other side of the time warp," Lakesh said. "Truly fascinating concepts…"

"He'll be healthy, right?" Kane asked. "I've been through a bad mat-trans jump…"

Morganstern subconsciously wiped some crust from the corner of his mouth, evidence that the mathematician's stomach wasn't used to being launched from wormhole to wormhole. "A good jump feels like a punch in the stomach, sir."

"Kane. I work for a living," Kane answered.

"Sorry," Morganstern answered. "A bad one…how's that?"

"Imagine your worst case of influenza," Kane responded. "Then compress that misery into five minutes to an hour."

Morganstern sighed. "Pure suckage."

"Indeed, friend Daryl," Lakesh agreed.

"So what about Grant?" Kane asked. "Did you get any data about his jump on the computers at Cerberus?"

Lakesh shook his head. "No. When the console shattered, we lost any uplink."

"What about the coordinates before everything was wrecked?" Kane asked.

"Nothing was programmed. Chances are that the mercenaries intended to just shoot them off blindly," Morganstern replied. "Or trap them in electronic stasis as pure data, like Sindri or Domi."

Lakesh shrugged. "We've been catching the Moon Base scientists up on what's been going on while they were asleep."

"They probably would have assumed that, with no target, the hostages would have been vaporized, and not have a clue that they were stored in computer memory," Kane countered. "Merkel and Allen didn't seem to be too nice."

"Fuck you, boy scout!" a snarl came from the doorway. Kane turned to see Sinclair crack the captive Merkel on the shoulder with her collapsible baton. Seeing the mercenary thug take a hit for his insolence didn't seem to be growing old for Kane, especially as Sinclair measured her strikes to cause pain, not to tear muscle or break bones.

"Sorry, Kane," Sinclair called out.

"Hey, it's every man's right to say what he thinks," Kane answered. "Just as long as he's willing to live with the consequences."

"Bastard," Merkel spit through a sneer.

The thwack of the baton on another part of Merkel's anatomy was good medicine for Kane's sour mood and worries. He turned back to Lakesh and Morganstern.

"Okay, what's this fascinating stuff Lakesh is blubbering about?" Kane asked.

"Well, Mr. Grant was pushed through the time stream during a trawl malfunction, correct?" Morganstern returned.

"That's why he's not here," Kane answered.

Morganstern nodded. "You already know about parallel universes from prior journeys and your encounters with Colonel Thrush. Those aren't dimensions, however, and Mr. Grant has traveled along a dimension."

"Except he hasn't traveled a length or a width, but a when?" Kane asked.

Morganstern's face brightened up. "Right. We're here in the third dimension. Most scientists agree that the fourth dimension is time, which ironically is the same dimension that we fold through when we mat-trans from one point to another."

Kane blinked. "I thought we went through a wormhole."

"This is all string theory, which means the wormhole is actually a point where the universe could be folded upon itself. In fact, according to string theory, instead of flat planes being bent to touch themselves and making a hole, reality is a string that can be folded over itself again and again," Morganstern explained.

Kane did something he'd thought he'd never do, look to Lakesh for a simpler explanation. Lakesh grinned.

"He is explaining it the simple way. Instead of strings, think of thin, flexible tubing as what the wormholes really are," Lakesh told him. "We squirt you through the tubing, and you extrude out the other end, which then closes the hole when it's sucked back."

"Like a flexible straw," Morganstern offered. "You hit the recall and…"

"So tell me again why this might be good for Grant?" Kane asked. "Because I saw Shizuka yanked through what looked like a column of water, and her body stretched through like something out of a cartoon."

"And at the same time Mr. Grant was disappearing as he contacted the event horizon?" Morganstern asked.

"Yeah…if that's what the freaky time field was," Kane said.

"It only looked as if Grant and Shizuka were being forced through a pinhole," Morganstern began. He shook his head. "Actually, they were probably entering a portal that was essentially only a few hydrogen radii across… but we're dealing with optical illusions. We can't really process how we look when we're moved through higher dimensions."

"Shizuka feels like she was stretched thinner than my patience," Kane said.

Morganstern cleared his throat, recognizing the veiled threat. "There would have been no actual physical trauma, as the temporal event was not caused by hypergravity, as in a black hole. A stellar singularity would literally stretch a human being into a long chain of atoms, while Mr. Grant and Ms. Shizuka's interaction with the temporal fold was a much more dimensionally elastic situation."

"In other words, because we're dealing with travel via a higher dimension's fold, my six-foot-plus buddy could fit through a microscopic hole," Kane said.

Morganstern nodded.

"So Grant will be feeling all right when he lands thousands of years ago in Mesopotamia?" Kane asked.

"Perhaps more than all right," Morganstern said. "He may not even be 'landed' all the way so to speak."

"Grant could show up as a ghost, like what happened when he appeared in Washington, D.C., the night Colonel Thrush sparked the atomic war," Kane suggested.

"Right," the mathematician agreed. "Or he could appear as some other dimensional shadow."

"Okay, because I can't see Baptiste having to struggle with a coat made of…shadow, you said?" Kane asked.

"Shadow. Image. Representation. Like a photograph is an echo of a three-dimensional world in two dimensions, Mr. Grant and his accoutrements will look real enough, but it's only what a two-dimensional world can display of the reality," Morganstern said.

Kane rubbed his eyebrows. "Thrush had no difficulty surviving the detonation of an earthshaker nuke, nor falling into a black hole. Though I thought that it was because he had millions of duplicates from other casements."

"Duplicates which themselves are tesseracts of an original entity," the mathematician noted. "A tesseract is…"

"A three-dimensional representation of something from a higher dimension," Kane said. "Baptiste told me that once. Grant could end up like Thrush?"

"Not in the whole 'conquer the omniverse with my big Galactus orb ship' way, but in that he could prove to be more difficult to harm simply by the dint that he's not entirely there," Morganstern explained.

Kane frowned, thinking of what Brigid had told him in regards to Grant's armored trench coat. It was unmistakably his, and hadn't appeared damaged or worn by the elements. Kane had been in enough cities to know that even a few hundred years of exposure would degrade clothing. Five millennia hadn't done one bit to rot the leather shell over the bulletproof, synthetic core…

"Okay, let me take a stab. Grant's coat has shown no signs of aging since it was stuck in the ruins thousands of years ago," Kane said. "That means aside from dust settling on it, time's taken no toll on it. No rot, no breakdown of the artificial fibers."

"The coat has become a tesseract. What we in three dimensions can see of the garment's shadow in our place," Morganstern told him. "It can be touched, felt and otherwise observed, but it's not interacting with reality."

Kane squinted. "So Grant could simply reappear in our time…unaged, unaffected by his trip?"

"Two problems with that theory. The world would have noticed an immortal person, especially someone as large and capable as Mr. Grant," Morganstern replied. "And just because the effects of aging on his coat have been minimized, we're not sure if Mr. Grant's tesseract in the other era is entirely immune to harm."

"But if only his shadow is destroyed, he should be fine," Kane said. "I don't die when someone obliterates my shadow with a flashlight."

"Nor do you come to harm when a flashlight is shone upon you," Morganstern told him. "Fire not only dissipates a shadow easily, but can destroy human flesh."

"And the Annunaki have plenty of firepower. Who's to say that they don't have their weapons calibrated to work on more than one dimension?" Kane asked.

"Brigid told me that she was under the assumption that's the reason Ullikummis's stone blade was formed from a material that, to her eyes, was indistinguishable from his own impenetrable hide. It's possible that such stone was the only material with the properties that could slay another Annunaki overlord. Presumably, this meant that there was some feature of these beings that made them impossible to harm by conventional means. Colonel Thrush and the Annunaki have all boasted of being creatures who exist in a multitude of planes of existence," Morganstern said. "While I doubt all of them made blades from their own bones…"

"It'd be why Enlil was not only so goddamn strong, even for his size, but how he survived a fall of several hundred feet," Kane said. "Ugh…this shit makes my head hurt."

"Congratulations. You've suffered your first quantum headache," Lakesh told Kane.

"So going back and just grabbing Grant isn't going to work. We'll only be bringing home a shadow," Kane said. "You guys have to funnel us to exactly where he is, not where his…tetra act?"

"Tesseract," Morganstern corrected.

Kane nodded. "That. So we could be stuck here trying to rescue him for a while."

"And there's no guarantee that we'd even encounter him in actual linear progression to his arrival," Lakesh added. "Friend Grant could be stuck in Urudug for weeks, months, even decades before we can retrieve him."

Kane's frown returned. "If we can get him back."

Silence once more fell like a curtain over the Chronos laboratory.

Chapter 6

They called Grant "Enkidu," which Shamhat had explained to him meant "man-bull." The months he'd spent as their captive, bound in chains he could not break or slip from, were long and frustrating. Since Grant had no memory of his own name, he simply went about calling himself Enkidu in his thoughts, figuring that it would have to do until…

Until what? Grant/Enkidu asked himself. Until I return to a world where I have my own name? When, Enkidu, would that be?

Wherever he was from, Enkidu/Grant was familiar with many of the creatures of this realm. He knew that the female escorting the small, cloaked freak was an Annunaki, though he didn't know her name. There was something vaguely familiar about the stone-mottled face looking at him from under his cowl, their eyes meeting through Ullikummis's veil of shadows.

The name Ullikummis seemed familiar to the burly captive, but Grant couldn't place where he'd heard it before. Mention of the name was an unusual bit of recognition that was made awkward because the face he saw didn't match the creature associated with the appellation Ullikummis. Those ancient Sumerian syllables conjured a giant made from hunks of stone that slid against each other, separated by veins of lavalike blood. There was something similar to the soulless black eyes of the Annunaki hybrid before him, and it had nothing to do with the creature's brother, Humbaba. How the similarity could exist when the Ullikummis of memory possessed eyes like white-hot coals eluded him, but there was something familiar about the youth. It was as if he was looking at an elephant; he could tell that one part was the tail of the beast because right now he saw the whole thing.

The others in the court of Urudug were long-lived creatures, but he could see them from a perspective that he was certain he'd never possessed before. Ullikummis, the young being standing before him, was a fluid, odd creation, something that possessed other forms, drastic changes from reptilian infant to a god carved from boulders. Grant tried to suppress his headaches, even as he tried the chains again, feeling their weight preventing the shrug of his powerful shoulders.

Ullikummis looked at him, a smirk of admiration bestowed upon the man, turning into a glare of derision pointed toward his half brother.

The visitation feast that Humbaba held for Ullikummis and his mother, Ninlil, went on for a long time. Grant gave up trying to gauge time here in the windowless, subterranean temple. It was more than simply a matter of not being able to see the sun; it was a function of his inability to gauge time at the same rate as the beings around him. For a time, Grant had mused that it was because these alien creatures simply weren't right in terms of their anchoring to time.

That was dashed aside when he was put with other human captives. Grant/Enkidu could see them as nothing a normal person could be like. Sitting with them, he was unable to speak their language, even after Shamhat tried to inject that knowledge into his brain via telepathic induction. Grant's mind resisted all but the gentlest, most subtle of psychic energies. Telepathic speech worked, but psychic probes into his past or future were rebuked by a psionic backlash that caused even the strongest of Igigi telepaths to cringe.

It was not just language that separated Grant from his fellow "apekin," as Shamhat and Humbaba had referred to them. Grant's senses were inundated with input. When he stood with them, when he tried to talk to them, when he interacted with them, he could see the present clearly, but he also saw shadows of moments ago and moments ahead. It was what had given the captive known as Enkidu the advantage in his initial combat with the Nephilim guards. The blurred shadows of movements to arrive allowed Grant sufficient warning to counter their moves with his own.

Physical touches were similar. He could sense that he would feel the caress of a female human slave or the sharp backhand of an irate Shamhat before they came. Smells and sounds had the same swooping-by effect. After four months, the oddness of the world around Grant had ceased to be a cause for concern. He was used to it.

The world was nothing but an odd dream, things arriving in slow motion and leaving echoes in all of his senses. At first, it was distraction enough to keep him cowed, but that had only lasted a week until he'd wrapped his chains around the throat of one of his guards, crushing the drone's neck. Even incapable of full movement due to his bindings, the man-bull had enough freedom to kill three more guards and injure a half-dozen more before he was beaten.

That was when the heavier, secondary-orichalcum chains had been placed upon him. His ability to struggle in them was limited by their great mass. For the past two months, Grant could shift somewhat in them, utilizing the few millimeters of slack that the manacles allowed him. There was no way he could ever break such bonds, but it was better than sitting helplessly between interrogation and indoctrination sessions.

The young Ullikummis had retired for the night, his mother following a short time after, so now the feast was filled with Humbaba's lackeys, all seeking the approbation of their bestial lord.

One of the Igigi, not Shamhat, cackled and grabbed a Nubian slave, twisting her arm off and tossing her toward Humbaba. "The greatest share for the greatest in station!"

Humbaba roared with laughter, catching the girl and hauling her up to his great jaws.

"No!" Enkidu bellowed, straining against the chains that held him.

It was too late. Humbaba's jaws closed, the slave's ribs snapping in half before the lion-god threw his head back to swallow. Stringy lengths of sinew and entrails adorned his bloody maw as he gnashed and chewed violently, seeming to take pleasure in the distress of a slave being devoured bloodily before him.

Grant/Enkidu felt Shamhat's attention, and a glance showed the Igigi slave master smirking with a realization. Grant didn't like that.

"We shall talk after this, Enkidu," Shamhat told him. "And you will finally be tamed."

The man-bull of Urudug fought to loosen his chains, struggling even as he knew that he was lost.

HUMBABA LET the guts of the human dangle from his leonine muzzle, sitting back on his throne. He waited for

Shamhat to return from Enkidu's cell, occupying himself with the sexual ministrations of a pair of slaves, their mouths making wonderful music in his lap.

The females were Semites, not Nubians like the young thing he'd torn into at Ohsad's prompting. Humbaba had found that the humans were nervous about tending to his desires if they were of the same race as one he had taken as live food. He rested one clawed paw on the back of the olive-skinned slave's head, the tips of two talons scratching lightly on her scalp. That elicited a yelp of dismay, and she nearly squirmed out of his grasp. Humbaba grimaced, realizing that he had to be careful with these fragile beings. Movements that would be a gentle caress for an Annunaki lover would draw blood and tear muscle with one of these delicate harlots. It wasn't that Humbaba cared about their feelings; they were as insects beneath the humans themselves. However, the god-prince of Urudug wished to complete his pleasuring before the slave girls were thrown into panic and slain for their transgressions.

Once he had been sated by their mouths and supple bodies, then Humbaba would have no concern about twisting them apart like loaves of bread and supping on their flesh.

Shamhat, however, picked the moment before Humbaba was to reach climax to enter his chambers, a crooked grin crossing his snakelike lips. "We have our leash on Enkidu."

Humbaba swiveled his angry, glaring eyes toward the Igigi slave lord. "Now?"

Shamhat chuckled. "My presence has never interrupted your enjoyment of the humans before, beloved master."

Humbaba tried to fight off the urge to grin, but the Igigi was correct. The Annunaki were creatures that were extremely long-lived. Experimentation in intimacy was another means of allaying the boredom of eternity. Lovemaking, conquest, conspiracy, scientific experimentation, all of it was just a dalliance, an attempt to keep at bay the growing dissatisfaction at the lack of purpose in their lives. They called themselves gods, and indeed they were powerful beings, long-lived, possessed of fantastic technologies that could hurl them across the galaxy as easily as a boat could ford a stream.

Humbaba himself had been such a distraction for his father, Enlil. By his half-Annunaki nature, he was given his own court to rule over, to plot in, and the charge of protection of the Cedar Forest, as the human Sumerians called it. The plants grown in this alien Eden-like garden were crops brought from Nibiru, fruits that succored the Annunaki, granting them the nourishment and enzymes that made their bodies last longer, be stronger, endure near impossible injuries.

Humbaba had long known that he was merely a guard dog, looked down upon by some of the pure-blooded brothers of Enlil. Still, his father's station granted the leonine godling a princely rank and authority over armies of Nephilim drones and Igigi servants. His physical power was sufficient to quell any sense of rebellion among the other minions of the Annunaki, and even some of the other children of Enlil's brethren. He was part of a grand game that played out for the entertainment of the overlords, a spectator sport where armies clashed and assassins skulked. Humbaba had played the bloodsport well enough that he was concerned that he had become less than entertaining.

When Ullikummis came of age, Humbaba wondered if they would be cast into conflict against each other. The natural power of a ten-foot half Anhur, half Annunaki warrior would be hard-pressed against Enlil's son as his skin grew more and more stony. The child, a mere eight years old, was as tall as most humans hoped to be, so a growth spurt would put the freak at least as tall as Humbaba, maybe even larger.

It would be a good game, the godling thought. Humbaba looked forward to their conflict, the test of sinew against stone, lion's blood against whatever would surge through the limbs of a living rock slide. Right now, however, Humbaba's boredom was such that he shoved his concubines aside to join Shamhat in Enkidu's cell.

The servant girls watched their gigantic master stride away from them, still in a state of arousal, but no longer caring for their seductive touch. Their eyes were wide with fear, wondering if his dismissal of them would result in their deaths, but in truth, Shamhat had prolonged their meager existences. Still, the scent of their fear was a heady drug to Humbaba.

"So, what leash can we utilize on this damnable aberration of a human?" Humbaba asked.

"This is a creature who cares for his fellow humans, despite the distance between them," Shamhat said. "Though they do not share language or even similar perception, his heart is tied to them. Should harm befall them, or the threat of harm, his will buckles."

"We assailed him with tortures, but he endured them endlessly," Humbaba noted. "It is compassion which has broken this wild steed."

The creature they called Enkidu regarded Humbaba and Shamhat with dark, baleful eyes. There was a rage surging behind those angry orbs, a fury no doubt incited by the spill of blood and severed body parts strewed on Shamhat's table.

"Compassion…such an underused term in this realm of apes," Shamhat mused, picking up a small hand off of his butcher's block.

Fuckers!

The thought was so filled with vitriol and rage that Humbaba took a step back. He'd lowered his telepathic shields in order to hear what Enkidu had to say, but this was a mental bellow that, if were uttered aloud, would have left eardrums ringing.

The half-lion god picked up a severed human drumstick and wandered closer to the imprisoned human. "Please, Enkidu, why are you—?"

"Shut the fuck up!" Grant/Enkidu shouted. "Give me that murderous snake-face, give him to me now!"

Even if Humbaba's mind hadn't translated the odd polylinguistic barks of the ape, Enkidu's meaning wouldn't have been clearer. Froth formed on his lips as he regarded the Igigi as he nibbled on the fingers of the tiny, severed hand.

"Snake-face," Humbaba repeated softly. The telepathic understanding of that word amused the lion-god. "Yes, that's what they are."

"I'll kill him. I'll kill you, too," Enkidu threatened. "Fucking murderous fucks."

"You try, the humans will suffer," Humbaba said, picking up on Shamhat's suggestions.

Enkidu's face screwed up in frustration, his eyes flitting between Humbaba and his Igigi minion. "You'd do it, too. I know your snake-face kind."

Humbaba rested his taloned hand on Enkidu's. "My face is not that of a snake, foolish ape."

"You told me you're Annunaki. The son of Enlil," Grant said. "And I know who and what Enlil is. He's the worst serpent of all."

Humbaba managed a smile. "You know my father, seemingly personally, and yet you are clueless as to who you are, what you are. How can I take a mystery like you seriously if you're so confused?"

"You're taking me seriously enough to wrap me in these chains. You've lost how many of your Nephilim to me?" Enkidu/Grant returned. "You try mind probes and other shit. And now, you assholes cut up women to get a rise out of me."

The seething anger flowed from the human as if it were sweat rolling off him in the course of combat. The man-bull's fingers flexed with the kind of strength that had allowed him to use steel chain as a garrote and twist off a Nephilim drone's head effortlessly. Normally, Humbaba wasn't impressed with physical displays of strength, but this was different. The odd human traveler *knew* who Enlil was, and was not intimidated by one who was the Annunaki lord's own progeny There were those who had their own sponsorship of Enlil's "equals," such as Marduk's child Harkul, renowned to be the strongest of all creatures on Earth, who had the courage and might to back up their willingness to engage Humbaba one on one, but Enkidu had fallen once in battle to the lion-godling, and had no such patron who would guard him.

Yet, what fear there was in the man-bull was drowned out by anger that Humbaba had not seen, even with the most painful; of tortures at the burning ASP projectors or the lash of steel cord whips on his back. Enkidu/Grant was not immune to pain; he had buckled and cried out for mercy as skin was burned, blood was drawn and flesh was flayed.

The fury over abuses of fellow humans, this was new. This was aggression unfettered. When he'd first arrived, he battled mightily, but only in self-defense. His slaying of the drones was an attempt to escape and to fend off others who sought to beat him down. There was animosity, but Enkidu/Grant had restrained himself. Now, the secondary orichalcum chains ground against each other, the metal singing as he strained against them. He'd never snap them, but the muscles and veins bulged down his long, powerful limbs.

Humbaba clubbed him in the crook of his neck, a chop designed to overwhelm his nerves yet render him unconscious with a minimum of damage. Normally, the impact would have dropped even the strongest of human soldiers, but the man-bull weathered it, only falling to his knees. Smoldering brown eyes glared up at the son of Enlil, Grant's lips curled in defiant rage.

Humbaba struck again, another nerve punch. Finally, the rebellious human slumped into unconsciousness.

"What manner of beast are you, Enkidu?" Humbaba asked rhetorically to the insensate Grant.

STEPHEN WAYLON REGARDED Daryl Morganstern with a cocked eyebrow.

"I'm just here because I can jury-rig a 3.2-gigahertz circuit board out of Styrofoam and tinfoil," he told the mathematician. "I work on things I can touch—understanding quantum physics is outside my realm. You want to reprogram this to do what?"

Morganstern rubbed his brow. "To be able to open a standing portal into the fifth dimension so that we can locate Mr. Grant's actual form, and not the tesseract projected into the third dimension."

Waylon blinked. "The fifth dimension is at a right angle to time, right?"

"More accurately, it's duration, according to my professor, Robert Bryanton," Morganstern replied. "The direction we're traveling through duration is known as time, so the opposite direction is antitime."

Waylon winced and pulled out a notebook and drew a few lines sloppily. "So duration is a length, the fifth is the width vector of duration, perpendicular, but still a flat plane. The fifth dimension is…the direction of alternate choice?"

"Called probability space, and it's highly fluid," Morganstern told him. "At least as far as we can experience it from our position along the time stream."

"It presumably becomes more stable when viewed from higher dimensions, right?" Waylon asked, leaving the notebook next to his tool roll.

"I'm still trying to work out the mathematical proofs on that," Morganstern answered. "I'm trying to reassemble the theories from the extant data that Brigid has pulled up for me."

"You're going to flaunt your relationship with Cerberus's Amazon princess, aren't you?" Waylon asked.

Morganstern smiled sheepishly. "Wouldn't you?"

"Heroines don't like being treated like trophies, my friend," Waylon answered. "Listen, I'm going to put this back together according to the design specs Lakesh provided for me. We'll work out what holes we want to open once this spaghetti and broken chips becomes coherent machinery again."

Morganstern nodded, and Waylon knew that the mathematician was disappointed at not being able to talk more about string theory and Everett's many-worlds interpretation at length with someone who had the scientific background to comprehend it. The engineer had work to do, however, and the conversation would only delay the return of Grant to the halls of Cerberus.

Waylon turned to the counter where he'd laid out his tools on a black nylon roll of pouches. It was a compulsive disorder symptom, but Waylon had developed it as a way to distract his attention from snickers and chuckles behind his back. Growing up African-American in Chicago with his eclectic and decidedly nerdy pursuits had left him with the need for mental and emotional armor against bullies.

Because of this obsessive attention to detail and demand for an orderly workplace, Waylon noticed that one of his screwdrivers was on the floor. Morganstern hadn't touched his tools; Waylon had drawn that line in the sand long ago. No one else was on hand to have moved his equipment, and it was highly unlikely that the implement had self-motivated. Waylon frowned as he looked at the screwdriver.

He pulled his pocket recorder—a boon he cherished since he often thought too fast to keep up with pen and paper—and turned it on. "I humbly request you not meddle with my tools, sir. If you wish communication, I have an electronic recording device present. Speak, and while you may not be audible to my ears, the digital media will be sensitive enough."

Waylon left the recorder running for a few minutes as he resoldered resistors to a stripped circuit board. Only the soft hiss of alloy dissolving under the heated iron tip met his ears, and he kept his breath low and soft as he worked. There was a brief instance of a man's sweat reaching his nostrils, overwhelming the scent of the solder wire. Waylon looked up, and watched a trail of smoke spiral toward the temporal-dilation platform.

"So you are done?" Waylon asked.

The smoke dissipated, and he rewound the recorder for playback. While Waylon was a man of science, he was also someone with a curiosity about things for which physics had no explanation. Among those were paranormal occurrences, things that had been tied to ghost or poltergeist activity. Key indicators of ghostly activity involved items seemingly moving by themselves and electronic voice phenomena. Since this was a time where telepathic seven-foot-tall aliens sought to usurp humanity's control of the Earth, Waylon was able to suspend his skepticism to give traditional ghost-hunting tactics an effort. As well, when it came to ghosts, Waylon had been open to the concept that their difficult to quantify and qualify existence had been a symptom of transdimensional contact. Morganstern had only spent a few minutes trying to point out that Grant was not in a traditional time-trawl destination.

Waylon took a few moments to review the audio recording. What he heard sent a bolt of nerve-chilling cold through his body.

"Mr. Kane!"

"Just…what is it?" Kane asked, dismissing his frustration at honorifics.

"Listen," Waylon told him, handing over the digital recorder.

The small speaker released a raspy, halting rumble. "Tell…Kane…lost…body…find me."

Kane shuddered. It sounded like Grant, except the voice had the odd echo effect of an Annunaki. He looked at Waylon. "Where did you get this?"

Waylon pointed. "I think it's an electronic voice phenomenon."

"Ghost speech," Kane muttered. He'd become familiar with paranormal activity while doing research on telepathy after his encounters with Balam, the Archon. Unfortunately, research on psychic ability was limited to magazines that shared article space with ape-men, ghosts and UFOs. Kane ended up reading those, as well, curiosity lured in by lurid titles and photographs.

The recorder continued to play, the eerie voice speaking again.

"Brigid…no! Away from…room…"

Kane whirled, activating his Commtact reflexively. "Baptiste! Baptiste! Report in now!"

Chapter 7

Mariah Falk did some mental calculations as they reached the bottom of the ramp before making her announcement. "Judging by gradient, distance and the rock content of the walls, we've gone at least two hundred feet down from the surface. What do the cuneiform say?"

"I'm not quite certain thanks to the syntax of this particular dialect," Brigid answered the geologist. "The symbols are familiar…"

"But the language is different. Like Chinese and Japanese?" Domi asked.

Brigid smirked. "How'd you know that?"

Domi blushed. "I asked Shizuka to read something for me. It was Chinese, and she explained. Went into something about two Chinese languages, too."

Brigid nodded, then looked to Mariah. "Two hundred feet below the surface?"

"Yes, but given that this is a narrow corridor, it's structurally sound," the geologist said. She swept the wall with her flashlight, frowning. "You two might think I'm crazy, but the air feels heavier down here."

Domi's ruby-red eyes glinted in the reflected torchlight, making it seem as if she was tapping some feral vision sense. That the albino actually possessed excessively light-sensitive eyes only added to the eerie chill running up and down Mariah's spine. "No fresh rot. Old tomb."

Mariah swallowed. She could tell that Domi was in fight-or-flight mode. The heroes of the Cerberus redoubt were legendary, their tales spreading and taking on mythic proportions, like tales from a lurid pulp novel. Personality traits like the clipped, primitive diction Domi dropped into when under stress were common knowledge among the scientists who came down from the Manitius Base. Her hand hovered close to the Glock she wore on her hip, her nerves on edge because she knew that she was the weakest link if mayhem should come. Unbidden, the memory of the "red shirts" in fiction came to her mind. She could easily see how she was just an incidental character who could be killed off.

"No movement. Just…strange," Domi said. Her eyes disappeared as she turned away. She was so far from the spill of the flashlight that she was a shadow in the darkness.

Brigid stepped from the wall. "The Cedar Forest?"

Mariah turned to the archivist as she spoke. "What?"

"The Cedar Forest. We're on the so-called staircase to the Cedar Forest," Brigid said. "As far as I can take from the cuneiform."

"Cedar trees make for a strange underground forest. Sure it's not some form of subterranean fungi?" Mariah asked.

"The translation is to a word that we call *cedar* now, but there is the possibility that we're looking at something different," Brigid said. "According to the tale of Humbaba, the fruit of the Cedar Forest granted those who ate it a form of immortal life. That's why Gilgamesh and Enkidu came to the forest and slew Humbaba."

Mariah frowned. "Eternal life? That never sounds good. Eternal youth has some draw, but you live a few centuries, while aging normally, you end up looking like a plucked chicken as your skin sags from gravity and your joints swell from erosion."

"You've thought about this?" Brigid asked.

"Just a mental what-if game," Mariah said. "As a little girl, I read about an item which granted you three wishes. Careless wording of wishes ended up in a dead child, and his mutilated corpse crawling out of a grave and knocking at a door."

"So you wanted to make sure that if you were granted such a wish, you didn't end up screwed by the jinni," Brigid surmised.

Mariah nodded. "As an intellectual exercise. Outwitting the little imps who want to ruin me."

"Did you ever decide the best wish to make?" Brigid asked.

"Yes. Get the hell out of my life and leave me completely alone," Mariah said. "And look where it got me. A two-hundred-year nap and waking up in a suburb of hell. Didn't even think the bastards existed, and they screw me for intellectual exercises."

"Your loss, sadly, is our gain," Brigid told her. "And hopefully, it's a boon to the rest of the world. We need smart people to rebuild."

Mariah nodded. "Well, it's not as if I can quit and go home. I couldn't have done it when I went to the Moon. Besides, while the neighborhood sucks, I like my new roommates."

The sudden flash of Domi's ruby-red eyes, glimmering like blood droplets in the glow of her torch, caused Mariah to flinch. "Found a door."

"Where?" Brigid and Mariah asked.

The geologist idly wondered what Edwards was doing now. Of course, he'd chosen to stay behind as his bulk would be difficult to fit into the tiny hatch they'd blown in the temple roof. Even if he could squirm through the hole, it would be hard to contact him as the Commtact he wore no longer had the ability to broadcast. Right now, he supplemented the cybernetic communicator with a handheld walkie-talkie.

"Edwards? Can you still read us?" Mariah asked.

"Still here, Falk," the big ex-Mag replied. "Remarkably good signal, as well."

Brigid frowned. "Any movement outside?"

"Negative. All quiet out here. Any signs of life down there?" Edwards asked.

"We're looking," Brigid answered. "Baptiste out."

Mariah wondered at the sudden grim tone that the archivist had taken when she heard the soft scritch in the darkness, from the direction of the door that Domi had discovered. She studied the feral girl's silhouette, noting that she had drawn both her pistol and the knife from her belt sheath.

"Not good," Domi grumbled.

"Not necessarily," Brigid replied. She turned on the flashlight attached to her Copperhead. "How big of a chamber can be on the far side of that door, Mariah?"

Falk ran through some mathematical figures in her mind, lighting up the doorway. It was carved from ancient wood, whole tree trunks utilized and bound together with steel bands. She released a low whistle, staring at a barrier that was easily forty feet tall. The cedar logs were two feet in diameter, and through uneven gaps between the trunks, she could see other logs resting against them.

"We're looking at a four-foot-thick pair of doors," Mariah said. "They're stretching...eighty feet wide?"

Brigid nodded in concurrence. "I'd say that."

Mariah looked to the ceiling, but it was so high up her light couldn't touch it. She swallowed, trying to return moisture to her drying mouth. "Last time I saw a door that big, there was a giant gorilla looking for a bride on the other side."

"Please focus, Mariah. We've handled all manner of apes before. What kind of subterranean caves can we anticipate down here?" Brigid asked.

Mariah frowned. "We've dropped another hundred, hundred and fifty feet on the slope down. And we're not looking at ancient peoples using primitive tools. We could be looking at something that makes the temple seem like a postage stamp…"

Mariah's flashlight fell on a shadowed alcove to the right of the door, where the scratching sound seemed to emanate from. The constant grating had not changed in urgency, despite all of the conversation. Domi crouched before it, like a pointer illuminating a nest of pheasant for a hunter to shoot down. Brigid took a few steps to the other side of the alcove.

"Maintenance hatch, presumably," Brigid noted.

"Presumably," Mariah agreed. "It'd make things easier than hauling those doors open, not that there seems to be any unlocking mechanism on this side."

"It wouldn't make sense to put the handles of a vault on the outside, where they could be easily manipulated," Brigid said. "There also don't seem to be any controls on this access hatch."

Mariah peered around the corner of the alcove. Her flashlight dimmed for a moment, as did the torch mounted under Brigid's rifle. "What the hell?"

"It got cold," Brigid said softly. "I feel as if something is pushing against me."

"Grant," Domi called out in a harsh whisper. "I hear him over my Commtact. Get away from that door."

"Grant?" Brigid asked. "Are you sure? There's no…"

"Brigid, *move!*" Domi urged. She rushed forward, small callused hands grabbing both Brigid and Falk by the wrists and tugged them with strength that belied her tiny size.

The scratching suddenly turned to pounding.

"What is that?" Mariah asked, leveling her Glock at the door as Domi whirled to face it.

"He can't say," Domi replied. "Worse than me."

"Edwards, can you read me?" Brigid asked over her Commtact.

"Blood!" Mariah pointed out. "Under the door!"

The three women looked at a growing puddle. On second glance at the thick, cloying fluid, Mariah had been generous calling it blood, it was more brown than red. Domi, however, pushed her back farther, keeping her pistol aimed at the door. The pounding hammered louder and louder, the door starting to shift against its jamb. Dust poured on the surface of the spreading mass of fluid, sticking to the surface as if it had a rubbery skin.

"What the hell is behind there?" Mariah asked, the strength leaving her voice, the Glock's glowing green front sight trembling as she aimed it.

"We're not staying to find out," Brigid said as the door's hammering increased. "Edwards? Can you hear us?"

The radio silence was an eerie counterpoint to the crack and crunch of the slowly failing door.

STRETCHED ACROSS TIME, Grant's consciousness was fractured. He cast shadows in different eras, different places, while his core being was trapped in an area where he truly had no means of interaction. As such, only thin spurts of information were able to be shared between his disparate tesseracts.

In his home time, the shadow cast from the dimension he was trapped in was a consciousness, an energy form that was the equivalent of a ghost, capable of manipulating small objects with the greatest of physical effort, and inaudible except to electronic devices. Grant had his identity there, the memories of himself and his loved ones and, as such, was tormented in that he could see Kane brooding and absorbed with concern.

He grasped helplessly, a phantom that couldn't tug at his friend's sleeve. He'd scream, and yet no one heard. It was only when Waylon, the scrawny little freezie from the Moon, pulled out the recorder that Grant had a flicker of hope.

That hope was dashed when Grant tried to speak but found his vocabulary gone. That part of his temporal shadow was hurtled back five millennia to where the far more solid tesseract existed. His words were shunted away from him, trapped in a body without a clue of its identity.

Grant wanted to hit something, but even at his strongest jolt of solidity, all he could do was affect a rapping. He didn't receive feedback; he felt nothing that he touched. It was a twisted nightmare from which he couldn't awaken. In frustration, he turned to someone who might know better. Brigid Baptiste was one of the most intelligent women that he knew, and simply thinking of her, he was whisked across the globe at the speed of thought.

Waylon had demonstrated that he could be heard electronically, and Grant, the ghost, tried to work with that. Domi and Brigid were together, and through that personal link, as well as the cybernetic communicators installed in their mandibles, Grant would have the ability to make himself heard.

He hovered around them, bodiless, speaking and not being heard as Brigid and Domi, accompanied by a woman he recognized as Mariah Falk, examined a huge pair of doors wrought from thick logs. Grant realized that neither of his friends could hear him. This barren tomb was different than the Operation Chronos laboratory.

Grant was trying to think, to concentrate in order to figure out why he couldn't be heard when Falk's light began to dim. Energized by a sudden influx of electricity from the flashlight's battery, the time-tossed phantasm had not only mental clarity, but a voice again. He was drawing power from the torch, something that not only allowed him to broadcast, but to think and make mental connections.

"Domi!" Grant called. "Brigid!"

The two women reacted to his cry. They tensed, acknowledging his speech, picked up by the acutely sensitive transceivers in their Commtacts.

Five millennia back down the time stream, the body of Grant, or at least the shadow trapped in that era, was learning. Information, related directly to the giant cedar gate, flowed across the chord that connected them to their base identity. The being that was called Enkidu by the ancient Annunaki who held him captive was brought to the massive doors to the "forest" beyond.

Grant, a man outside of time, realized that Domi, Brigid and Mariah were frozen, like a pause frame, as the experience of his past shadow caught up with him.

Grant had no face, but he grimaced as he knew he had no means of communicating back with his time-lost body.

ENKIDU/GRANT RESENTED the leash of black steel links around his neck as he was led by Shamhat, the Igigi slave master, toward what the reptilian called the garden of cedar. It was a symbol of his defeat at the hands of the godling who had "tamed the man-beast."

"What is that?" Enkidu asked, looking at the massive doors. It was comprised of thick logs, and he didn't think that anything short of teams of oxen could pry them apart. Again, the amnesiac hated that he had all of this intelligence but was completely in the dark about his own identity. He could gauge the mass of a pair of doors, but his parents' names and his home city eluded his faculties. Even as he spoke, he heard the "pre-echoes" of Shamhat's voice, the words flowing slowly, echoing in his ears in a manner he knew wasn't right but couldn't correct.

"The gates of the garden, man-bull," Shamhat answered. "I intend to ask a boon of you, and as such, we need you at your strongest."

Enkidu/Grant glared at Shamhat with hatred sharp as the knife he wished he'd possessed. He could easily imagine the Igigi's internal organs spilling between scales parted by an unforgiving blade. "If I get strong enough, this little piece of jewelry won't save your scrawny neck."

Shamhat's reptilian lips curved up in a toadlike smirk. "Upon my death, thirty children will be thrown into lye."

"Fucking bastard," Grant retorted.

Shamhat tilted his head. "You seem to think of a term for fornication as a verb, an adverb and a noun, and it's an insult. What a remarkable four letters you brought from your time."

"I brought a lot more, but the curses are the only spite I can hurl at you which won't end in murdered people," Enkidu replied.

"Fuck," Shamhat repeated. "It is a guttural, sharp word. It requires emphasis, and it feels cathartic. So far, it amuses me, beast. But such amusement only goes so far."

"You're taking me into your garden?" Enkidu/Grant inquired. "For what?"

"The taste of a fruit necessary for you to deal with Gi Malesh," Shamhat told him.

Enkidu's frown was buried behind a shaggy beard and an overgrown, drooping mustache, but it was blatantly evident in his eyes and brow. "Gi Malesh. Who is he?"

"She," Shamhat corrected. "She is Humbaba's rival, and you shall slay her."

"Another snake-face?" Grant asked.

"Annunaki," Shamhat admonished him again. "You shall speak of your betters with respect, not derision."

"Petty motherfuckers like you don't even approach inferiority," Enkidu growled. "You've got numbers and you've got firepower. I'd be stupid to fight with you with all of that, but I don't have to admire the Annunaki's so-called noble fucking birth."

"They rule your world," Shamhat warned. "They control the fate of your people."

From beneath a wrinkled brow, the man-bull regarded the wielder of his leash. "So you say, but the weapons and clothing you took from me are evidence that we have our own strengths, and we've somehow put you behind us. I knew the Annunaki and the Nephilim, but I'd never heard of no Iggy-pop."

Shamhat's yellow eyes narrowed at the implication.

"You fuckers are extinct in the world I come from. Not even a footnote, otherwise—" He was going to say that someone would have told him, but even as he felt the impulse to say the name, to relay that memory, the thought tumbled away, fracturing under the act of observation. "Otherwise, I would have heard about you."

Shamhat saw the pause, saw the frustration of his amnesia and laughed. "Says the man with holes in his memory."

The doors rolled open, shoved by gaunt figures who were more dead than alive, skin gray in pallor. A few looked up from their task of moving the great cedar gates, the remnants of a spark in otherwise black, glassy eyes. Enkidu had seen such creatures on only rare occasions before. The name for them was apparent.

Zombies.

"More unlucky bastards taking bites from your garden?" Enkidu asked.

Shamhat chuckled. "Same patch of land, but different fruit. We have given them the sup that will ensure their eternal servitude in conditions your kind would succumb to."

Dozens of them had set to work pushing doors three logs thick, and countless more toiled, working in the darkened depths of the garden. Lights were sparse, tiny islands of glow visible to the human's eyes, but probably fully illuminated for the alien creature beside him.

"I take it these zombies don't have to see," Grant said.

Shamhat shook his head. "Not for their duties here. They serve in perpetuity, needing naught, thanks to their last meal. They till the Earth, care for the plants of the garden, and they will swarm and defend it with what passes for their lives."

The warrior that used to be Grant saw that though they were slender and sagging, their limbs still retained power, and they moved tirelessly. There were dozens at the door, and scores more visible around the dim stars of light in the garden. In the shadows, there could have been five for every one he'd seen. It was a literal army.

"Worry not, Enkidu. They will not turn upon me, and as you are with me…"

"Worried?" Enkidu countered. "Just counting."

In the glow, he could see the plants they were working on. Some of them resembled giant mushrooms, and some instinct told him that the other odd, bulbous growths were similar types of fungus. Here in the catacombs beneath the court of Urudug, spores from distant stars grew easily without sunlight or rain. Enkidu looked through the eyes of Grant, adapting to the shadows, and saw the reflected glints of glassy black eyes, spread out like a sea of stars in inky darkness. The time-lost human lost count of the pairs, and knew that anyone who stumbled into this subterranean garden would face a horde of implacable rage.

With that thought, Enkidu/Grant's head swam, as if something had reached into his skull, scooping out the realization and dragging it away. It wasn't a psychic assault. He'd already been assailed by some of the strongest minds in the region. He wanted to howl, to call out to the thing touching his brain, but as soon as the wave of dissonance passed, his contact with what could be his identity was gone.

He glared at the ghouls in the fungal garden, realizing that whatever knowledge he'd now experienced was pulled forward, perhaps to his home time.

"Godspeed," he whispered as the tingling subsided.

DOMI'S WILDERNESS-TRAINED SENSES made her far more attuned to subtle undercurrents of sound, and she could hear the sudden rise of a low-frequency set of moans and groans with the soggy slaps on the access hatch beside the gigantic cedar gate. Her muscles were drawn tight in her arms and legs, instincts kicking in. The fluid seeping under the door was bloodlike, but it was something that smelled old and rotted, something ancient and horrible. If the heightened adrenaline of combat mode allowed her to articulate, Domi would warn Brigid and Mariah Falk that whatever was "bleeding" on the other side was something that hadn't been human for years, if not centuries.

As it was, the albino warrior woman kept herself between the failing barrier and her friends, her heart hammering inside of her petite chest, her already white knuckles stretched even more taut as she grasped her Detonics .45 and combat knife. The Copperhead slung across her back might have given her the advantage in firepower, but the two weapons she clutched tightly were things that she knew intimately. In her feral war-state, she could naturally work them both. They were akin to the claws and fangs of a mountain lion, instinctive weaponry that didn't require much thought to operate. They were parts of her, and the groans of the horde battering at the door had awakened the deep-down knowledge that she'd have to be at her absolute fighting best.

The stone slab cracked in the center, already shifting violently.

A whine pierced Domi's eardrum as the Commtact released a high-pitched note, a tone that reminded her of Grant despite it being an electronic squeal. Images shot across her mind's eye, moving too quickly for her to comprehend except that there was something evil, soulless on the other side of the collapsing door.

"Tell me something I don't know," Domi growled as she backed up, keeping herself as a human wall between her friends and the unknown threat that was destroying a chunk of stone that had stood for thousands of years.

Eyes stretching out like a sea of stars glared back out of her imagination, black, glassy orbs set in gaunt, gray, pallid faces. They were the visages of dead things that still moved with unnatural vitality.

Domi turned, and saw that Brigid and Mariah Falk had reached the base of the ramp. Teeth gritted, the feral warrior girl continued backing up.

"Domi! Come on!" Brigid shouted. "Grant showed me…something. We can't fight it!"

"Go!" Domi countered. "Be after you."

The slab split and came apart. Mangled limbs flailed momentarily, their owners collapsing to the floor, trampled by the tidal wave of semihumanity surging forward behind it. Dark, oily-skinned figures stumbled out of the bottleneck of the access hatch, staggering for balance.

Domi glanced back. Brigid and Mariah were gone. Would they have enough of a cushion to get away now?

She studied the spastic movements of the soulless puppets as they jerked toward her. They stared at the albino girl with gibbering rage, but most of them were slow, dragging broken limbs. Something leaped from the group, however, possessing a speed and energy rivaling the living.

Gnarled, clawlike fingers raked the air, seizing at Domi as she swung her knife to fight off the bestial humanoid. Others of similar swiftness broke off from the staggering horde to fall upon her.

Chapter 8

Edwards grimaced. Something had suddenly drained the batteries on his walkie-talkie, as well as the spares he had pocketed as a contingency. Whatever had sucked the electricity out of them had produced a couple of odd squeaks on his Commtact—it was capable of receiving, not transmitting. If he were a more curious sort, he'd have pondered the mystery of the dead cells. Instead, Edwards knew that if he was out of contact with Brigid Baptiste and Domi, then it was a full-blown emergency.

The gap he'd cut through the stone was nominally large enough for him to squeeze through, but in practice, with his gear, he was having a devil of a time pushing into the hole. He'd shoved his pack and rifle through, discarding the dead walkie-talkie as superfluous. His first try showed that his equipment harness was hanging up on the lips of the opening. Luckily, since it was combat gear, it had secure but quick release snaps. The belts and suspenders of the load-bearing vest came off. Without magazine and equipment pouches slowing him down, Edwards slithered through, grunting as he shifted his wide shoulders enough to get the largest part through the hole. Hanging on to the lip with both hands, he twisted until his feet were free and he dropped to the floor.

Edwards pulled on his battle harness and had taken a few steps when a familiar voice called out.

"Edwards!" He turned and saw Kane, framed in the hole he'd just come through.

"When did you arrive?" the CAT Beta member asked.

"A moment ago. We can't contact Baptiste and the others," Kane said.

"Get in here, then," Edwards grunted. "My radio's batteries died, even ones just in my pocket."

Kane didn't have the struggle that Edwards suffered through, slithering into the temple without doffing any of his gear. Sela Sinclair was on his heels, their weapon lights clicking on as soon as they hit the floor. "Something sucked the juice out of your walkie-talkie? Did you hear anything over your Commtact?"

"Something, but it was just noise, a howl," Edwards said as Kane took the point.

Sinclair took up position at the opposite point of the V formation from Edwards. "Kane's Commtact picked up Grant."

"Wasn't he sent back in time?" Edwards asked.

"It's not that easy to explain," Kane returned. "Hold up…"

As if the lean, wolf-muscled Kane had anticipated the sound, Edwards could hear the distant shout of Brigid Baptiste. In fact, Edwards didn't doubt that Kane had some kind of strange, almost doomsayerlike powers. Most of it was simply sharply tuned senses, but there were instances where Kane's intuition went beyond natural ken.

Edwards knew Brigid's voice, and her sharp cry was a name he knew well.

"Domi!"

Kane led with his Copperhead as the point of the group's spear. "Move it! Get some grens ready."

Edwards didn't question Kane's request. From the grimness in the ex-Magistrate's voice, he was in combat mode. Something monstrous was unfolding in the lower tunnels, and Kane wasn't looking for nonlethal, riot-control measures. The unmistakable boom of Domi's .45 faded to a throaty pop, thanks to the distance, telling Edwards that conflict had been joined.

The three Cerberus warriors picked up speed, driven on by the urgency of Brigid Baptiste's call of concern.

KANE REACHED the far end of the submerged temple, two hundred yards away, and was at the top of the downward ramp when the stench of sickly sweet rot met his nostrils. After the reanimated mummies of Aten and Papa Hurbon's, the stench was all too familiar.

It was the rot of something that had no business moving. The chatter of an automatic rifle and the boom of a heavy-caliber handgun reverberated up from the depths of the ramp. The gunfire, with an undercurrent of bursting meat and low groans, simply confirmed the opposition that Kane dreaded.

Kane saw Mariah Falk backing up the ramp, Glock aimed down into the darkness below. He took her by the shoulder. She let out a yelp of terror, but she had the presence of mind not to turn her pistol toward him. "Get to the entrance."

Falk looked with breathless relief to Kane. "Domi's fighting monsters…"

"I know," Kane answered, giving her a shove in the right direction. He heard what could only be Brigid's Copperhead chattering away on full auto and charged toward the sound of the gunfire. As he neared the bottom of the ramp, legs pumping hard at a full run, he saw Brigid's weapon light burning over the entire scene.

Domi was in the fight of her life, her ghost-white face, hair and hands the only flashes that Kane could make out amid the dark gray figures that clawed and lunged toward her. Domi's knuckles and weapons were splattered with thick, brownish blood as she whipped the razor-sharp point around, sprays of molasses-colored gore having struck her face, sticking to her cheeks like macabre freckles.

Kane shouldered his Copperhead rifle and took a quick examination of the scene. He knew that Domi was too packed behind a wall of groaning, clawing creatures for him to immediately drop automatic fire into the fight. The rush of two gaunt, shambling figures that galloped along with their arms flailing like dropped reins caught his attention. Their unnatural swiftness brought them into a circle behind the feral albino girl in a blind spot as she wrestled with another of their lot. Kane lit the two creatures up, 4.85 mm rounds slicing into their chests.

Their naked, dark torsos ruptured, exposing purple inner flesh and white bone within. The impact of the high-velocity slugs knocked them to the ground, and Kane gave the two unliving assailants another pair of short bursts to make certain they were anchored to a permanent form of death. His encounters with previous reanimates made him especially aware of how difficult it could be to permanently neutralize such beings without sparing a few rounds for their brains.

Kane realized he needn't have worried as he saw Brigid Baptiste blow one in half with an extended blast of Copperhead fire. The submachine gun cored the creature's chest, shattering its ribs. The monstrosity's limbs lost their unnatural vitality and it collapsed.

"Some are fast, some are slow," Brigid announced. Her face was freckled with brownish gore from where the single-minded horde had lunged at her. Fresh bruises were on her jaw, and her hair was a rat's nest from where the snarling beasts had plucked at her. Her shadow suit didn't show any signs of actual damage, thanks to its elastic properties. Most of them could only sense Domi, or perhaps they saw the smaller creature as easier prey. As it was, every time her Copperhead's weapon light splayed in the face of one of the zombie horde, its attention was drawn to her immediately. Fortunately, such attraction occurred just as the flame-haired archivist was aiming at one of them.

"I noticed," Kane said, slipping up beside her. He handed over a pouch of spare magazines, noting that the archivist had five empties littering the ground near her feet. "Domi! Break off!"

The albino outlander's ruby-red eyes glared at Kane as if glowing with animalistic fire. It was a glare of frustration with Kane, a statement of the obvious. The opponents she was dealing with were having trouble, tripping over each other as they rushed toward her. Unlike the sluggish creatures whom Kane had faced under Papa Hurbon, these things had short-range speed, lunging quickly after shuffling into position. Had it been only two or three gaunt, dark gray assailants, Domi could have been overwhelmed, but when it was a half-dozen attackers at once, they got in one another's paths. Long, slender limbs snarled together, giving Domi enough of a breather to drive bodies against each other before tearing into them with her gun and knife.

Kane knew that with such a mob of creatures, seemingly endless as they spewed out of the door beside the giant cedar gates, he'd have to carve a path through them to get Domi out of the melee. He could see that the sticky brown blood was cut by the same sweat that matted her bone-colored hair to her scalp.

Behind him, Edwards and Sinclair cut loose with their own weapons, hosing the horde as it stumbled out of a doorway beside the largest pair of gates that Kane had ever seen. The two CAT members' assault rifles cut through bodies, but for each gray figure that collapsed to the ground, split apart by high-velocity bullets, two more were forcing their way into the open.

The number of slow shamblers had dropped off as the crowd streaming out of the portal no longer had been smashed and flattened, limbs crushed as they hammered on the broken slabs of door that were visible at their feet. Other trampled forms squirmed on the floor, crushed by their brethren without concern, feral eyes glaring at the intruders in their realm. With four people at the bottom of the ramp that led to the surface, the horde had something new to draw them. It took some of the pressure off Domi, though she was still cut off from escape. The dark gray monstrosities turned their attention toward the rifle-armed humans, surging forward despite the high-velocity bullets slicing into their number. There were enough of them that the submachine guns did little more than scratch the surface. Each one that fell soaked up bullets that could have stopped five behind it. Rounds that sliced through the corpses only caused minor injuries that did little to slow the implacable mob.

Kane grimaced and let the Copperhead dangle from its sling. He was going in to rescue Domi, who was in the midst of a full-blown riot of the dead things. He drew his knife, a foot-long piece of razor-sharp steel that had sufficient weight to carve through a healthy man's arm and sever it. Kane lopped off one of the zombie's arms with a powerful swing, using the butt of his Sin Eater as a club to cave in the skull of a second creature. With each step, Kane dropped two of the snarling gray attackers, either with blade, bullet or blunt force.

His march to Domi's assistance was relentless, and she struggled back. None of their allies dared to provide covering fire; the melee was too tangled, and a bullet meant for a zombie could have struck one of their own. Certainly, both Kane and Domi were protected by the shadow suits, but their heads were exposed.

"Come on," Kane growled as his elbow smashed out the teeth of one of this tomb's defenders.

Domi slithered past Kane, her Detonics .45 booming as she blew the head off another of the monsters. "You move, too!"

Kane brought his knife around in an arc, the long, deep belly curve of the blade sweeping across a half-dozen faces and throats, driving the gray-skinned, ancient guardians back. "Just go!"

There was a dull, hollow silence that rushed in on Kane's ears amid the groans and the impacts of hand-to-hand combat. It didn't take more than a fraction of a second to realize that Brigid, Sinclair and Edwards had gone from using their Copperheads as assault rifles to using them as clubs. For all the swiftness that he'd been able to slice through the crowd, the zombies' numbers had recovered.

"How many of these assholes are there?" Kane growled as he lurched, using his elbow as a battering ram to plow through a pair of the gaunt, dark figures.

"Lots," came Grant's ghostly voice over his Commtact.

"Thanks for nothing," Kane growled. In truth, he had never felt the need for his friend at his side so dearly as he did now. If any fighting man on Earth could have turned the tide in this battle, it would have been the solid column of muscle and fury that was Grant.

Now Kane swam in a hostile sea of reeking flesh. Instead of being slapped by waves, jagged nails and knobby knuckles swung at him. His cheek and forehead were opened up by the splintered talons of the living dead, while his shadow suit cushioned the rest of his body against pounding fists. If Kane hadn't been wearing the skintight jumpsuit, his clothing would have been snagged and torn by the grasping enemy, slowing him down, making him more vulnerable to their assault.

"Gren," Grant urged over the cybernetic implant. It became an incessant chant rumbling through Kane's head as he hammered back at the feral beast-men who surrounded him. The Sin Eater had cycled empty, and there was no way that Kane could spare a moment to insert a fresh magazine. Somewhere along the way, the combat knife had been lodged in the rib bones of one of the angry creatures lunging at him, so now all he had was his fist and the weight of the folding machine pistol as weapons.

"Cool it, Grant!" Kane shouted, punching and clubbing at the implacable mass swarming around him.

"What's he saying?" Brigid called. She must have been twenty feet away, but the reanimated monstrosities made it feel as if she were miles away.

"He says to use a grenade!" Kane replied. Slender limbs suddenly looped around his head and neck, dragging him off balance. The creatures were no stronger than a normal man, but there were many of them, and their numbers would have provided enough leverage to bring him down had it not been for Domi grasping him by the wrist to keep him from hitting the floor.

Kane didn't want to imagine the force of hundreds of feet stomping and trampling him into the ground. The shadow suit would have become a simple tube, and he could see himself being forced out of the neck and sleeves as paste.

The albino girl's wilderness-honed strength was enough to keep Kane on his feet, though she had the assistance of one of the monsters, whom she clung to like a tree trunk. Kane struggled to break the grasps on his neck, but there were too many of them.

A thunderclap erupted behind Kane and Domi, a wave of hyperpressure squeezing their eardrums and eyeballs under the sensation of a massive weight. The detonation of an implode grenade was unmistakable and overwhelming. The two Cerberus fighters were staggered, but so were their enemies. Used to the near impact of the high-powered blast, Kane and Domi were just a hair quicker at recovery, taking three steps before the rotted enemy's fists and claws returned to battering them.

Now it was only feet through a wall of darkened flesh. "Now what?"

"Gate!" came Grant's eerie whisper, picked up by the electronics in Kane's Commtact.

Kane swung a hard backhand around, felt jaws shattering under the force of his slashing fist. He cut himself enough room to pull another implode grenade off his harness, whipping it toward the entrance at the side of the cedar gates. He hoped that he'd gotten Grant's meaning, despite his lack of vocabulary. The miniature bomb split the darkness like a thunderbolt, severed limbs flying as dust and pebbles peppered his bloodied face. The earthshaking implosion rolled across the crowd of gray figures.

This time Kane couldn't remain on his feet, nor could the horde surrounding him. The packed chamber was bowled over as if it were a row of dominoes.

"Kane!" That was Brigid, her yelp of concern knifing through the blast-induced ringing that had seized his ears and brain.

"Close the hatch!" Kane roared at the top of his lungs.

Domi struggled to her feet, throwing off clawing hands as she broke from the toppled creatures around her. Arms slithered around her slender legs, but the albino girl kicked away from them. Her knife flashed as it rose and fell, hacking at wrists and forearms, chopping them away from her knees and calves. Kane struck with abandon at the carpet of writhing rot around him. Prone, he didn't have the leverage to escape as readily as the slender, smaller albino girl, who had less body mass to hang on to.

That's when the cadaverous men started biting Kane on his legs and chest. Blunt, ancient teeth closed on his skin beneath the shadow suit, and the ex-Magistrate grimaced in pain. The high-tech cloth offered protection from rapid shock and impact, as well as the slow, relentless force of jaws. The natural resistance of the dense fabric and its low friction coefficient kept those relentless mouths from tearing his flesh.

That kind of protection wasn't going to last for long from the dozens of mouths closing on him. Kane brought up his knees, pumping them alternately against faces. Jaws dislocated, noses crunched and heads bounced, but the creatures continued to lunge at him. They were attacking with whatever weapons they had. The cadaverous creatures weren't looking for sustenance; they were making use of their teeth to attack when their fists and nails were not enough. It was a primitive, animalistic strategy, and it was working.

More thunderclaps resounded through the antechamber, high-powered grenades going off violently. Bodies crumpled and tumbled, cartwheeling past Kane and knocking his attackers aside. The same wheeling corpses hammered at Kane himself, but because he was prone and besieged by a dozen enemies, he was shielded from the brunt of their assault.

Kane struggled to his feet, his opponents swept away. He could feel dozens of bruises all along his body, as well as blood drying on a number of scratches on his face. Shell-shocked zombies swayed uneasily as they stood, an equal number of their brethren squirming on the stone floor where they'd been flattened by the thunderous blasts.

One of them had recovered enough of what senses it retained to jump at Kane, but this creature was not motivated by an intact consciousness, and it wasn't used to combat amid explosions. Kane's reflexes were honed by countless hours of training and actual experience. With a deft movement, he grabbed the lunging zombie by its forearm and pivoted. The slender limb snapped, bones shattering as Kane used the creature's own momentum and mass against it. The thing sailed over the prone forms of its brethren and crashed face-first into the stone wall. It trailed an oily black smear, chunks of bone and skin sticking to the sandstone bricks.

Others worked their way toward Kane and Domi, but they were slowed by their dead or fallen kin, unsteady legs snarled in masses of limbs and torsos at their feet. Kane and Domi, not driven by a primal, ancient programming and feral hostility, but intellect and skill, weren't prone to tripping when dealing with their attackers.

"Kane!" Edwards bellowed. "Catch!"

Kane turned and snatched the tossed combat knife out of the air. Behind Edwards, a handgun cracked rapidly, bullets slicing into the creatures who had been assailing him. He could make out that the gunner was Mariah Falk, unwilling to abandon the warriors of Cerberus when she heard the gunfire cease. A smile crossed Kane's face at the thought of the courage that he, Brigid, Grant and Domi had instilled into the Manitius Base staff.

Falk was no soldier, but when the battle had grown eerily silent, her sense of duty had drawn her back, despite the orders given to her to run away. She was willing to stand beside her friends, and that instilled a surge of pride into Kane.

It was just the amount of motivation that turned a worn and sluggish fighting man into a dervish of zombie destruction. His foot-long blade hacked and carved viciously into the monsters surrounding him. Heads and arms flew off under his and Domi's assault, adrenaline surging as Kane's revived enthusiasm infected Domi.

From the ramp, Brigid, Sinclair and Edwards had been given enough of a breather that they were able to pull their sidearms. Out of the corner of his eye, Kane could see that the three Cerberus combatants had taken their own beatings. Their rifles had run out of ammunition, so they'd had to resort to using the Copperheads as clubs, swinging them to break in heads and snap necks. Edwards had been at the forefront of the conflict, his great size and strength making him the center of the wall that had kept the monstrosities from chasing Falk.

Sinclair hadn't used her SMG as a club; she'd turned to the collapsible baton she wore on her hip. The once shiny high-tensile shaft was now drenched in blood and bent from hammering at the living dead. Brigid cut loose with her little 9 mm pistol now, her flame-red tresses clawed at, clumps missing from her curls.

It was a war zone, and it hadn't died down yet. Kane looked to the hole from which the horde had crawled, and it had been collapsed by the force of the implode grenades. The stone had caved in, thick and immovable. To Kane's surprise, however, the cedar gates had simply been scorched, the hardened wood unstripped by the nearby detonations.

As Kane split the face of a rotted enemy, he gave a sigh of relief as he realized that the enemy's numbers wouldn't increase, not unless they could somehow operate the huge cedar gates.

That was unlikely, he hoped.

"Can't open," Grant grumbled through the Commtact.

"Now you get all talkative," Kane grunted back.

There was a murmur that Kane couldn't make out over the cybernetic implant.

"Kane! Come on!" Falk shouted.

He and Domi looked at each other, then raced over the fallen forms. Kane could feel bones shatter beneath his boots, while Domi leaped and scurried from body to body, as if she were crossing a river on stones. The barefoot, feral girl and the ex-Magistrate had their own means of cutting out of the chamber, moving to the relative safety of the ramp. As they crossed the final fifteen feet to their allies, Sinclair and Edwards hammered 9 mm bullets into the writhing mass behind them. Nothing was going to chase the pair.

"Move, climb, climb!" Kane urged as he skidded to a halt. He stuffed a fresh magazine into his Sin Eater and raked the crawling crowd of trampled zombies. Heads and torsos burst open under fire, slowing them down as Domi reached into her belt for another grenade.

The albino made certain that Brigid and the others were out of blast range when she pulled the pin and dropped it into the struggling floor full of creatures. Kane and Domi were running as soon as the grenade left her hand, charging up after their allies. Groaning monstrosities were cut short as the blast enveloped the horde at the bottom of the ramp. Shredded chunks of rotted meat pelted them with wet slaps, but now it was over.

Kane rested his hands on his knees, panting. If anything had the ability to stand up and come after the Cerberus explorers, then Kane gave the creature full credit. As it was, they weren't being followed.

"What the hell was behind those gates, Baptiste?" Kane asked.

Brigid looked at Falk for a moment, then sighed. "A wish for eternal life gone badly. How did you know to come?"

"Grant told me," Kane said. "Can you still hear us, buddy?"

Brigid pointed to the chemical light stick she had dangling around her neck. "Grant can't summon up the energy to communicate over the Commtacts. He's drained batteries in an effort to transmit. Your flashlight is probably dead now."

"So, to hear what he has to say, we've got to get to a place with a lot of available energy?" Kane asked.

Brigid nodded. "That would help, but we're not going to get much conversation out of him. He can only use one or two simple words at a time."

"So his brain is fractured," Kane said. "At least that's what Waylon said."

"More like his consciousness is spread over two levels. Like a shadow cast on an uneven surface," Brigid said. "Here, he's a ghost, pure ego."

"And in the past, his body is running around with... what?" Kane asked.

"A good vocabulary, but not much memory, going by our encounters with Grant," Brigid returned.

"So Grant's not operating at his best," Kane said.

He could read his own face reflected in Brigid's concerned features.

"We'll find him. We'll bring him home and make him whole again," Brigid said.

Kane squeezed his eyes shut, then looked down at the darkened pit where weak, helpless moans rose. He didn't want to think of what horrors Grant had to face, five millennia in the past.

Chapter 9

Shamhat regarded the creature he knew as Enkidu the man-bull as he whispered a soft phrase. For a moment, the Igigi sensed that the human had expanded, a funnel pouring from his forehead, stretching like an undulating worm before it disappeared into nothingness.

Enkidu looked at Shamhat.

"What was that?" the Igigi asked the human.

"What was what?" Enkidu returned, as if shutting the door on further conversation.

Shamhat frowned, his reptile scaled lips scraping against each other at the man-bull's willfulness. "I saw you. I saw something tap into your conscious memories."

"You can't tap my brain. Nor can any of the Annunaki," Enkidu/Grant taunted in reply. "Who can read my mind when the most powerful intellects of this age are blunted?"

Shamhat's slitted yellow reptilian eyes narrowed. "You can."

"Then why can't I remember who I am?" Enkidu asked. It was a taunt, the dangling of knowledge that the nonhuman couldn't grasp despite his biological superiority.

Shamhat grimaced. "Taste of the fruits of the Cedar Garden, human. It shall be your only chance to survive the task we set before you."

"Only chance?" the man-bull asked. He seemed hurt at the implication that there was an opponent who could put him down. It was the first sign of arrogance that Enkidu had displayed since Shamhat had exerted his will over the man.

Shamhat reached out, plucking a red gourd hanging from a web of plasticlike fungus. It took a twist of the Igigi's wrist to pry it loose, the stem snapping with the crack of shattering bone. Enkidu looked at the offered fruit.

"Taste of it," Shamhat said. "Before the freshness of it fades."

Enkidu hefted the gourd, staring at it. "This isn't something which will enhance my strength."

"Eat!" Shamhat shouted. "Or do—"

"All right," Enkidu answered. "You complain like that, you'll…"

"I'll what?" Shamhat asked as Enkidu's teeth burst the sleek skin of the fungal polyp. Red juices trickled down the human's chin, soaking into the long, drooping mustache that looped down strangely under his jaw.

"Another false-start memory of something," Enkidu admitted. "I'll figure all of this out someday."

"What will you do to celebrate?" Shamhat asked.

Enkidu took another bite of the fungal fruit, crimson pulp squirting as his dark eyes bored into the Igigi. He lowered the gourd and smiled, looking akin to Humbaba when the half-lion god had rooted around in the entrails of a human.

"Maintain the delusion that you shall live so long, Enkidu," Shamhat told him.

"Poison?" the man asked, throwing the gutted gourd at the Igigi's feet.

"Not as you would assume it," Shamhat replied.

"Let me guess, my blood would be poison to Gi Malesh, who has something in common with Humbaba?" Enkidu asked.

"She is his sister," Shamhat admitted.

Enkidu nodded. "It sounds just like the snake-faces. Petty, backstabbing bastards."

"What you consider petty…"

"Just give me a break. This attack is a suicide mission," Enkidu growled. "She kills me, and she takes her prize, maybe eating my heart. Humbaba gets rid of his sister without having to do anything himself."

"Except for breaking and imprisoning you," Shamhat returned.

"They call that bait where I come from," Enkidu/ Grant said. "Except even then, the fisher still has to reel in his fish. Humbaba, for being so big, is just another coward, a tyrant who—"

"Still your tongue, lest you sacrifice another life," Shamhat warned.

Enkidu frowned, glowering eyes locked on the Igigi, but his silence was assured.

Shamhat and his prisoner left the garden behind the cedar gates in silence.

IT HAD BEEN two days when Enkidu/Grant had reached the forest from where Humbaba and his people had taken the wood for the great cedar gates. The road was easily traveled, paved and delineated by years of effort. Rib bones of dead slaves adorned the sides of the trail where corpses rotted or skeletons were stripped clean by scavengers.

With a sneer, Enkidu thought of the Annunaki and how he was so familiar their callous disregard for human life. His trek across country to battle Gi Malesh was just another example of how their kind considered people as tools to be used up and disposed of. These beings were alien, foreign visitors to a world where they meddled and let the pieces fall where they may. They had taken on the title of gods, but in reality, most of their forsaken breed were nothing more than glorified demons, miserable creatures so bored by eternal life that their only pleasure came from shortening the already brief existences of other people, usually in the most excruciating means possible.

Enkidu didn't remember much, but he had a deep-down, almost instinctual feeling of hatred for the Annunaki. That Malesh shared the genetic material of the scale-faced "gods" was more than enough of a reason to do everything within his power to destroy her. Another name danced on the tip of his tongue, another woman of the Annunaki who had inspired loathing within him.

Another Annunaki torture, he mused. The lack of memory, the familiarity of an enemy's name yet skittering away, taunting him with a clue to his true identity—it was frustrating. How many months had passed here? And how much time had gone by in that future he'd been plucked from?

He rubbed his brow, trying to put aside the jumble of thoughts regarding his identity. It hurt his brain too much, as if he were pushing his tongue against a sore tooth or picking at a scab. His mind had a wound, a rift that had pried him apart from himself. Such deep introspection was rooting around inside an open sore, exacerbating the injury.

Enkidu unshouldered the pack he carried and laid it on the ground. Shamhat had given him prepared packages of the red gourd to replenish the potency of its poisonous effect on him. Enkidu tossed the packages in a hole in the ground, then stamped it down. That was one thing he didn't want to worry about. Too much exposure to the fungal juices might have bad effects on him.

If it was poison to an Annunaki, he didn't want to think of what it could do to a human over the long term.

It had been a long day of marching down the road, so Enkidu decided to find a spot to rest and make camp for the night. He had his sword belt, a three-foot-long *kopesh* that looked like a vaguely straightened question mark. The curve of the blade just under the spike-wedge tip was a fat belly that was capable of lopping through limbs as if they were made of butter. Enkidu frowned as another type of aggressive slashing blade came to mind. The *katana* was a finely forged, heavily reinforced sword that achieved its slashing ability with a straight edge. However, the *kopesh* he had been given was one of the most successful swords of the Bronze Age.

He began to talk to himself about it. "I know what the tribe of Israel used to hack apart the Egyptians and the Philistines, and can compare it to a sword from a nation on the other side of the globe…"

Enkidu sighed and cupped his forehead. "Goddamn hole in my brain!"

Even as he cursed his situation, he grimaced. Complaining out loud wasn't especially productive when you were trying to make certain you were settling in a safe area.

Enkidu at least had the saving grace that he was cursing in his own language, which he knew was North American English. North America. Japan. Israel. All places that had never been mentioned by the other people, at least those he could understand. The Igigi, who could communicate mentally with him, were creatures that didn't exist in his time.

Still, distracting himself in enemy territory wasn't something he wanted to do. Sure, he was almost seven feet tall, wearing a sleeveless tunic that was under a bronzed chest piece of armor and a heavy, leather-strapped skirt that would turn aside a spear or sword from his groin and the juncture of vulnerable arteries there. With a spear and sword of his own, Enkidu was an impressive giant. A small troupe of what could have been bandits had eyed him as they passed on the road, and from the look in their eyes, they knew he was not going to be prey for them. Predators wanted something soft and easy to attack, to minimize the energy spent and the risk to themselves. Even looking at the body of Grant was enough of a pause, his unclad arms as thick around as young tree trunks, a barrel of a chest wrapped in cloth and shaped bronze and long legs making him akin to a demigod as he trod across the Earth. Couple that with his weapons and the grim countenance of a wary warrior, and no thief or marauder wanted to test his mettle against Grant.

Enkidu ran his fingertips across his armor, a wistful memory bubbling, elusive as smoke. The hard chest plate was familiar, but it was the wrong color from what it should have been.

He frowned as terms came to mind.

"Polycarbonate hard shell. Helmet implanted with night-vision and infrared optics, as well as encrypted radio communications. Guaranteed to resist 5.56 mm NATO rifle rounds with minimal cosmetic smearing," came the spiel from Grant's vocabulary.

"He is from a future time," he remembered Shamhat saying. "The firearms he carries and the clothing he wears are of materials beyond the scope of current human technology. That's not counting the cybernetic implant installed in his jaw."

All pretty words and terms, but without an identity, a history to hang them all on, they were worthless. The items mentioned in those words were also useless now. Not only did he not have the batteries to power the electronics sensory systems in the helmet, but he also had no one to transmit and receive from in this era. Polycarbonate left thousands of years away was less useful than his own feces. At least he could use his turds to maintain the integrity of the fire pit he was forming. It wasn't the most pleasant process, but caking firewood together with his crap was fairly sanitary given that Enkidu wasn't suffering from any intestinal infections and the heat of the flame would kill any microorganisms quickly.

"All right, maybe the knowledge isn't all worthless," Enkidu muttered, thanking himself, Grant, for at least having that data stored in the Swiss cheese he called a brain.

With his attention divided between setting the fire and ensuring the security of his camp, Enkidu had a reprieve from the relentless hollowness of a lack of identity. It was good, hard work, and at the end of it, he reached for a wineskin in his pack. He decanted a cupful, which he diluted with water he obtained at a stream. The alcohol in the wine would deal with any bacteria or other "bugs" in the water—clean water was a misnomer considering all the animals and humans who bathed and relieved themselves in the streams. The use of wine with every meal was a survival tactic to prevent dysentery. The skin full of fortified wine was less for getting a buzz than guaranteeing good health.

All in all, Enkidu/Grant would have preferred an ice-cold bottle of beer, something that would probably only be found in northern Europe, but only if he could wait five hundred years.

"While I'm wishing for shit, I'd like to have a pony. No, a full-size horse," Enkidu muttered. He managed a smirk of satisfaction. Whoever he had been, he had an appreciation for sarcastic wit. Being a grouchy smart-ass was something that transcended his rifted identity.

There was the rustle of movement beyond the clearing he sat in. Enkidu squashed the urge to reach for his sword or spear. It could have been a small forest animal, or it could have been someone curious about him. There was no direct sign of hostility, and given his "Doppler effect" sense of time, any assault on him might as well be happening in slow motion. No one had been able to surprise Enkidu in his time here. Even Humbaba hadn't been able to surprise him in combat, but his Annunaki speed and strength were just too much even for pre-warned reflexes.

The thought that Malesh might be a similarly formidable opponent danced in his mind, but Humbaba had accomplished his overpowering of the time-lost human in close quarters. Events in a hand-to-hand battle occurred in milliseconds, and even slowed to a third of its normal pace, those brief instants were too swift to compensate for, not with the reflexes of Humbaba. The standard Nephilim that Enkidu/Grant had resisted weren't as quick and dangerous as one who bore the blood of the Annunaki, especially Enlil.

Malesh, however, would be that fast, though again, Enkidu would have distance and time on his side to react to one of her charges.

Famous last words. The thought rose from Grant's experience as he settled in for the night.

ENKIDU'S SLEEP was short-lived, only a few moments before the snap of twigs in the forest aroused him. His fingers slid around the pommel of his knife, an almost imperceptible movement in the darkness, backlit by the fire he reclined near. His eyes were slitted open, in case someone was watching from the other side of the bonfire. Stealth and combat reactions were ingrained into his nervous system, a hardwiring that came from what must have been years of experience. Enkidu could tell that he wasn't a young man. Indeed when he'd arrived, he had a slight paunch, and he could see gray hairs growing on a skull that had been shaved close, a shiny form of faux baldness that must have either been a concession to conceit or to keep enemies from snatching his locks in combat.

It had been a few moments since the snap of the twig that had awakened him, and now the only sound he could make out over the crackle of the fire was the rush of wind through the leaves. Of course, there was the dissonance from reality that the only wind seemed to be going through a narrow corridor of air among a series of bushes just behind him. Enkidu/Grant rolled over in a flash, realizing that such localized clamor could only mean a fight. He lunged for his sword, scooping it up deftly.

At that moment, a hard thud, stretched at three times of what would be its usual duration, heralded the sudden arrival of a lithe, feminine figure. Enkidu barely had the time to throw himself away from her path as she skidded backward, clawing at the ground with one hand, digging in her feet to stop. Dirt and grass flew from the earth at her passage, and the fire was snuffed, drowned in flying dust, its kindling scattered.

Grant/Enkidu received a good look at the figure before the glow of the flames were extinguished. It was a woman with a golden brown mane of hair, her arms and legs long and wrapped in corded muscle. She was definitely feline in aspect, but not so grossly leonine as her brother. She was also smaller, only around Enkidu's height. There was a slight pause, her back and shoulders flexing as she wound herself up to lunge back into the forest. Emerald eyes regarded him coolly as she looked over her shoulder.

There was a flash of something. A reminder of another lean, beautiful warrior woman, a tumbling forward and backward vision, akin to the view he had seen of Ullikummis, the young mottle-skinned freak he'd met in the court of Humbaba. There was a "worm" of existence, rolling through time, unfurling ahead, uncoiling and turning into different iterations.

It was an odd, discordant bit of recognition, tendrils of futures and pasts splitting and reintegrating, forming a loop. Something seemed to unfurl, reaching out to him almost as a lover's caress. A wan, golden-skinned face appeared before him, lips moving uncertainly, dark almond-shaped eyes wide with recognition and confusion. Enkidu wished that he could draw up the name of the ghostly image, but then she was yanked away, her cry echoing through eternity, or at least through his brain.

The link to his future retreated just as phenomenal leg muscles rocketed the tall, golden silhouette back into the tree line. Enkidu pushed himself to his feet and took off after her, scooping up his spear to supplement the sword. There was only one creature in the world that this could be—Gi Malesh herself. Such lightning-quick reflexes and sheer physical power were indications of whom he had been sent to kill.

"Get this job done fast, and return," he muttered as he accelerated after the young goddess.

He lost half a step, instinct slowing him down, overriding his urge to slay the half-Annunaki. The identity of Malesh that knew him, that reached out with loving tenderness.

You can't kill that, came the resolute thought to his mind. She's important.

Enkidu's slowed half step turned back into a full run, his powerful form slicing through brush and undergrowth, his stovepipe legs hurling him over low shrubs and roots that would have snarled his path. Experiencing time at one-third of its conventional rate, Enkidu was able to guide himself to a sure-footed landing and avoid snarling himself on an obstruction. He was able to keep pace with Malesh's golden shape as it wove between trees in pursuit of an enemy.

Enkidu spotted something in his peripheral vision, a humanoid shape impaled on a branch. A six-inch-thick shattered limb jutted through the dead thing's rib cage. He noticed the shimmering scaled flesh of a Nephilim warrior, and paid the corpse no mind. Shamhat had sent shadows to make certain his prized slave wouldn't stray. That was what he'd sensed in the woods just beyond his campsite.

Malesh had noticed them, too, and she had decided to take care of the Nephilim before observing the lone human sent to the forest that she'd controlled. Enkidu/ Grant didn't know how many Nephilim had accompanied him on this journey, but Malesh was busy with at least one more of them. The lifeless drone, long left in his dust, was only one small part of this mess.

Enkidu had his memories of conflict with the soulless creatures, knowledge of their combat style burned into his reflexes. While one of them might have been able to send a normal-size human flying, Malesh looked easily as massive as the time-lost Grant. Those factors, coupled with the enhanced strength that came from the Annunaki and whatever other genetic heritage she possessed, meant that a mere Nephilim could have struck her hard enough to drive her backward, requiring a three-point stance to slow herself down.

Something else was out here in the shadows, which meant that Enkidu could quite easily be thrown into a battle with a force he wouldn't be able to handle.

Deep down, the thread of Grant's stubbornness pulsed like a throbbing vein, urging him to race even more quickly in the shadows.

MALESH HEARD the crash and stomp of the human's feet behind her as she pursued the more monstrous of her brothers' intruders. This creature had nearly felled her with a blow that only her quickness had blunted. The nails on her left hand and her toes' claws were splintered by the effort to decelerate from that unholy impact. Now, she was left with only one set of talons with which to engage the horned thing that plowed ahead of her.

Trees snapped in half ahead, indicating that whatever was on the run was simply giving itself room where it felt it could battle with more freedom. That gave Malesh a countdown, a small cushion of space and time where she could catch up to Humbaba's beast and bring it to the ground. Five claws and her fangs would have to do.

Even now, her legs and arms hurt as she had gone full quadrupedal, using the entire length of her lithe, powerful frame to spring ever faster. With catlike bounds and bounces off the broken trees dropped by her horned opponent's passage, she ate up the distance between them quickly.

This was going to be too easy, for this monstrosity was a hundred yards from the closest clearing that provided any combat stretch. As she kicked off a shattered trunk, she saw the ebony form of a minotaur standing like a pillar in front of her. Malesh tried to twist out of the way, but the enemy had picked this moment to ambush her perfectly. She'd committed to her lunge, and despite the fact that Malesh would always be able to land on her feet, she didn't have the power to change her trajectory midleap.

The creature brought down its heavy fist, more hoof than fingers wrapped in a knot, and clubbed Malesh between her shoulder blades. The blow slammed her to the ground, knocking the wind from her lungs.

Malesh's brain swam crazily, laid low by the power of the massive attacker. She tried to focus her vision, even as the beast brought its foot down, trapping her arm beneath its weight. Without any leverage, the daughter of Enlil was trapped, though thankfully her bone structure was dense enough that the fifteen hundred pounds of muscle and sinew pressing on her shoulder joint hadn't cracked bone and cartilage like a twig.

"Strong one," the bull growled. It shifted its weight, drawing up its other massive hind hoof. While the monster's weight wouldn't break bone, it was a certainty that a full-power kick would easily separate her head from her shoulders.

Malesh's green eyes flashed with furious defiance. The goddess would not face her end whimpering for mercy.

As she glared at the thing about to kill her, she noticed that a heavy shaft of bronze-ring-wrapped wood jutted from the creature's upper chest. The minotaur toppled, thrown off balance by the sudden addition to its body weight, bright blood frothing from the humanoid's nostrils.

Malesh glanced back to see the human, sword glimmering in the starlight.

"The snake-faces sent me to kill this woman," came the stentorian roar of the tall human. "Fuck off!"

The minotaur swatted the shaft of the spear, shattering it off so that it didn't jut too far. Its eyes twisted, pained from the shifting of the nine-inch leaf of razor-sharp bronze in its shoulder. Its lips curled back, bloody streams trailing from its enlarged nostrils. It had no intelligible response, but its counterchallenge was unmistakable as massive lungs bellowed out a ferocious crack of thunder. Malesh winced at the sound, a painful spike through her keen hearing that registered sound far above and below normal human range. The reverberations made her eyeballs quiver in their sockets.

However, she was still beneath the creature's hoof, pinned to the earth, at least for a moment more. Then the minotaur was gone from her, charging the dark-skinned human who leaped with equal rage.

Malesh could only look on as the most physically powerful human she'd ever seen threw himself into conflict with three-quarters of a ton of genetically engineered killing machine with only a few feet of sharpened bronze to make up the 1200-pound difference in their mass.

Chapter 10

Enkidu inherited a sentence from Grant, something that had been said countless times before, but there had been enough times when the statement had been directed at himself.

Another fine mess you've gotten me into. It was a quick thought, just before gravity took over from the force of his leap, pulling him toward the would-be god killer who would have done the job he'd been sent to do. Instead of sitting back to watch the minotaur kick Malesh's skull a country mile away, Enkidu knew that there would be no honor in this kind of death, and no answer to be gotten from a decapitated corpse. Malesh was somehow entwined with Grant, the unknown section of the identity that was pulled from him in his temporal displacement.

That was why his forearms ached from his bronze sword stopping cold midway through the minotaur's heavy collarbone. Enkidu jammed his feet against the giant's chest to push himself out of the way of the sharpened war horns of his bullish opponent, but even with his altered time sense, an inch of one point sliced the skin of his arm from shoulder to elbow.

A shrug of the three-quarter-ton monster launched Enkidu off its chest, but the human turned in midflight, tucking his limbs in tight in order to minimize his inevitable impact with the ground. He hit with a roll and tumbled, getting a few feet ahead of the massive fist that had dropped a goddess like a rock. The ground shook behind Enkidu as he twisted to his feet, knife flashing from its sheath.

Black eyes blinked at the quickness of the human, the minotaur letting loose a spray of bloody foam that would have blinded Enkidu had he not seen the squirt of gore and froth coming. Rather than get mucus in his eyes, the human dropped his shoulder and charged at the larger humanoid. It was as if he had tried to tackle a brick wall, and the minotaur had moved just as much, but Enkidu whipped his knife around, parting the beast's thick cowhide to saw open muscle from sternum to midchest. He knew that he couldn't get to the creature's vital organs, not with rib bones such as the one that stopped his sword cold. However, Enkidu knew that a stronger opponent could be brought low if its strength was sapped.

Chest muscles slashed open, the minotaur grunted. Now, along with the pain of nine inches of spear point in its shoulder, the creature's right arm hung like a leaden weight. It could have summoned the strength to slap Grant/Enkidu aside, but the minotaur was unable to swivel its left arm to connect with the human. Enkidu jammed his knee into the huge humanoid's groin, just below its abdominal muscles. The follow-up strike was more than enough to weaken the bigger foe's stance.

Enkidu scurried around the minotaur's weakened right side, using body positioning to keep out of the monster's line of fire. He tried a few quick lashes with the bronze knife, but the creature's legs were just too tough, powerful leather across muscle sheets as dense as tight steel cable. The minotaur twisted hard and smashed its uninjured fist down, and Enkidu backpedaled just enough to avoid having his head pushed out through his anus. Rather, the discomfort that the human did feel were jolts of vibrations up both of his legs.

Enkidu grabbed for his sword's handle and jerked back hard. Bone grated, but refused to surrender the bronzed blade. He let go and dove aside as the minotaur's elbow whipped around in a vicious arc. The breeze whipped up by the monster's shrug was phenomenal, but the heavily armored knuckles of the beast struck Enkidu's knife and launched it spinning through the air to sink into a tree trunk.

The wickedly sharpened war horns swiveled, following the minotaur's eyes, and he lunged forward to make a head butt that would have pinioned the human, rupturing his chest under their twin impacts. Enkidu slapped against the horns, as much to deflect them as to push himself out of the way. The point of one nicked his side, drawing blood from a shallow but painful gash. Enkidu whirled uncontrollably as the minotaur's shoulder struck him far more solidly than the swooping horns. He struck the ground hard, but the momentum of the giant man-thing carried it away from the stunned human.

Grant/Enkidu rolled to all fours, scanning the clearing for something to even the odds, as his knife was gone. His gaze fell on the brass-ring-wrapped shaft of his broken spear. It was fifteen feet away, which would have been only a few steps and a leisurely scant moment to reach…if 1500 pounds of solid muscle weren't snorting right behind him, grunting in rage and pain. Enkidu pushed off against the ground, snapping his legs straight to lunge for the staff. The thunder of a hoof slamming into the ground signaled that the minotaur sought to recover its footing. Scrambling on all fours was not a natural movement for the time-flung Grant, but he covered the distance between himself and the broken shaft in record time. His fingers wrapped around the fire-hardened handle by the time he heard the second hammer blow of a hoof striking the ground behind him.

Enkidu twisted and swung the shaft up. He rolled partially out of the way of the minotaur's charge and used the momentum from his spin to increase the power of the staff's swing. The minotaur seemed to hover in midair, Grant's vocabulary bubbling up the term *piñata,* a Mexican village's candy-filled construction hung on a rope and beaten with sticks for celebration. This time, the piñata's treasure was a mouth full of teeth shooting in every direction as a heavy ball of brass that weighted the end of his spear connected. The minotaur was knocked loopy, its head whipped about as Enkidu rolled away from the falling monster. The ground shook heavily as the man-beast struck the ground, stunned.

Enkidu leaned against the pole, pushing himself to his feet. The dislocation of the minotaur's jaw had bought him moments to recover his strength. A trickle of blood crawled down from his ribs, but Enkidu's right arm was soaked from shoulder to wrist. Luckily, the designers of the Persian war spear had anticipated soldiers needing to grip the weapon, either slick with blood or rain. Ribs of pounded metal provided a nonslip surface for Enkidu to hang on to.

He searched the clearing, looking for Malesh. He'd only announced seconds ago that he had been sent to slay her, although the challenge to the minotaur had been in American English, a language that he doubted either of the genetic supercreatures could understand. Still, if he'd learned anything from the Annunaki-blooded it was the telepathic ability to translate the words of any in their presence. Still, if she could read his thoughts as well as his words, Malesh might not be concerned with Enkidu's murderous intent. There was something that bonded the two beings, some tendril that stretched weirdly across the ages, a connection that was visible to the time-lost human simply because of his disjointed connection to normal time.

The cat woman was still on the ground, not moving, her voluptuous curves glimmering in the starlight.

A snort drew Enkidu's attention.

"Not down for the count?" the human challenged as he watched the minotaur rise to all fours. Its black eyes mirrored the dark rage in Grant's brown irises. The powerful giant ripped the sword from its collarbone, then dug its fingers into the wound to pry the leaf-bladed spear point from its shoulder.

The sharp bronze blades clattered on the ground at the tall beast's feet. The thing was easily three yards tall, even with its head sagging from pain and exhaustion. The minotaur and Enkidu had thrown everything at each other in an attempt to end this battle, and the creature's cowhide, rent in several places by sword, knife and spear, showed that it had taken significant pounding. Bloody drool strung from broken lips, evidencing the powerful shot that had stopped it cold for a moment.

Enkidu took an inventory of Grant's powerful body. He was already a mass of bruises, bleeding from two injuries, and just now he was feeling his knife hand stiffening from where the minotaur had broken at least one carpal bone. This was all a flurry of activity that was done in the space of half a minute. If the conflict lasted to all of two minutes, neither of them would be able to lift a finger, provided they survived.

In defiance, Enkidu whirled the broken spear, then pointed the blood-spattered pommel at the minotaur. The humanoid bull responded, lowering its head and digging at the dirt. No quarter was going to be granted in the next few heartbeats.

Muscles tensed, flexing as each combatant loosened and optimized his position to launch at the other. So far, they had engaged in feral, undisciplined combat, at least so far as striking out of rage and going for their maximum impact. Grant's martial-arts skill had bled through to Enkidu to allow him to make the most of lack of balance and unsure footing, as well as to aim his blows efficiently. Now Enkidu was listening to that knowledge, bathing in it. He would need every ounce of accuracy as well as the might of his thick, melon-size shoulders to bring down the minotaur in the end.

The bull-thing's head lowered, black eyes locking solidly on the human who had been called a man-bull by Shamhat. The creature's fifteen-hundred-pound frame seemed to ripple, undulating as it began to send its might into a leap that would allow it to gore Enkidu through the torso, ripping him apart with brutal efficiency. At the moment he had registered the minotaur's motion, Enkidu accelerated toward his opponent, taking advantage of his limited precognitive experience of time.

It was unfair, but then, Enkidu had been outweighed by a factor of more than five to one. What he couldn't match in strength and destructive ability, he'd have to compensate for with speed and precision. And that precision was going to be assisted by his foe's own forward momentum. The brass knob that was the bottom striking surface of his spear, specifically made for if its point had been taken off, whistled through the air, propelled at lightning speed. Enkidu felt Grant's shoulder and back muscles wrench with the violence of the swipe, aimed directly between the eyes of the killer bull-creature.

Three-quarters of a ton, accelerating at phenomenal speed, met the metal ball. The physics of the impact were akin to a small truck blasting at full speed toward a brick wall. The wall would have lost, but four pounds of forged, dense metal struck a tiny section of bone between the minotaur's eyes. The humanoid's skull shattered, splinters of its brow whirling like scythes through its brain.

All that concentrated energy had initiated an instantaneous kill upon the genetically engineered killing machine, but on the other end of the staff, Enkidu's body shook violently, vibrations from the blow rocketing through the wood and forcing waves through his arm muscles up to his neck. The jolt rocked the human's brain, and he was left limp, the only reason why the tumbling corpse of the minotaur didn't crush him. As it was, the freight train of dead bull lifted Enkidu off his feet and hurled him a dozen feet until he was stopped by a tree trunk in the middle of his back.

As his eyes blurred, consciousness starting to descend upon him, Enkidu looked up to see Malesh stand over him, bloody and battered but able to stand, light-years ahead of his own weakness.

His eyes closed despite his struggle to keep them open. Enkidu accepted that they might never open again, if only because he had done the right thing and spared the woman looking down upon him.

LAKESH, BRIGID BAPTISTE, Bryant and Morganstern were all assembled around the table, looking at the offsite diagnostics of the time trawl, trying to make heads or tails out of the data. Lakesh furrowed his brow as he analyzed the disjointed signals on the portable tablet computer he pored over.

"Suddenly, I am no longer enamored of science that requires alternate dimensions to allow varied phenomena to even out," Lakesh muttered.

"If that's a veiled reference to the physicist Kaluza informing Albert Einstein that the equations for light and gravity are resolved in the fifth dimension, you're reaching in terms of jokes," Brigid told him.

Morganstern and Bryant both chuckled at the thought, however. Lakesh managed a smirk, and said, "I'm playing to the scale of the crowd."

"Many of these signals do not make sense in the conventional scheme of things," Bryant said. "If anything, we have to consider that we're looking at alternate means of movement. Physically, Grant was present in ancient Sumeria, but he's also haunting this time. According to that weirdness, he's a ghost and a zombie all at once."

"Or simply two different forms of shadows, intersecting two eras at once," Morganstern explained. "Which means we need to be able to send Kane and Sinclair to three points in the multiverse."

"I'm going, as well," Brigid said firmly to the mathematician. The meek scientist looked up to the woman he considered a superheroine, brown eyes swimming as his efforts to protect her were rebuked. He lowered his gaze, duly admonished by her tone of voice.

"Damn it, Brigid, no wonder you can't get a decent tumble," Kane's voice boomed from the doorway. "You're a bully."

Brigid rolled her eyes. "Give me a break, Kane. We're working on high-level dimensional physics."

"And we're going to have to jump into that rabbit's hole to retrieve Grant," Kane concluded. "Why do we have to travel to three different places?"

"Frankly, the problem is not where Grant is, nor when, but a whole different question that hasn't been invented," Bryant explained. "Call it a where/when/how."

"I can get the where and when, but…" Kane paused before the next part of his sentence, knowing it didn't sound right even as the words left his lips. "How does the how apply to Grant's position?"

"We live in a multiverse involving all forms of reality. Casements are splits off the trunk of history formed by random events and decisions, so that you can have not a thread of reality, but entire cables composed of millions of such temporal fibers," Morganstern said. "We're situated, swimming along one thread, which we are steering through time and space by everything we say or do, or even the conditions amenable to an accident."

"The ghost Grant is somewhere between the threads? Or is he on another thread?" Kane asked.

Brigid raised an eyebrow.

"What, Baptiste?" Kane asked her.

"You're catching on to this quickly," she mentioned.

Kane shrugged. "The cable-and-thread description makes my head hurt a lot less than when Lakesh tries to lay it out, and hell, I've been to those other 'fibers,' as Daryl calls them. We both have, and it ain't new to Grant, either."

Brigid nodded. "God, how jaded are we that parallel universes are old hat?"

"I wouldn't say old hat," Lakesh interjected. "Even with the computational power of our recent discoveries, I haven't been able to access another dimension."

"Maccan did," Kane said. "And he damn near dropped a Martian pyramid on our heads when we slammed that door shut."

Kane groaned with a sudden realization. "Great, we might end up stumbling our way to where we exiled that pointy-eared freak."

"It's unlikely. The spaces between space-time threads are probably quite vast, despite the analogy of tightly wound cables," Morganstern said.

"If you're right, I'll owe you one, kid," Kane replied. "Bad enough that Maccan was furious with us when we caught up with him. Just imagine if we dropped into his lap."

"Bad," Lakesh said. It was rare for the physicist to use only one word when ten would have sufficed, but then, it had been a rare instance where he had been kidnapped and held prisoner by a malevolent force with little regard for him. He'd been in enemy hands before, but they were usually a "friendly" enemy like Erica van Sloan. Lakesh regretted his dalliances with the "dragon queen" when they had both been returned to relative youth by Sam the Imperator's technology. Yet for all of her attempts at worldwide conquest, she was still a human woman with allegiances to humanity, not the last of an ancient race driven insane by his loneliness and imprisonment.

"We'll close that door once we nab ghost Grant," Kane said.

"You can't put up a wall in transdimensional space, friend Kane," Lakesh countered. "It'd be like trying to stop a Manta at fifty thousand feet by putting a ten-foot-tall brick wall in its flight path."

Kane sighed. "I'm trying to reassure you, Moe. Maccan isn't coming back."

"Just like Thrush wasn't coming back? Or Sindri? Or good old mummified Enlil?" Brigid inquired.

"So we sit on our damn thumbs while one of our own is lost in the same whatever hole that we dropped a Tuatha asshole?" Kane asked.

"I can steer you close, given the information stored within the diagnostics," Morganstern replied, speaking up to cool down the raw nerves. "Given that Maccan was dimensionally shunted a year ago, and millions of miles away, the likelihood of you entering the same point of seventh-dimensional space is closing on impossible."

"But clearly not impossible," Lakesh said.

"I'll risk it for Grant. Besides, we're not going through without the right equipment, correct?" Kane asked.

"That's if firearms operate in such a dimension," Bryant said. "We are talking about alternate states of physics, and it's quite possible that the shadow that Grant's casting to this era has no physical component... and neither would you in that environment."

Kane squeezed his eyebrows together, then realized the different bodies he'd been when he was bouncing between parallel universes. Suddenly the concept of being a ball of energy wasn't so strange.

"If that's true, then what are we going to do to grab Grant if he's not grabbable?" Kane asked.

"Presumably, you'd be composed of the same form of energy as his shadow casts. It could be quite possible that all you have to do is return on your tether signal, and he'd piggyback on you," Morganstern said. "Whether he becomes corporeal or is a voice in your head when you return is academic at this point, but you will have made contact and retrieval."

"Any option on which would be better, a physical body or Grant bouncing around in my head?" Kane asked.

"Given that Mr. Grant would be entirely composed of ego in this particular shadow, I think we'd prefer him be a disembodied voice," Morganstern said.

"He'd be only a fragment of the Grant shadow left in ancient Sumcria. You'd probably have a drooling, insensate amputee or a withered skeleton," Bryant added.

"Right. Annoying voice good. Body bad," Kane answered. "Then we head to Sumeria and pick up the body?"

Lakesh nodded. "But even with a mental and a physical aspect, they are simply two shadows of the true organism. We need them, though."

"There'll be some kind of tether that can lead us to the original, right?" Kane asked.

"In a best-case scenario, yes," Lakesh replied. "In Egyptian mythology, there is a figurative silver thread linking the *ka* and *ba* of a being…the spirit and body of an immortal pharaoh."

"Spirit and body," Kane muttered. "Just like we have now."

"Supposedly, when the *ba* and *ka* are reunited, they recombine to live again," Lakesh said. "Who would have thought that this could be a mythical allusion to what we are experiencing here."

Lakesh frowned as he realized the irony of his statement. Over the past several years, the Cerberus explorers had encountered an entire litany of supposedly mythological beings and creatures that had been all too real. The concept of a mummy's body and soul being indicative of Grant's time-lost status suddenly didn't seem so far-fetched, especially given the addition of tesseracts—shadows of a being or object passed down from a higher dimension. The concept of the afterlife was hardly unique, and the Egyptians had the highest recognition of the nature of such a realm, storing servants, pets, food and riches for their god-kings who had passed on. The actual items themselves were inert, lifeless things without nourishment or actual worth to a dead man, but to a shadow, the shades of those items could be useful in a higher dimension.

It went with Lakesh's experience of how the Hindu religion understood the cyclical nature of the universe and the multiverse, an ever-renewing state of being drawn together. To the Hindus, the "discovery" of the Big Bang, the primal event where the universe was forged, was nothing new, something that had been told in the stories of Siva in his facet as Kali, dancing the death of an old world and a restart. In Lakesh's time, there had been a discussion of whether the universe would collapse on itself or continue expanding until entropy snuffed every erg of warmth and energy from the final atoms of reality. The entropic view had been winning, as there was no known means of creating a gravitational force that would draw far-flung galaxies back together into a primordial superatom.

That had been before preliminary evidence had been discovered about dark matter—a substance that possessed sufficient mass and subsequent gravitational pull to cause an aeon's distant collapse of gravity.

"Forgive me. Apparently my youthful clarity and vigor are failing me worse than I had thought," Lakesh lamented.

"You're still sharper than my combat knife, no matter how ancient you are," Kane replied. "So no excuses of diminished faculties, at least until we get Grant back."

"I'll never give up looking for our friend," Lakesh promised. "And if I personally have to walk through Maccan to do it, then I'll bring all I've got."

Kane nodded, clapping his friend on the shoulder. "I'm not interested in fighting him, either, so don't feel bad. You're smart not to want to throw down with that freak. It's all right to be scared. Scared sometimes makes you fight smarter."

"And here I thought your courage was blind stupidity and your success came from dumb luck," Brigid noted.

Kane locked her with a glare.

"If you're done flirting in here, Mr. Kane," Morganstern squeaked. He cleared his throat, surprised at his challenge to the hero of Cerberus. Kane could tell that there was more than a little bit of jealousy in his interruption.

"I'll go. I know you'll point me in the right direction to find Grant," Kane said. He smiled as he did so, trying to allay the mathematician's nerves about his status with the tall, beautiful archivist.

The four scientists continued to examine diagnostic code, line by line, searching for the formula that would be able to launch a rescue party for Grant.

All the while, they wondered how long their friend had been trapped at the beginning of history, and how much he had suffered.

Chapter 11

Enkidu wondered how long he had been unconscious as his eyes fluttered open. Tentatively, he moved the arm that he remembered had been gashed open in his conflict with the minotaur that had been dispatched as his shadow. It moved smoothly, without a hint of pain. He brought the fingers of his other hand to touch it, and realized that his hand, once broken, had its limberness and dexterity back. His fingertips met smooth, unscarred flesh, his bicep as firm and strong as it had been before the fight.

He reached for where his side had been rent, and that wound had been healed, as well. Flexing his wrist and making his fingers dance, he realized that if broken bones had been stitched and torn flesh had grown back together, he must have been out for months.

"You have been asleep for two weeks," a husky feminine voice said from the doorway of the cave he was in. "Without access to a cask, I was not able to mend your injuries swiftly, so I had to do it the slow way."

Enkidu sat up, looking to see the magnificent figure of Malesh, seven feet tall and carved of golden, nearly feline beauty. She was unmistakably human in her form, except that her apparent slimness was in proportion to a body that was stretched tall. Her limbs would have been willowy twigs on a woman of five-and-a-half feet, but at seven feet in height, the truth was that she was a powerful example of superhuman perfection. Dark hair with golden streaks poured down over her shoulders.

Though Humbaba had said she was his sister, the resemblance was merely in the eyes. She could have passed for a normal woman, if humans naturally grew to seven feet or more in height. The only signs that she had alien blood were her cold, yellow cat eyes and a slight flatness to her nose, which could have simply made her African in origin.

"You understand me, or I understand you," Enkidu said numbly. "That means…"

"I knew your meaning when you challenged my brother's beast pawn," Malesh said slowly. She milked each word of the sentence, every one a measured intonation that held both seduction and threat toward the man. "Of course, the very fact that you traveled from Eridu to my forest was an indication of your hostile intent."

"So what kept you from eliminating me?" Enkidu asked, pushing himself to his feet. He had been lying on a mat that bore the contour of his body. He must have lain there, immobile, for the entire two weeks to have created such a perfect impression. Either that or the mat had been molded especially for him, a perfect cradle for an injured, unconscious human.

He had no symptoms of stiffness, no bed sores from lying stationary for two weeks, so it was likely built to his specifications. This was not the technology of a woman who had been exiled to the primitive backwoods of a preindustrial planet. He winced as such an assumption hurt his brain due to its familiarity. Someone he had known in another lifetime had said such things, almost on a regular basis. Thus, he knew what he was talking about, but the lack of identities, either of himself or the cherished friend who had spoken those words, reminded him of the gaping wounds in his memory.

"Concentrate on something else, Enkidu," Malesh whispered softly. "Pay no mind to matters which no longer have concern to you."

Enkidu looked at the goddess at the cavern entrance. She was sufficient distraction from his psychic scars, though her presence raised a whole new set of questions.

"Like I said, why am I still alive?" Enkidu/Grant asked.

"You protected me when you could have allowed the beast to slay me," Malesh said. "You protected me at what could have been the cost of your life. When I laid you there, you were moments from your last breath."

"Still doesn't change my mission," Enkidu replied. He realized that he was completely naked, though the clothes he had worn, or suitable replacements, were folded on a table in the corner. Strangely, he didn't feel any shame, as if concern over his own nudity was dispelled.

The hole in his memory yawned in his consciousness once again, this time exacerbated by the temporal shadow of Malesh, who had recognized him. What Enkidu could not know was that Grant initially had shown reluctance to bathe naked with the samurai leader Shizuka during their first few days together. The boldness of the beautiful Japanese warrior had shocked him, and Grant was uncomfortable with such brazenness.

Reluctantly, he stayed, perhaps strengthened because he had already been attracted to Shizuka. She also seemed to pay no mind to what Grant had considered a flabby mess of middle-aged nudity. It had taken months, but Grant had grown to be completely comfortable with himself in her presence. He was still critical of his own appearance, but Shizuka had purged him of his shame of being exposed. What Enkidu also couldn't know was that the ghostly tendril, the tesseract that had reached out to him, was Shizuka.

Still, there was an instinctual recognition. Malesh and Shizuka were physical opposites, his samurai lover being petite yet hard muscled, while the goddess was huge, her musculature subtle beneath olive skin. But beneath the skin, from a perspective that only a displaced being could have, the two women were identical twins—warrior souls unafraid of a world bent on their destruction.

Enkidu took a couple of deep breaths, trying to control the flutter of Grant's heart.

"I tried to peer into your mind, but it is unattainable. All that I can do is comprehend your words, as if your vocabulary were the only piece of your intellect here, everything else hidden behind an impenetrable veil," Malesh explained. "It's interesting that your identity is hidden behind that veil, as if parts of your mind are not here, not formed."

"I appeared in Urudug, Humbaba's home, and was captured," Enkidu admitted. "He sent me after you, after he learned what leash to pull to control me."

Malesh narrowed her eyes. "What hold does he have over you?"

"My fellow humans," Enkidu said. "If I fail, dozens will be tortured and killed because of me."

"They would die anyway," Malesh said. "My brother sees humans as playthings, nearly inconsequential."

Enkidu's frown followed his drooping gunslinger's mustache. "Things aren't as clear-cut as I thought. I've been gone for weeks?"

Malesh nodded, her black-and-gold locks brushing over her smooth, muscular shoulders. "It is likely that you failed to protect those people."

Enkidu closed Grant's fists, tendons popping as anger bubbled from the core of his being. "You saved my life, but it really doesn't matter. I've failed."

Malesh tilted her head quizzically. "Who were these people?"

"Slaves. Innocent people toiling in the court of Urudug at Humbaba's pleasure," Enkidu said. "Women, children, old men, the kind of people I'm supposed to protect."

"Supposed to?" Malesh asked. "How well did you know them?"

"Not at all. I couldn't even speak their language, but I have my duty," Enkidu returned. Grant's upper lip curled up in a sneer. "Humbaba took my compassion and used it as a knife in my gut."

As if on cue, Enkidu felt a tremor of the muscles in his abdomen rippling up through his chest and down his densely muscled arms.

"What will you do?" Malesh asked.

"Go back," he told her, turning to gather his clothing. It took a few moments to strap into his sandal-bottomed boots, thick leather strips protecting his feet while metal braces ran from just above the ankle to just below his knee. With a flourish, he wound his kilt around his waist over the undergarment that protected his groin and thighs from the chafing thick lengths of studded leather.

Malesh rested a hand on his shoulder. "It's a suicide mission."

He turned, a cold, dark rage smoldering in Grant's eyes. "Let me go. This isn't your fight."

Malesh started to squeeze, but the Doppler effect of Enkidu's time-lost senses warned him of the firming of her grip and he wrenched himself free, feeling the sharpness of her nails leave shallow scratches on his skin. "Enkidu, you…I demand you stay here."

"Don't push your luck," the human growled. "Or I'll forget that you kept me here for noble reasons, not to allow your brother to murder more innocents."

"They were slaves. It was their lot to die. You…are different," Malesh said. Despite the reserve she held in her voice, he could sense an underlying current of frustration at his defiance. "You are a warrior…"

"And a warrior is fucking worthless if he can't protect the helpless," Enkidu grumbled. "Humbaba's slaves are the most helpless of all, and because I threw down with a goddamn hunk of livestock, two dozen women and children are dead, or tortured damn close to it. Get the hell out of my way before I knock you out of it!"

Malesh surged forward, hand winding back for a slap across the face. Enkidu saw the windup even before it began, and he plunged his foot between her feet, ensnarling her legs. He caught her by the wrist and pivoted, hurling her to the floor, using her strength and momentum against her. It was a maneuver that Grant been on the wrong end of in sparring with Domi and Shizuka, but Enkidu didn't know that. All he knew was that he'd derailed Malesh's assault, and in three swift strides, he was at the cave entrance.

With a suddenness that even his time-warped reflexes couldn't compensate for, Malesh snaked a strong arm

around Enkidu's throat. Forearm muscles as hard as
cedar beneath velvet-soft skin squeezed over his windpipe, pulling his head back. Enkidu had no time or leverage to slip out of the grasp before it had closed, but he
was able to bring up his own forearm to block the fist
that was going to press against the arteries in his neck
to finish the sleeper hold.

The swiftness of his reaction startled and distracted
Malesh long enough for Enkidu to take advantage of her
momentary slack to bring his elbow back into her ribs.
The blow knocked the breath from her lungs, further
loosening her hold. With a swift pivot and a firm grasp
on the goddess's forearm, he spun behind her, pulling her
hand up between her shoulder blades. He threw all of his
weight into slamming her against the cave entrance, but
Malesh was not without her own considerable reflexes.
She put her knee against the wall, giving her the leverage
necessary to keep her from banging her head against
unyielding stone. Enkidu grimaced and compensated for
her maneuver. He drew up both knees into the small of
the seven-foot goddess's back and yanked on her trapped
arm, twisting it.

His weight unbalanced Malesh, and she stumbled
backward, her resistance to his hard shove now working
against her. Enkidu tucked his legs up higher, his naked
back striking the stone floor as the two combatants toppled. On his back, he kicked out with all the power in
Grant's mighty legs, releasing the warrior woman's arm
as he did so. If he'd held on, he knew that the leverage
would have been sufficient to snap even her arm bones.
As it was, Enkidu wasn't interested in crippling Malesh,
simply tossing her aside, and she launched hard, her face
slamming into the ceiling of the cave before she bounced
to the ground, stunned.

Enkidu rolled to his hands and knees, looking at Malesh as she lay on her back, face out of sight so he couldn't tell how out of it she was. He rose to his feet, his head leaning closer to look over Malesh. "I'm not interested in breaking you apart. And I am grateful for your—"

Enkidu felt but didn't see the goddess's leg sweep across his ankles, so he didn't have the same reaction time his Doppler-effect senses could have given him otherwise. By the time he was reacting to her touch, he was cartwheeling in a spin caused by the force of her kick. Enkidu managed to catch himself on his hands, lowering himself to the ground to keep him from breaking his head on the cavern floor, but Malesh whirled fluidly to her own feet just as his touched the ground.

This time, Enkidu saw her coming, and in doing so, launched himself from all fours, his shoulder catching her in her smooth, tight stomach. Her abdominal muscles flexed under the impact, and she released a grunt of surprise as she was lifted from the ground. Malesh, once more on Enkidu's blind side, connected her elbow with his right shoulder blade, a powerful impact that jolted the strength from his legs. It didn't matter to the goddess, as the two people had combined to create enough momentum to jar her senses when they hit the wall. Those bamboo-strong abdominal muscles provided a safety cushion so that Enkidu didn't snap Grant's clavicle, but he still crashed to his knees, stunned by the double impact of Malesh's elbow and the wall.

"Save your gratitude, impertinent ape," Malesh panted, rubbing the ribs on the right side of her body. Her crash had done more than knock the wind out of her lungs, and it showed in her beautiful, faintly feline features.

"That's the trouble with you fucking aliens," Enkidu sputtered through Grant's lips, backing off. He had been restraining himself against the outlaw goddess, but there was no doubt that the reins were slipping on his control. If Malesh was holding broken ribs, then he'd gone too far. "Not a goddamn concern for humans, think you're so much better."

Malesh hadn't moved from leaning against the cavern wall, and Enkidu struggled against the battering he took, finally rising to his full height. "Are you okay, Malesh?"

Her head lowered slightly, her knees wobbly, and Enkidu almost took a step forward to offer aid when he noticed that her feet ground into the floor, getting traction. He preempted Malesh's ambush by bringing up his cupped hand to the side of her head. The cuff struck her over the ear, producing a burst of pressure that left the goddess reeling before her spring-steel muscles could snap in reaction to him. Malesh's head bounced off the wall again and she stumbled forward, staggered by the attack.

"Don't get in my damn way," Enkidu growled. "I don't like doing this—"

He was cut off as Malesh backhanded him with all the power of her right arm. Corded muscles propelled her fist across his jaw. Had he not noticed the swing coming, Enkidu knew that Grant's jaw would have been shattered like a crystal goblet struck by a sledgehammer. As it was, even though he'd buckled and rolled with the force of the impact, his head was still swimming, sloshing against the sides of his skull. Enkidu felt cross-eyed after that punch, and he could only claw at the side of the cavern, struggling for a handhold to keep standing. Blood poured over his split lower lip, nerves misfiring in the juncture between neck and brain.

Malesh's golden cateyes swung toward him, feral rage bubbling to the surface. The time for reason had passed; Enkidu had overridden her intellect and released the animal within. He'd defied her and caused her mind-splitting pain. Against such anger, all Enkidu could do was fight as ferociously as she did, for she was fighting to the death now.

Malesh whirled, fingers curled into flesh-shredding talons, pointed canines flashing through her open mouth. Enkidu responded, snapping a hard left into her face. He felt her nose cartilage crunch under his knuckles, and she stopped, her flowing black-and-gold mane pouring around his forearm as her forward momentum bled through her tresses. Enkidu grunted, feeling his knuckles crack, as well, the impact of her near three hundred pounds rolling up his arm and jolting his left shoulder.

The two figures bounced away from each other, but Malesh raked her clawlike nails down his extended forearm, leaving four bloody furrows in his skin. Enkidu was lucky that she didn't have the presence of mind to dig deeper as she fell back, but even by happenstance, she'd drawn blood easily. Enkidu lifted his foot, planting his sandal sole in her stomach with all of his weight on it. Malesh flew back, tumbling on the hard cavern floor.

Even hammered violently with a punch and a kick, Malesh had the grace and agility to somersault backward, landing in a low crouch, snarling on all fours. Enkidu flexed his fists, tendons popping. His left hand hurt like hell, but he continued to maintain a strong grip on that side. He still had his few human weapons.

Anger rumbled in his stomach as he knew that every minute fighting Malesh was a threat to finding out about his past, and a chance of crippling injury that would prevent him from destroying Humbaba. Right now, though, he didn't have the luxury of holding back. Malesh sprang forward like a great beast, claws extended to peel the flesh from his bones. Enkidu lunged at the same time, swinging his uninjured forearm up under Malesh's jaw as he wove between her extended talons.

Jarred in the throat, Malesh gurgled and choked, eyes bulging. Even so, she clawed Enkidu's back, a flaying double slash that left blood pouring down his back like a waterfall. Enkidu knew, however, that the sheets of muscle and heavy bone of the human back had been enough to turn a grizzly bear's lethal paw swipe into merely a painful, bloody gouge. He was cut but he wasn't crippled as he snapped his forehead into Malesh's jaw, the heavy dome of his skull driving her mandible back into her neck and the junctures of nerves just behind the hinges. It was an impact that would have left a lesser foe insensate, gasping for breath on the floor, but Malesh had the blood of inhuman races flowing through her long, lean limbs. The head butt floored her, but she still managed an animalistic howl of rage, sounding more like a mountain lion than a beautiful woman.

Enkidu kicked her, driving his heel into her upper chest hard enough to bounce her head off of the cavern's cold, stony floor. Even that stomp didn't keep Malesh from lashing out with her claws. The leather straps of his boot were carved away, his shin guard clanging on the ground. If it hadn't been for the thick strips protecting his calves, Enkidu knew that he would have had half of his leg torn off. As it was, he had to kick off the sandallike remnant to keep from tripping over the slashed boot.

Malesh brought up her second handful of cutting blades, and Enkidu brought up his other shin, intercepting the disemboweling swipe. Nails clattered against the bronze plate protecting Grant's leg, buying him enough time to grab her by the wrist with both hands.

Malesh pulled back with a strength that Enkidu almost didn't believe, but as he yanked on the powerfully muscled limb, he hopped and wrapped his legs around the arm, his ankles scissoring around her neck. Using every ounce of muscle in his rippling torso, Enkidu rolled until Malesh was pinned, chin to the ground, her free hand flopping helplessly as she couldn't reach under her torso or behind her back to reach him. The scissored ankles squeezed on Malesh's neck, a variation on the sleeper hold that had been meant to tame Enkidu earlier. Malesh thrashed, yowling and spouting curses in unknown, blasphemous languages.

"Calm down!" Enkidu bellowed. Though he had leverage and all of his weight devoted to keeping Malesh's right arm immobilized, she still had enough strength to flex it. If not for the pressure he was applying to her neck with his feet, she'd burst free easily. As it was, Enkidu held on, twisting with all of his might. She wasn't going to escape, because the moment she did, he'd be out of options. She was simply too strong and too fast for him, even though he operated at three times the normal passage of moments. The half-Annunaki continued to rail against him with unholy cries.

Enkidu yanked, pulling, twisting on the arm to keep it trapped, knowing as he flexed his spine and knees to hold her steady that he was applying neck-breaking force to her. He felt her vertebrae grinding under his naked ankle as leather straps ground against the flesh of her throat. The yells were choked off now, raspy gurgles signifying that he had her in a stranglehold.

"Pass out," he whispered, half praying, half begging the outlaw goddess in his trap.

Malesh writhed on the stone floor of the cave, her struggles ebbing as she was running out of the oxygen necessary to keep her muscles strong and vital. Enkidu hoped that her air was exhausted before he applied enough force to break her neck or permanently cripple her shoulder. He felt as if he had been fighting and praying for a half hour when finally she slumped, limp on the ground.

Enkidu relaxed his grasp instantly, even though he was aware she could be laying another trap for him. So far, he hadn't felt any indication that she'd suffered spinal damage, and the few pops her shoulder made sounded more like tendons snapping rather than the joint cracking.

"Damn it, woman, don't be dead," Enkidu whispered as he felt for her pulse. She was unconscious but still alive. He rolled her onto her back, gently, looking for signs of permanent injury.

Enkidu didn't want to think what kind of blood loss he was going to deal with, nor the chance of infection he risked thanks to the bloody wounds her talons had inflicted upon him.

Malesh's hand shot up, wrapping around his throat, her eyes snapping open and focusing on him. The grip was strong, her left hand's fingers as rigid as iron, the sharp points of her nails pressing on his skin.

"Could kill you…" Malesh whispered.

Enkidu couldn't say anything in response, both from shock at the sudden grab and from the force of her grasp around his windpipe. He let his shoulders sag. She loosened her grip.

"Speak…" Malesh croaked.

"Do what you want," Enkidu rasped. "You'd be putting me out of my misery."

Malesh let her hand slip from around his throat, and she sighed. "Just…so we understand…each other."

Enkidu crawled and slumped against the wall, leaning his shoulder against it.

He didn't want to go through another fight with Malesh again.

Chapter 12

Kane had stepped through the time trawl's event horizon, and everything stopped making sense. He could smell colors and touch sounds. He turned to look at himself and saw his body trailing behind him like a gigantic worm, a pulsing, throbbing artery stretching back across years and lifetimes. Nausea filled him as he looked closer at the turning segments, seeing different people as slices in the time stream.

Most were too far out of sight to make out details, but there was one, a tall, grim man dressed in sixteenth- or seventeenth-century garb, a tall hat atop his long brown hair, a large, fat belt with a buckle across his waist. Two flintlock pistol handles jutted from the heavy swash, a sharp saber hanging in its scabbard. He leaned heavily against a tall staff adorned with a crystal held in an unnatural-looking cradle. The image stalked along, and only momentarily looked up, facing a shadow through time. There was a moment of linkage, recognition, the Puritan's face looking concerned and studious as it saw the future shadow. The moment passed, and Kane writhed, swooping through what should have been a void, but more resembled a purple haze, crisscrossed with odd briars of unusual colors and arches formed of crumbling and reassembling rock.

Kane tried to concentrate on the area, looking for landmarks, but the terrain was fluid, an ever protean environment that melted and flowed into new appearances.

Another "timeworm" undulated, sidling up against him. As it neared, Kane recognized Brigid Baptiste, other women trailing back through the ages. He tried to speak, but his mouth didn't seem to work. If anything, it didn't even seem as if he could control his limbs, as if they were glued to the afterimages spiraling down his trail.

Think, Kane. That was Brigid's voice, and suddenly Kane became calmer.

We're telepathic here? Kane asked.

It's relative. Here, will can be power. We are operating with physics that even I have trouble understanding.

Kane glanced back down Brigid's timeworm, seeing a kaleidoscope of different women fading back through the odd space they'd entered. The archivist had as many incarnations as Kane had, but this was nothing new to the Cerberus explorer. Once, he'd assumed that the dreams he'd experienced in mat-trans jumps were feverish concoctions of his own mind, hallucinations induced by the disruption of his molecules. Now, he seemed to feel that this was the kind of space he and Brigid had been squirted through by the power of Lakesh's inventions.

Here was where Kane had felt and touched his past, his consciousness rolling down the core of the spine of his history as he traveled between points in space by leapfrogging through this dimension. It was something that created a weight on his mind, something solid and firm when the timeworm faded from existence.

"What's going on?" Kane asked. He was shocked that his voice worked, and realized that he was a whole and normal entity, despite the fact that he floated in the odd, ever-evolving null space. A green globe buzzed past him, smelling of berries and chiming away with tinny music.

"It took some effort and concentration, but I taught you how to ignore the distraction of our temporal dimensions," Brigid said.

"You taught me…the telepathy, right?" Kane asked.

"Indeed," Brigid responded. "That is as good an excuse as any. It seemed like it took a few years…"

"It probably did. Remember, we're where time doesn't really have meaning," Kane said. "At least that's what your boyfriend said."

The corner of Brigid's mouth rose in a wry smirk. "Are you certain you aren't jealous? You keep calling him my boyfriend."

"Isn't he?" Kane asked. "Either way, I like the kid."

"We're looking for Grant, not discussing my relationships," Brigid said. With that, she disappeared, seemingly stretching to the horizon of this odd void before being sucked toward it.

Kane blinked. This place did work oddly. He tried to figure out how to duplicate such a step, then dismissed it. Brigid had told him that will was reality here. He felt himself suddenly accelerate, blasting across the distance between himself and his fellow explorer, soaring like a Manta, only with even more control and dexterity. He wove around the odd briar bridges and avoided the strange spheres and hovering puddles hanging in the purple-backed world. In moments, he was at Brigid Baptiste's side.

"We need to get you a red cape and boots if you insist on traveling that way," Brigid muttered.

"You've got your style, I have mine," Kane replied. "Did you see Grant? Or were you just avoiding small talk?"

"I didn't see him," Brigid answered. "However, I am following the mathematical course laid out for me."

"Ah," Kane exclaimed. "We'll find another time to talk about the kid."

"You're not much older than he is," Brigid grumbled.

"But he's so small," Kane replied.

Brigid pressed her palm to her forehead, sighing. She regained her composure, and pointed. "That direction."

A small light flared in the distance as she pointed. She added. "Second star to the right, straight on till dawn."

Kane left before she could take one of her seven-league steps. The between space rolled past him as a blur. He enjoyed doffing the grip of gravity and flying under his own power. He knew it was simply his mind translating the experience of this realm into something he understood. Kane was drawing from his time behind the controls of the transatmospheric Mantas, itself only a more intense version of his time in the swift and deadly Deathbird helicopters.

At the same time, he realized that his banter with Brigid was simply a means of anchoring himself. He was focusing on the mundane in order to keep the expanse and protean nature of this "between" realm from stressing his sanity.

He landed at the beacon location, Brigid stepping in just after him. This particular location was a murky void, flickering stars winking to life before fading into oblivion.

"Not a friendly place," Kane muttered. Brigid had willed a flashlight into existence, its piercing beam slicing through the dark, actually carving wounds in the shadows that bled dark purple blood before the darkness closed, healing.

"That…is unusual," Brigid noted, shutting off the light. Instead, she created an oil lantern and hung it on an imaginary hook. The void was illuminated now, bubbling and hissing, but no longer acting as if it were being slashed apart. "I wonder what this could be."

"Just as long as it hasn't eaten Grant," Kane said, running his fingers along a membrane that had just winked into existence.

The membrane parted at Kane's touch, and he saw a Greek man; at least he resembled their friends from New Olympus. The man sat on a bench, brow wrinkled as if he was deep in thought. Kane could see that the man's thighs had grown to be a part of the stone. He was rooted to the spot.

Surprisingly, the man wore a purple tunic that hung over his shoulders and was cinched around the waist with an ornate leather belt with pouches wound around it. The tunic had a gold-thread design running around what would have been a hem, shaped in squares that were reminiscent of continuous waves. Sashed over one shoulder was a cloak, held in place by a large pin, hanging so that if the man was cold, he could wrap both arms easily. The whole style of dress was at once primitive yet highly refined, natural cloths woven together with skill. The Greek's eyebrows rose in response to Kane's arrival.

"Greetings, stranger. I am Theseus of Athens," the man said, his words translated by the realm. "You are…?"

"Kane, of the Cerberus redoubt," he answered.

"Cerberus, then you have been sent by Hades to release me from this torment?" Theseus asked. "No, wait, even as you speak the name of the watchdog, I know you speak of something completely different."

"My home is named after that three-headed dog," Kane replied. "What happened to you?"

"I came on a journey. Have you seen my friend Heracles?" Theseus asked.

"No," Kane answered. "I'm looking for a friend of my…"

Kane had to clench his eyes shut as he experienced a powerful surge of déjà vu. As he opened them, he saw a pulsing, almost electrical circuit, joining the two of them. He reached to touch it, but the Greek snatched at Kane's wrist.

"I would not tamper with that, Kane," Theseus replied. "In this place, such manipulations would be detrimental to both of our healths."

Kane looked back to see that Brigid was nowhere in sight. He looked down at the cord between them, recognizing it as another representation of the timeworm, as he'd named it. The Athenian and Kane were two points along that line.

"No wonder we can understand each other," Kane stated.

"We are two points along a continuous stream," Theseus replied. "Amazing."

A bulky, thickly muscled form appeared at the other side of the bench. For a moment, Kane was certain that it was Grant. Both men had the same height and build, and even his voice had the deep timbre of Grant's, but he was a few shades of bronze lighter than his friend, with a full beard and head of dark curls.

"Theseus, enough of your thinking," Heracles spoke. For a moment the giant glanced at Kane, and again the Cerberus explorer felt that this *had* to be Grant. "Your family misses you, it is time to go home. Who is this?"

"He is your friend," Theseus replied. "Perhaps you may be able to assist him."

Heracles raised an eyebrow, evaluating the man from the future. "For a moment, I thought you were talking to yourself. Then I thought he might be an impostor, but this is something...different."

"We seem to be on related quests," Theseus said. "However, unlike you searching for me, I am looking for you..."

Heracles looked between the two men. Only now had the muscular titan noticed the tether between the two. "Very strange. I shall help you, but I would appreciate your help with this bench."

Kane looked as Heracles took one of Theseus's arms. Kane gripped his friend the same way. "How do we know we won't rip his legs off?"

"We shall free him. Should he be able to walk, that will be a great boon," Heracles said. He began to pull, powerful arms swelling with incredible might. "Theseus seems to believe that you and he are the same."

Kane grunted as he pulled on his end. "We are linked...but we're hardly the same."

"We are in Hades, and in such a realm, we can see each other's souls, as well as his flesh. The two of you, in that aspect, are the same shining beacon of leadership and resourcefulness," Heracles explained. "Pull harder, Kane."

Kane looked up with disdain, leaning back harder. It felt as if he was trying to drag a Deathbird through a porthole. But slowly, surely, he was starting to feel the bench begin to surrender Theseus. His counterpart's upper arms and shoulders were now straining, the skin drawn taut over muscles that flexed in an effort to pull himself free. The tug-of-war against the bench felt as if it was against a living thing, despite the fact that he saw it had been simply stone.

"This is no mere couch carved of marble, Kane," Theseus said. "It is a tool of Hades. I felt the need to stop and think, and next I knew, it had grown to absorb me. This is no more inert stone than…aggggh…"

There was an ugly ripping sound. Theseus looked down, watching as flesh was pulled off. However, instead of a grisly display of blood and torn muscle, this seemed to be clay shorn from one clump to rest on another. The two men pulled harder to release the third, and finally Theseus came loose from the bench. The Athenian winced, then clutched the back of his thighs.

"Zeus's thunder," Theseus whispered. "I'm surprised I have enough leg left to stand on."

"As I said, anything more would be a great boon," Heracles said with a throaty chuckle. "Aha! Look, your legs are of the same lean build now."

Kane looked down. He hadn't changed, but apparently Theseus's thighs had been thicker before. Idly, he remembered the lean limbs of the Puritan with the odd walking stick. It couldn't have been a coincidence, Kane thought.

"You seek my counterpart from your realm?" Heracles asked.

"His name is Grant," Kane said.

Heracles folded his thick arms across his barrel chest, rubbing his bearded chin.

"I felt something accompany me since I trod my first steps in this odd realm," Heracles told him. "Grant…is that you?"

A deep sigh resounded in the chamber before a whispered "Yes" met Kane's ears.

Heracles smirked. "'Tis not often that I solve a problem through observation and thought, but when I do think…"

He winked to Theseus, who chuckled. The Athenian rested a hand on Heracles's shoulder. "No one ever called you dim, my friend."

"So what are we going to do?" Kane asked.

"Just as my brother in blood was able to seek me out through the bonds of friendship, your Grant can now reach out to you," Theseus replied.

"Sounds like a bunch of mumbo jumbo to me," Kane muttered.

Theseus pointed to the bench, which had two strips of pink flesh, then to the pulsing line between them. "We are not on our Earths. This is another world, one where gods live."

"Will to power," Kane repeated Brigid's earlier statement. "Physics doesn't work the same here."

"Perhaps we are all gods somewhere," Theseus said.

Kane reached out to Heracles. "I'll take Grant for now."

Heracles looked to the offered hand, then gripped it with a gentle firmness that seemed to be in contrast to his awesome build. Perhaps the huge Greek, who knew he was so strong, knew he had nothing to prove with a handshake. There was a spark, long after their palms touched, indicating that whatever was happening, it wasn't a matter of static electricity between the two men. The spark turned into a long humming jolt as Grant flowed like water between Heracles and Kane. Kane drew his hand back, flexing his fingers, feeling as if his lower right arm was stuffed with lightning, arcs crackling across spaces between his arm hairs. It wasn't pain so much as pressure and warmth, and eventually his forearm hair lay back down. It had turned into a throbbing pulse, locked deep within his bones.

"Well met, friend Kane," Heracles said. "May your journeys always bring you home."

"Good luck to you, Herc—" Kane began, then blinked in recognition of the powerful figure before him. "Hercules?"

"Heracles," the Greek corrected. "Though I've been called that by others, so I take no offense."

Kane looked down at his forearm, then up to see a new membrane floating across the room. He glanced at Theseus and his mythic friend, and as the membrane flowed around him, this spot in Hades faded, replaced with the nonspace of briars and floating orbs.

"Kane! Where have you been?" Brigid Baptiste snapped, floating toward him. The woman was disheveled again, and she gripped her flashlight as if it was a broken sword. The lens on the torch was broken, and the butt cap had fallen off. "What's wrong with your arm?"

"I found Grant, I believe," Kane answered. "Was Hercules ever known as Heracles?"

"What does that have to do with anything?" Baptiste inquired, annoyed as she ran her fingers over Kane's right arm. She touched it, and heard Grant whisper, "Hello." At the utterance, she recoiled in surprise. "Oh, my."

"I met with two men named Heracles and Theseus, after I'd gone through one of the membranes hovering around here," Kane said. "What happened to the inky blob we were in?"

"It moved on," Brigid said. "It didn't like my flashlight."

"It attacked you," Kane murmured. In the distance, he could see what appeared to be a cloud and an inchworm, squeaking along through space. The ex-Magistrate smirked. Whatever the puddle of darkness had thought of human prey like Brigid, it had learned a painful lesson. The archivist was not an easy meal for predators, in this or any universe.

Brigid closed her eyes, and a moment later, she was perfectly coiffed, cleaned up from her ordeal. Even her flashlight seemed to recover. In between the threads of time's onward flow, the power to turn imagination into reality was limited only by willpower, and Kane had to remember that the torch she held was a construction of her thoughts. "You're telling me that you went back in time?"

"I didn't say that. I said that I'd entered a membrane which took me somewhere else," Kane said. "A place that Theseus called Hades. He was trapped on a bench—"

"He had sat down to think and couldn't get up. His flesh had grown to its surface, and when his friend Heracles came to rescue him, Theseus left a portion of his thighs behind. Since that time, all Athenian men have had slender thighs," Brigid Baptiste said. "Where did you read that story?"

"I didn't. I lived it," Kane told her. "I was also linked to Theseus, just as Grant had gravitated toward Heracles."

Brigid frowned as she looked at Kane, his arm pregnant with energy that felt like Grant. "That's a big claim, but then, Theseus had much in common with you, if the myths have any basis in reality. He was a trickster, as well as a fighter."

"I suppose the similarities between Grant and Heracles are obvious, as well," Kane muttered.

Brigid suddenly seemed lost in thought. Before her appeared two tiny images of Kane and Grant. The figures split, the Kane forming himself and Theseus, while Grant begot Heracles.

"Yes." Grant's whisper resonated around them. "Yes. More."

"What are you doing?" Kane asked.

"We discovered what may have been the court of Humbaba in the city of Eridu," Brigid replied.

As if she'd summoned it, a small tabletop diorama of the underground temple exactly like the one in which Kane had rescued her appeared. He half imagined swarms of ant-size zombies, then stepped back as they suddenly appeared, spilling out of the sides of the model. Their diminutive forms tumbled through the empty void.

"Kane, be careful," Brigid admonished. "Brush yourself off. The last thing we need are bug-size zombies coming back through the time trawl."

Kane nodded, dismissing the creatures completely. He made certain to think of each of the creatures that spiraled into the null space, locking on each and returning it to the nothingness of this realm. As he completed the destruction of the phantom miniatures, the tiny temple swelled in size, surrounding them. Except for the increased lighting, a glow that was provided by lit torches in metal cages bolted to the wall, it was exactly how Kane had remembered it.

"This is impressive," Kane said. "One of the benefits of that endless memory you have."

"Partly a gift, partly a curse," Brigid replied. She strode toward a corner of the temple floor, intently focused on something. Kane wondered what when he realized that this structure was changing before his eyes.

"When we entered, the floor was bent," Brigid explained. She pointed, and a crack hinged in the ground, pushing up.

"I remember," Kane said. "It had been buried, right?"

"It had always been built underground," Brigid noted. "Something had pushed the floor up beneath the court of Urudug, crushing the wall we'd entered through, burying Grant's coat."

"Huh?" Kane looked and watched as the floor rose, smashing the wall inward, creating a pile of broken stone. "Right, where we'd come in."

"This was where Humbaba stood as the guardian of the Cedar Forest," Brigid said. "Humbaba was slain by the great hero Gilgamesh for the fruit of eternal life, hidden behind the very gates where we fought those zombies."

"That kind of eternal life isn't the kind of existence I'd want," Kane muttered.

"That's what Mariah had said," Brigid returned. "Gilgamesh had a companion."

Kane noticed that Brigid still had her images of Kane, Grant, Theseus and Heracles. Now they had split again, another pair appearing before her, but only split off from Grant.

"I presume that's Gigamush and the buddy you were talking about," Kane noted.

"Gilgamesh had dared to oppose the Sumerian gods," Brigid told him. "In an effort to stop that rebellion, they sent a man-beast, a powerful humanoid who had been an untamed wildman, to battle the outlaw."

Kane looked at the duplicate of Grant, this time cast in the role of a Bronze Age Sumerian warrior. The other figure was a clean-shaven man, himself possessed of great height and power. "That's Gig."

Brigid nodded. "And the man-bull sent to battle him was named Enkidu. A being sent by the gods, but who turned against those same beings because he had developed a love for Gilgamesh."

"Grant's straight," Kane said.

"History is patriarchal. There was a pharaoh who lived her life as a man, but was actually a woman in disguise," Brigid mentioned. "In Britain, the Romans who tried to denounce the rebel queen Boudicca said she was actually a man who dressed as a woman. That bit of revisionism was erased from the history books, however, and Boudicca became a fabled folk heroine. Who is to say that Gilgamesh might not be a woman?"

"That's why you didn't split Gig off from me," Kane said.

"Together, Gilgamesh and Enkidu defied the will of Enlil and slew Humþaba in order to gain access to the Cedar Forest," Brigid continued.

Kane grimaced. "Enlil. Let me guess, Humbaba was another one of his rotten kids."

"Not all of his children are bad. Don't forget Fand," Brigid said.

"So what happened to Gig and Grant after they offed Humbaby?" Kane quizzed.

Brigid winced. "We're not certain that Enkidu is Grant."

"Baptiste, what happened?" Kane snapped.

"The gods took him," Brigid said.

"Took him," Kane repeated. "What happened?"

"Gilgamesh didn't know. He sought him across the whole of the world," Brigid explained, speaking softly, as if holding back.

"Did Enlil kill Enkidu?" Kane growled.

Brigid took a deep breath. "The story says that Enkidu was taken away, never to be allowed to see Gilgamesh again."

Kane scowled. "Enlil killed Grant."

The temple crumbled away around them as Kane felt a terrible pang in his heart.

Chapter 13

The two figures waited by the side of the road, crouched in the long grass, concealed beneath cloaks of woven grass blades. They watched as the convoy grew closer. The target was an army in transit to protect recently captured slaves who would be sent to Eridu to toil under the lashes of the slave masters of Urudug. Though most of the soldiers appeared human, there were a few who concealed their heads and arms beneath cloaks, leggings hiding their thighs and calves. The hoods did nothing, however, to disguise the fact that these soldiers were nearly a half foot taller than the people they were escorting, and none carried a spear or sword.

Enkidu leaned closer, mouthing words, but Malesh could hear him though his "spoken" thoughts. The sharpest of ears couldn't pick up on their conversation. "Look at what's on their wrists. Either they're wearing too much jewelry, or they've got ASPs."

"The arms of Enlil," Malesh returned with her telepathy. "Humbaba is desperate if he is allowing the Nephilim to mingle with men while wearing plasma projectors."

Enkidu/Grant looked down to the bow that lay in the grass beside him. He'd spent a couple of weeks designing and constructing the weapon, working from memories of what he had known. He wished that he had the ability to forge steel and mix gunpowder to create an analog to the Sin Eater and Calico taken from him in the court of Urudug, but that kind of chemistry and iron working were unrealistic under the circumstances.

However, the body dynamics of archery, especially combat archery, were stored in his mental files. Construction was simple. Even finding a proper cord to serve as the bowstring had been easy after "borrowing" some horsehair from steeds liberated from Humbaba's soldiers. The convoy was mostly on foot, evidence that setting horses loose into the wild had been a drain on the court's resources. It had been a month since Enkidu and Malesh had begun the raids, and trying to recapture the horses in the forest ruled by Malesh was too hard for Humbaba's forces, especially with their guerrilla tactics.

"How desperate would you like to make him?" Enkidu asked, tightening his grip around the center of the bow.

Malesh's smile was as wry as it was subtle. "Let fly, man-bull."

Enkidu didn't rise but remained kneeling. The top curve of his bow sticking up from the long grasses looked more like an extralong leaf or a ratty, stripped stalk or sapling. His powerful arms and shoulders swelled as he drew back the string, an extralong arrow necessary because of the prodigious spread of his limbs. The composite wood creaked under the strain, and only a half second was needed to lock on target. He released the string, the bow's struggles to return to straightness rewarded. Energy transferred from string to shaft, and in a heartbeat, the lead Nephilim jerked violently. He half turned, two feet of bloody arrow jutting from the back of his head, stringy lumps of brain attached to the arrowhead.

The reptilian drone's hood had been plucked off its head, and soldiers screamed as much in surprise at the monstrous creature's appearance as at his violent demise. Their shock froze them as two more of the Nephilim whirled to face their leader. A third one had the presence of mind to look to the field for the source of the lethal assault.

Enkidu pulled a second shaft from his quiver and nocked it in one smooth movement. As quick as he was, Grant's experience told him that he was by no means the fastest of archers. However, his phenomenal strength was sufficient to keep the bow steady and accurate. The draw and fire movements were still swift enough to catch the alert Annunaki slave through the chest before he could locate Enkidu and Malesh's position. The Nephilim looked down, not understanding that Enkidu had used finely chipped obsidian glass to form the arrowhead.

The volcanic stone could be ground down to an edge that was finer than most cutting surfaces available in this or even the modern world. The slicing surface was only a few molecules thick, and more than strong enough to part even the toughest of hide. This arrow didn't penetrate quite as far into its target, but that was because the obsidian had been shattered on impact with the heavy trunk of the alien's spinal column, as opposed to the relatively thin facial bones and through the concave inner surface of the back of its brother's skull.

The destruction of the obsidian arrowhead created a sheet of shrapnel that whirled violently through the Nephilim's lungs, severing vital blood vessels. It hadn't helped that the aorta had already been torn violently by Enkidu's arrow, hemorrhaging heavy gouts that flooded his thoracic cavity. Red syrup burst from the dying creature's mouth and it collapsed backward, its ASP discharging a sinuous, pulsing stream of energy that outshone the sun.

Soldiers were torn between standing their ground and fleeing. When the fiery release of the wrist blaster split the sky, half of the Sumerian soldiers broke and ran. Such weapons belonged to battling gods, and mere men had no place in the midst of such conflict.

Enkidu looked to see if Malesh was still there, but the outlaw goddess was on the move, already only a few feet away from the two Nephilim looking over their first fallen comrade. The ASP bolt searing through the air had wrested their attention completely away from Malesh, who, despite her own lightning quickness, moved with slightly less noise than a gale of wind through tree branches. By the time the hooded drones were aware of the rush of air coming up on them, Malesh was past them both, her fingers steeped in blood and torn flesh from their throats.

Nearly decapitated, the Nephilim couldn't do much more than reach up to stanch their wounds. The loss of major arteries feeding their brains made such movements pitifully inadequate, and both alien soldiers toppled into lifeless heaps of scaly flesh.

Enkidu couldn't understand a shouted command from one of the convoy, but he could tell that it was a human commander with more courage and duty than he'd seen so far. There was a moment of guilt as he looked for the man, knowing that by killing him, he'd be able to break the will of Humbaba's remaining loyal guards. Enkidu didn't like the idea of killing another human; he knew he was a time traveler, and he didn't want to have an effect on the history of the world. There was no guarantee that someone he'd cripple or kill wouldn't be the ancestor of a vital person later in time. On the heels of the sudden shout, a flight of spears arched into the sky, a rain that sailed toward him.

"Damn," Enkidu cursed. With a surge, he charged toward the convoy, feeling the spears pluck at the grassy mat that had camouflaged his shoulders. Thanks to his altered experience of time, Enkidu had barely avoided being turned into a pincushion. To return the favor, Enkidu nocked and fired a third arrow into the chest of yet another Nephilim warrior. The shaft sliced through him.

That was the last of the disguised alien drones, but now the bow was going to be useless in close combat, not like the spears the human soldiers carried. Enkidu tossed the bow to the side, unsheathing his sword in the same smooth movement. He whirled the *kopesh* in an arc, lopping through a half-dozen spear shafts in one powerful swing.

"Malesh! Their leader's giving them hope!" Enkidu called out.

"I see him!" the outlaw goddess returned.

Enkidu glanced over to see Malesh push two grown Sumerians aside as if they were rag dolls. She had been ruthless in ripping the throats out of the Nephilim, but she was filled with reluctance to use those same inhuman talons on the men sent to oppose her.

There had only been one human who had been brave enough to stand against her in combat, and that man was now battling at her side. Enkidu, on the other hand, didn't feel regret at having to put down soldiers trying to kill him. Even so, the *kopesh* flickered to and fro, causing only injury with the flat of his blade, not fatal gashes in limbs and torsos. The good thing about the *kopesh* was its hooked nature, its concave blade blunt and heavy spined. It was perfect for knocking heads and scooping people off their feet. So far, he'd been able to batter the fight out of people by being a living whirlwind, flooring opponents so quickly that they couldn't recover their senses.

A spear sizzled through the air, its bronze point aimed at Enkidu's heart. With a pivot, he swatted the weapon off course with the *kopesh*. As he returned to his course, he brought up his forearm to chest level, just the right height to smack three men in the head, bowling them off their feet. Enkidu found it easy to keep his human opponents at bay, though he knew that something as minor as a hand injury could mean the end of a soldier's life. His reactions were far faster than those he battled, his combat training from a world that had developed fighting into an art form, so his precision was more than sufficient.

Malesh pounced on the chest of a man, driving him to the ground with a double kick that threw up a cloud of dust that obscured the two people for a moment. That must have been the commander of the cadre, and Enkidu worried that if she landed on his ribs, she'd have driven them through his heart and lungs. It took a moment for him to remember that it was Malesh who had implored him to employ less than lethal force against his fellow humans.

Malesh stood over the commander, who surprisingly was still conscious. She glared at the spearmen around her. They had frozen in shock over their leader, fallen in battle.

The outlaw goddess hissed the men's native language, a sibilant tongue that sounded even more sinister when spoken as a grim threat. Enkidu didn't need her to translate for him. The spiel had been the same as every other battle they'd had with Humbaba's slave caravans and supply runs. She was offering them freedom and safety if they abandoned the armies of Eridu and forsook the court of Urudug.

If any had wished to fight alongside Malesh and Enkidu against the beast of the Cedar Forest, they were welcome. Several had accepted the offer, though the two rebels hadn't taken them out on missions, preferring to utilize their growing army to safeguard the freed slaves of Humbaba. Such guardianship was as vital a chore as encountering the convoys, especially since both Malesh and Enkidu were skilled enough so as not to endanger lives on these raids.

Enkidu/Grant stood his ground, prepared in case there was a secondary force waiting in ambush. This convoy had pack animals but no slaves. That was something of a blessing, especially since there were more than enough hungry mouths in the forest at this time. Sooner or later, the outlaws were going to have to establish livestock and crops to keep themselves sustained. Cherry-picking from Humbaba's convoys was enough to stave off starvation, but it wasn't going to keep people healthy.

"Enkidu, we have some more friends," Malesh said, extending her hand to help their leader rise.

Worry wrinkled Grant's brow as he looked around. This was too easy, despite the numbers against them. The Nephilim had acted swiftly, but surely Humbaba was smart enough not to underestimate his sister. After all, the half-Annunaki bastard had the foresight to send a genetically engineered monster and a small squad of Nephilim as a backup to Enkidu himself.

Maybe it was just all the months of lost memory, living in a world that was familiar yet alien. He'd reached levels of paranoia that once had been vital to survival, but could be wearing thin. Enkidu didn't think that a big, brawny brawler such as himself would have been much for logic, and yet he listened to the nagging voice of common sense whenever it piped up.

Keep focused, Enkidu told himself. You lose faith in your senses, Humbaba will eat you for lunch.

"Enkidu?" Malesh asked. "Something concerns you."

He had his ears peeled, but he didn't know what for. He hung his sword on his belt and retrieved his bow, looking at one of the fallen Nephilim. He was tempted to retrieve one of the alien drones' powerful wrist blasters, but he didn't know how much time he had. "Malesh, get these men to cover now."

"Cover?" Malesh asked.

Something glinted from behind a cloud, and suddenly Enkidu remembered the unnatural brightness of the ASP bolt that had discharged into the air. "Hide!"

Malesh looked up, recognition dawning on her golden bronze features. Her black-and-gold hair flew as she whirled, snarling out a warning in the soldiers' native language.

Enkidu's temptation to take an ASP wrist blaster was now all consuming. It was his only option in the face of the sleek, silver-skinned skimmer craft. The disk-like aircraft were rarely seen through history, but they had been noticed. In the twentieth century, such silver flyers were called UFOs, unidentified flying objects. Enkidu knew, from Grant's vocabulary, that they were also known as skimmers and they were deadly aircraft, though not unstoppable.

Indeed, he seemed to remember wielding something called a rocket launcher, blowing the skimmers out of the sky with nothing more than a conventional warhead.

Unfortunately, Enkidu also knew, from Grant's practical knowledge, that a reliable rocket launcher wouldn't be invented for at least three thousand years, though the Chinese had far cruder explosive gunpowder loads about five hundred years before that. All of this knowledge was academic, except to inform Enkidu that he wouldn't be completely helpless. He pulled the *kopesh* from his belt, ready to lop off the Nephilim's arm at the elbow in order to retrieve the ASP blaster. Its charged energy crystal would have more than sufficient juice to get off a couple of skimmer-damaging shots, if he was lucky. Light blazed in Enkidu's face as the Nephilim at his feet was hammered with a bolt of energy. It was the same kind of plasma as utilized by the ASP blasters, except on a slightly larger scale.

The bolt had landed ten feet in front of Enkidu, and it had been intended to at least deny the human access to the dead Nephilim's weapon. The heat flash was blinding and stinging, arriving at the speed of light so that even his time-altered reflexes couldn't respond quickly enough. Enkidu stumbled backward as the dead alien drone was incinerated by the plasma stream.

"Enkidu!" Malesh cried out.

"Run!" he bellowed, pushing himself to his feet from where he'd crashed in the dirt. The cloud released by the skimmer bolt's impact was all obscuring, which was a blessing as now the human was invisible from the air. Unfortunately, the flying dust was sticking to Enkidu's charred skin. He was going to be suffering when the numbing embrace of adrenaline faded from his system, which would be minutes if he managed to avoid further skimmer fire.

Enkidu raced through the cloud, broken-field style, zigging and zagging in the dust as he rushed toward the spot where he'd remembered another dead Nephilim's position. He knew that the pilot of the shiny disk might have targeted the other bodies on the ground. He remembered targeting systems from his time; he even recalled being in the interior of one such craft. Even through the dust cloud, if the skimmer's guns were locked on to certain positions, they could easily hit the dead drones repeatedly. He was certain that he'd either flown one of the skimmers or he had worked on a finely crafted simulator.

Enkidu closed in on where he knew the next closest Nephilim body was, and he reached down, hooking the corpse's shoulder, continuing at a full clip in an effort to get out of the path of the skimmer's guns. The weight of the Nephilim was more than enough to slow Enkidu by a half step, but a rain of hurtling plasma bolts ripped through the dust, searing holes through the cloud with their passage. One of those power streams slammed into the earth where he'd been a second before. Only the fact that he crossed a yard with each stride and he was five strides away from the corpse's original resting place had protected him from being caught in the heat flash, sparing him more burns.

Already, he could feel the skin curling and tightening where it had been dried out. Most of his injuries were relatively minor first- and second-degree burns, but he had at least one third-degree burn that was cracking with each movement. It was on his chest, and while running and jumping for his life, there was no way he could hold his torso still so that he wasn't causing damage to seared epidermis.

Enkidu/Grant leaped into the long grass, knowing that it was a poor substitute for cover. It would only provide concealment from the hostile skimmer, and he knew damn well that there were optics and sensors on the ship that could peer through foliage as if it were glass. He didn't have much time, and the air thundered as the skimmer burst through it, slicing over the clearing. The sonic boom rattled Grant's teeth, and he knew that it was just a softening tactic. Even if Enkidu had possessed a weapon capable of bringing down the ship, there was no way he could have tracked such a high-speed object, at least under normal circumstances.

Enkidu drew his knife and swung it against the elbow of the dead Nephilim, hearing the clank of metal on his bronze blade. The *kopesh,* which had far greater cutting power, was lost back where he'd been caught in the heat wave. He'd been only two yards away from where he'd have been suffering deep-tissue burn damage rather than one major and several minor burns. Panting, he knew that he might never have enough time to hack off the smart-metal armor that encased the Nephilim's right arm. With a frustrated snarl, he raised the curved blade and brought it down with all of his might. The metal resisted, only two inches of surface being cut. Blood started to seep from the cracks in his chest, thanks to his exertion. Another rise of the blade and its drop split more of the metal skin. A squirt of blood sprayed into Enkidu's face as his knife chopped all the way down to bone.

"Come off, damn you!" Enkidu snarled, chopping a third time. Metal clanged, bone crunched and flesh was parted. He was halfway through the arm, and he knew that his time was running down.

The bronze knife was blunted, its edge chipped and warped as it hacked at a material that it was not designed to defeat. Its metalurgy was insufficient to hold up to more than a few swings, unlike the nearly monomolecular edges of his obsidian arrow. His only real hope was that the compromised weave of the armor would allow him to tear the forearm loose.

The concealing cloud of dust had been snuffed by the supersonic passage of the skimmer, taking away what protection it had provided. High in the air, he saw the skimmer as a bright flash, a brilliant star in the daylight sky. It was looping a mile over the battlefield, swinging around for a fresh chance to strafe the time traveler out of existence.

Enkidu jammed one foot into the armpit of the corpse, dug his fingers into the forearm and twisted with all of his might. The joint popped loose immediately, muscle ripping under the force of his leverage. The armor itself released a rasp as compromised links popped apart. Another two or three tugs, and the arm might actually come loose, then he could peel the ASP from around the corpse's wrist.

The air crackled as more plasma rounds hammered into the grass. Enkidu rolled away, panic giving his feet wings, and he didn't let go of the partially severed forearm. A bolt's impact struck the ground, releasing a heat flash, pressurized air rolling over the two figures, providing just enough energy to pop corpse and outlaw apart. Enkidu slammed into the dirt, rolling in the grass as smoke roiled into the sky, the skimmer disappearing behind choking gouts.

It took a moment to realize that he hadn't surrendered the body part. With a wrench, he broke the Nephilim's wrist, crushing hand bones in order to make things easier to pull off. For a second, he wondered why he just hadn't cut off the corpse's hand, but then he realized that he knew he'd be more likely to slam the edge of the *kopesh* into the ASP itself, rather than lop through the finger bones in the way. A damaged, high-powered energy emitter would have caused him even further burns, possibly even fatal injuries. At the very least, he'd end up with a sword that wouldn't have been able to cut mud.

"Don't second-guess yourself, asshole," Grant/Enkidu snarled to himself, yanking the ASP free from its mounting on the forearm armor. The metal itself, no longer plugged into the smart node at the base of the Nephilim's neck, was still hard to cut, but was as flexible as silk. It slid down the hand along with the ASP, tinkling to the ground as it was now freed.

He looked around. Malesh and the other slaves were nowhere to be seen, but with the grassfire started by the skimmer, they could have just been thirty feet away, roasting in the flaming foliage.

"Malesh!" he called.

"Be at ease, Enkidu," came Malesh's telepathic response. "Clear your mind and I will guide your aim."

Enkidu knew that he wouldn't be able to hit a supersonic ship if he couldn't see it, even with a hand-portable plasma blaster. It took a few moments for him to slip the energy weapon around his right wrist. The ASP was made of a trio of burnished, gold-colored coils that all slid around his forearm like a noose, except comfortably. The three heads of the coils were flattened, looking akin to snakes, cobras to be exact. Concealed under a lump of the coils was a charged energy module, a crystal that throbbed with the power necessary to generate a deadly bolt.

Enkidu flexed his fist. He'd seen the weapon in use before, and somehow, he'd actually tested a captured model. It just wasn't the same as the Sin Eater, the gun that he'd worn when he'd first arrived. That, too, had been strapped to his forearm, and was a natural part of his body, stored in reflex memory. The wrapping of the ASP around his arm was something Enkidu did on autopilot, following Malesh's telepathic admonition to clear his mind. The sky was suddenly clear overhead, and he could see the thick, churning clouds gouting up from the grassfire.

That was Malesh's point of view, and thanks to her psychic contact with Grant/Enkidu, she was able to pinpoint him. He now had an estimate of where he had to shoot, though the hostile skimmer was hovering hundreds of feet up and away, just outside the range of the ASP, he presumed.

"Of course, you're not going to make this easy," Enkidu said with a sneer. "You're going to hang back until the smoke clears."

The fire also was interfering with the skimmer's infrared optics. There was no way that he was going to be an easy target soon, but thanks to the power source of the skimmer, it could hang in the sky for hours. Enkidu didn't have that kind of patience to deal with the Annunaki's deadly little scout. Exploding into a run, he charged toward where he'd estimated the edge of the fire was.

He was going to make himself an easy, tasty target.

Sure enough, as soon as Enkidu was in the open, the skimmer took the bait. It dived out of the sky, plasma bolts ripping from apertures in its hull, searing the ground in his wake. The enemy pilot swung the ship around closer, its aim homing in on the time-lost warrior.

Chapter 14

Lakesh was intrigued at Kane's and Brigid's reappearance. The two were bewildered, having returned from the dimension between dimensions, a pocket in space time that was just outside of the reality he was in.

"How was your journey, friend Kane?" Lakesh asked.

Kane opened his mouth, then shut it. He looked over at Brigid Baptiste, their eyes meeting. "Please tell me at least you have some recollection of where we were."

Brigid grimaced, concentrating on their travels. "How long were we gone, Lakesh?"

"An hour," the Cerberus head scientist replied. "How long did it feel like?"

"I don't remember," Brigid admitted, her cheeks reddening. "For once in my life, I can't access something I've experienced."

"What about the rest of your recollections?" Lakesh inquired.

"Still perfect. I'm just fuzzy on what happened…are you certain we went in?" Brigid asked.

"We projected you through the time trawl utilizing an experimental mathematical equation," Lakesh answered. "We scanned the globe for signs of you via your biolink transponders…"

"Not a sign of you, boss," Edwards said, directing his comment to Kane.

"So did we even get…" Kane trailed off, looking down to his lower right arm. "Grant?"

Kane's Commtact sighed through his mandible. "Yes."

From the looks on the others' faces, those who had an operating Commtact, which excluded Edwards, Morganstern and Waylon, had also heard his friend. Kane rubbed the limb. It felt as if it was stuffed with heat packs from survival kits. He frowned.

"You retrieved him! Wonderful," Lakesh exclaimed.

Kane grunted an agreement. "No one is happier than I am. Grant, do you know what happened to us?"

"No," came the slow response over their implanted communicators. There was a hesitancy that went beyond the difficulty of communication from his disembodied form.

Brigid blew out a stream of air in frustration. "Apparently, while we might have had experiences in that dimension, our intellects were unable to deal with it. We are three-dimensional beings, and we were operating on a higher plane where information doesn't translate into our current methods of visualization."

"In English, Baptiste?" Kane pleaded.

Brigid pursed her lips before going on. "We don't have any way to describe where we've been simply because there's nothing here that matches the dimension we had entered."

Kane nodded. "But I know we went somewhere."

"As do I," Brigid concurred. "Perhaps if we had a means to access our subconscious minds, we'd have more information about the exploratory nature of our journey. It'd be an exciting…"

"Baptiste," Kane growled. "Grant's stuck somewhere near the beginning of time, and he's in danger. In fact, I've got a strong urge that he has a timetable where he'll live or die."

Brigid winced, but not from Kane's anger. It was a spasm of memory niggling at her brain. She touched her forehead, using the pressure of her finger as a point to concentrate all of her external sensations.

"Brigid?" Lakesh spoke, getting ready to touch the eidetic archivist.

Kane snatched up Lakesh's wrist, holding him up. "She's concentrating on something. What I said must have flagged something in her subconscious."

"How—?" Lakesh began, but he stopped himself. If there were two people on Earth who knew each other completely, it was Kane and Brigid Baptiste. If Kane believed that Brigid was sifting through the layers of conscious and subconscious, then that was the task that the woman was attempting.

Kane grimaced as his lower right arm throbbed. It appeared as if a hot wire was glowing just under his skin. Lakesh looked on in awe, noting that the lights above them were flickering, the power being drawn from their bulbs. A hiss of static was shooting through all of their Commtacts.

"En…ki…du…" Grant said over the Commtact. It was a painful rasp that grated on Lakesh's and Kane's nerves. There was no sign that Brigid had heard; she was still deep in concentration.

"Damn it, Grant!" Kane snarled, clutching his arm as it stopped glowing. He felt as if he'd plunged it into a fireplace, though the skin and muscle beneath showed no signs of actual heat damage.

"Amazing phenomena," Lakesh muttered, his eyes wide.

"Not so much amazing as hurts like hell," Kane grumbled. "How come you can say yes and no without turning my arm into kindling, but you say a weird name…"

"Perhaps the power drain and channeling was necessary to access information that hadn't been normally available," Lakesh said. "He said he couldn't explain what happened there."

"But when it comes to information to save his fat ass, he lights me up," Kane muttered.

"How many times have you said you'd give your right arm for Grant?" Lakesh asked.

Kane looked sheepishly down at the limb. "Well, at least it's still attached to me, in that case."

Brigid rose from her self-induced trance, green eyes flitting between Kane and Lakesh. "Did Grant say something?"

"You were a little preoccupied. I heard…*an key do*." Kane winced, realizing that the nature of electronic voice phenomena meant he couldn't quite make out the exact sounds of Grant's whispers.

Brigid's eyes flashed with recognition despite what Kane knew to be a mispronunciation. "Enkidu, companion of Gilgamesh."

"Who are those people?" Kane asked.

"Gilgamesh is one of the first heroes in written record. There's some dispute between he and Beowulf, but—" Lakesh began.

"A myth?" Kane asked, looking for clarification.

"Supposedly he had offended Enlil for killing the guardian of the Cedar Forest," Brigid said. "This makes sense in terms of my reconstruction of my memories."

"What did you remember?" Kane asked.

"Apparently I was able to use the protean nature of the null space to construct a simulacrum of the temple at Eridu," Brigid explained.

"Zombie central," Kane grunted. "Cedar Forest? We saw a pair of giant gates made out of logs. I'm no expert on carpentry, but do you think those could have been cedar logs?"

"It's possible," Brigid replied. "What do you think?"

"Well, what was so special about the Cedar Forest that it needed a guardian?" Kane asked.

"I see what you're getting at," Brigid said. "Supposedly there was a fruit within the forest which was capable of granting eternal life."

"Hence the zombies swarming out from a side door," Kane muttered. "Do you think that Cedar Forest could have been slurred from cedar-gated garden?"

"An underground garden. It is likely that the Annunaki had hydroponic farming in that era," Brigid said.

"Hydroponics, or they could have utilized a form of gardening not reliant on photosynthesis," Lakesh said.

"Mushrooms," Kane said.

"This is moving off track. Enkidu was a man-bull who had originally been sent to slay Gilgamesh, or tame him. They battled to a standstill, and developed a deep friendship," Brigid said. "Together they attacked Humbaba, the creature whose temple we were in. As punishment for that crime, Enlil took Enkidu from Gilgamesh."

"Took him?" Kane muttered. "Wait, he suddenly pops up, and then after a fight against Enlil's personal sentry…"

"His son, in many myths," Brigid corrected.

"Enlil's son," Kane muttered. "And we discovered Grant's coat in Humbaba's temple…"

"We may have located Grant, then," Lakesh said. "And the identity he had taken in that era—Enkidu."

"So he's working alongside a primitive rebel against the Annunaki hierarchy of that time," Brigid said.

"Can we program the time trawl to send us there?" Kane asked.

"We would need to narrow things down," Brigid said. "Plus, we don't want to mess with history."

"History, as far as we can tell, tells us that when Grant and Gil make a move on Humbaba, the gods take Grant away. The only gods in that time are Enlil and his rotten buddies," Kane spit. Anger seethed in him.

"If we go too soon, we may not even get back the right Grant," Lakesh told him. "Or the pieces won't be in place."

Kane took a deep breath, reining in his frustration. "If we don't set it up for Grant's ego and body together in one spot, we might never get them back together?"

"We'd have to look for other temporal nexus points, a search akin to seeking a needle in a haystack," Brigid said. "Right now, we can calculate exactly where Grant will be by the apparent date of the temple's damage."

"So what does that mean?" Kane asked. "You know when that would be?"

"Right now, no," Brigid said. "We're going to have to return to Eridu and go back into the temple."

"You know that the basement is full of very angry creatures who beat the shit out of you and I," Kane reminded her.

"I know, but we've sealed off the Cedar Garden, as you've renamed it," Brigid told him. "Anything still left outside of the cave-in won't be ambulatory."

Kane nodded. He turned to Edwards. "Get full kits. You, me, Domi and Sinclair are heading in first to begin mop-up procedures. I don't want anything squirming up on Brigid while she's looking for Grant."

"Hot and heavy, not expeditionary?" Edwards asked.

"Exactly, Edwards," Kane said, clapping the big ex-Magistrate on his upper bicep. "Bring out the fun toys."

Edwards managed a crooked grin and headed off.

"Just to make certain," Kane told Brigid.

"I can't blame you this time," she answered.

THE PLASMA BOLTS LANDED with peals of thunder, superheated air crackling violently as its molecules were hurtled about like balls on a billiard table. Enkidu was in a full run, charging toward the skimmer as it leveled down out of the sky, a sliver of silver in its sleek profile spitting sparks that grew into seething tendrils of charged energy. The enemy pilot was on a strafing run, but by running toward the craft, Enkidu was keeping the skimmer's guns constantly adjusting. If the pilot wanted to take out Enkidu, he would have to plunge directly toward his human target, slicing into the ground because the skimmer would be unable to pull out of its dive.

The skimmer swerved, powering straight up into the sky, disappearing into the clear blue. Enkidu skidded to a rest and knew that he'd have to stay still, giving the skimmer something to hunt for. In the meantime, he needed to communicate with Malesh. He cast out his thoughts.

"I've got a moment. How are things on your end?" Enkidu asked.

"I've got the soldiers heading toward one of the warrens we've set up. The skimmers won't be able to spot them," Malesh answered telepathically.

"What about you?" Enkidu inquired.

"Humbaba has sent his ships after me before," Malesh replied. "No Nephilim has the skill to keep up with one who has the glory of both Anhur and Annunaki flowing through her veins."

Grant's distaste for the Annunaki made Enkidu's face twist in revulsion at the thought. Malesh had proved to be a courageous and noble ally, a woman who could truly earn the name goddess because of the battles she fought against the tyrants who turned people into slaves. That she had pride in her Annunaki heritage was the one flaw that stabbed at Enkidu's conscience. He and Grant shared a spite for the scaly alien overlords that was hard to kill. Both men despised themselves for having surrendered to blind prejudice, but neither had personally encountered a snake-face who behaved as anything more than a despot who enjoyed toying with human lives.

"Do not judge my kind because of the actions of a small expeditionary force," Malesh admonished over their psychic link.

"If you are judging me, look deeper," Enkidu said.

"You know that I cannot," Malesh said. "Anything but our shared conversation is a locked secret to me. Enkidu…beware!"

The human warrior looked up, then exploded into a frantic run. The plasma bolts weren't lasers, so they didn't move at the speed of light. The charged streams erupting from the diving skimmer betrayed themselves even as the apertures on its hull flared with the opening shots. At three times normal human speed, Enkidu was able to escape the initial volley of high-powered energy before it connected with the ground. Flaming clumps of grassy sod tumbled through the air, raining down.

Enkidu knew that he wasn't going to have an easy time of things as he baited the Annunaki fighter closer to him. His forearm muscles flexed, preparing to fire the ASP blaster wrapped around his wrist. The squeal of the plasma searing through the sky was evidence that the silver-skinned ship was still on his trail. This time, the craft's angle of attack was calculated to herd Enkidu away.

"Come on," Enkidu grunted, leaping and dodging, powerful legs launching him along at a triple pace. He knew that his body wasn't meant for such extreme rates of movement, and even through the pain-numbing effects of adrenaline coursing through his bloodstream, he could feel Grant's thigh muscles burning.

Suddenly, the skimmer veered, its trail of plasma fire straying off from Enkidu's wake. There was only one reason why the Nephilim pilot would have foregone a target as easy as Humbaba's errant slave—Malesh had shown herself in the field. The Nephilim drones had the capability for individual thought only so far as was necessary to carry out their orders. The creatures were clones, a ready-made army of disposable drones who were sent by the Annunaki on missions where they knew all of the creatures wouldn't return. The Nephilim had the urge for self-preservation only so much as to complete their objectives. Other than that, they were not afraid of death as they had no concept of self.

Something shuddered inside of him, the link between Grant's body, a tesseract of the original stuck somewhere in the boundless reaches of interdimensional space. The true Grant, thanks to its tenuous link to the body, suddenly had a realization due to the inner ruminations of the Enkidu identity. He thought of the uniform look of the Magistrates, how their faces were hidden behind the anonymity of jet-black armor and helmets, their names stripped down to a family name, and then only for the sake of identification. The Annunaki, back when they were in their form as the hybrid barons, had instinctively formed their corps of defenders into near duplicates of the Nephilim drones. The forearm-mounted weaponry— ASPs and Sin Eaters—the Magistrate's polycarbonate armor, and finally the lack of identity—soulless clones and identity-stripped policemen—was too great a set of coincidences for Grant.

It was an epiphany that ultimately did little to help Enkidu as he looked frantically for the outlaw goddess Malesh. Grant could only watch himself helplessly, scanning between the eras of the postapocalyptic society and the Annunaki-dominated realm of the dawn of recorded human history.

One of Grant's tesseracts was now literally part of Kane, residing in him after retrieval from the space just beyond his home time. It was a beacon, a tether that held him in the void where he was. The other tether anchor, the body now called Enkidu, was once more chasing after a skimmer. Grant realized that he had been similarly aggressive in his time, literally leaping onto a flying Deathbird to take out the murderous gunship. Still, he looked at himself as stupid and headstrong, grown far too reckless due to his work with Kane and

Brigid Baptiste. There was no way around it—had he not partnered with the younger man, his life would have been much more boring.

And lonely, he reminded himself. Grant had ended up in this mess, this featureless, wide expanse of void far from his home, because of love. He had literally wrested Shizuka from the clutches of the time warp created by the malfunctioning trawl, just as he had risked his life to rescue citizens of New Edo from attacking Magistrate forces. That wasn't rash foolhardiness. That was courage and compassion driving him. He put himself in the path of bullets for the sake of others. He found himself torn asunder and cast across time for love.

Grant wished that he could reach out to Enkidu to guide him. From his vantage point, in a dimension where all of time and temporal probability splayed out before him like a road map, he wanted to tell Enkidu not to feel ashamed for being attracted to Malesh. The outlaw goddess was linked to Shizuka by spirit. Malesh was the child of three worlds: Earth, the Anhur home world and Annunaki. Her earthly spirit had intertwined with Malesh, a case of an old soul reincarnated, combined with a byproduct of Shizuka's entry into the temporal void. Malesh's soul had been infused from the spiraling tendril of the samurai's spirit.

Her identity had been cast as a shadow back in time, where Grant's body and volumes of non-identity-aligned memories had been deposited. Grant wanted to shout as he saw the skimmer swerve toward Malesh. His high viewpoint, from out of time, gave him plenty of opportunity to see divergent time threads. In all but one, Malesh was charred into a lifeless husk by a direct hit from the skimmer's guns.

"Enkidu!" Grant bellowed to his tesseract, in a desperate attempt to reach him. The roar produced ripples in the colorful transtemporal void he was trapped within. Just as he had when he reached back to Enkidu during his trip to the Cedar Garden, Grant stretched himself to contact his body.

With the touch of his true self from beyond the pale of space, time suddenly slowed even more. Something was intervening, and Enkidu had a sense of it. The skimmer seemed to hang still in the air, plasma bolts moving more like melting wax than superheated ions.

Enkidu wasn't one to look a gift horse in the mouth. He brought up his ASP, focusing it on the silvery disk of the skimmer. Hot streams of energy poured from the three cobra heads, writhing streaks of lightning that stretched out between Enkidu and the hostile fighter craft. All three beams struck the silvery hull, boring into the perfect, mirrored surface.

Grant grimaced as he concentrated on his body, accelerating its reaction time, knowing that he couldn't slide Enkidu out of the time stream completely, lest his ASP blaster have no effect. Still, speeding up time for himself was a strain, an effort simply because he was hauling on the tether between himself and his shadow.

The belly of the skimmer ignited, flames spitting out as yellow fingers of hot energy clawed at the silver disk. The plasma guns on the craft stopped firing, and both Grant and Enkidu could see Malesh racing into the open, galloping along on all fours to get the most speed out of her long and powerful limbs.

The skimmer tumbled in the sky, mortally wounded. Grant released Enkidu's tether, allowing him to slide back into what had been his "normal" state of experiencing reality as a constant flow of Doppler effects.

The Annunaki fighter slammed into the country-side, a mushroom of flame rising from the wreckage as Malesh and Enkidu embraced, each realizing how close they had been to losing the other.

Grant could only watch as his shadow kissed Malesh for the first time. He wondered if that was the closest he would ever get to being with Shizuka again as he focused on his tesseract. The life of Enkidu was the only thing keeping Grant from being swallowed by the madness of nothing around him.

SHAMHAT LOOKED at the monitor as the skimmer disappeared from view. The supply convoy had been their latest ploy in the effort to bring down Malesh and her new consort, the renegade slave he'd named Enkidu. This ruse had cost them an Annunaki skimmer and several Nephilim. Shamhat ran an emergency diagnostic in order to determine whether it was a glitch in the system or the loss of the silver disk. Even as he initiated the diagnostic program, he knew deep in his dark, reptilian heart that Enkidu or Malesh had accomplished the improbable—the destruction of an armored transatmospheric craft armed with plasma launchers.

Either one or the other had gotten hold of the Nephilim's ASP weaponry, turning it to their defense. Shamhat cursed himself for not thinking that the Annunaki's own technology could be turned against itself. Self-recrimination wasn't going to solve anything, though he dreaded the thought of approaching Humbaba with his failure.

The Igigi rubbed his hand across his forehead, the callused plates on his palm scraping and clattering against the scales of his forehead. He didn't sweat, but with this manner of epic failure, Shamhat was certain he could easily learn how to.

At that moment, he felt the caress of Enlil's mind to his.

"Shamhat, how goes the war between my scions?" Enlil asked, entering the Igigi's mind. It was more a means of mental small talk, as Enlil's features drew dark and ominous as he absorbed the latest bit of conflict. It had been six months since Enlil's last contact with Shamhat, and in that time, much had occurred in the court of the Cedar Forest.

"How did you allow this to get so out of hand, Shamhat?" Enlil asked. "A human from a future time, dozens of Nephilim lost and now a skimmer? The gods do not openly rule and air their battles so publicly. It is why we are gods."

"If you will note, the future human was never allowed to learn the language of this era," Shamhat said. "As well, his knowledge of his own identity is somehow missing."

Enlil ruminated over the human, evaluating him and the mysteries of his technology for several moments. The firearms, the clothing material, even the cybernetic implants were nothing that the Annunaki had not already mastered and even discarded for newer, more powerful implements or personal psychic skills. The man, while unremarkable save in his size, had strength more than most humans, and a speed that matched the reflexes of even the most pure-blooded of Annunaki warlords.

With a sneer, Enlil wove off his examinations, Enkidu's avatar dissipating. "Shamhat, I will distract my son, lest he cause irreparable damage to my eyes within his realm. You will survive what brief punishment he subjects you to."

"Blessings unto you, my lord," the Igigi said in relief.

"Humbaba has crossed the line, engaging in vulgar displays of power. It is time he learned his lesson," Enlil pronounced. "However, utilizing this new slave, such rebuke should be easy."

Shamhat sighed. What Enlil considered easy was never gentle or kind. There would be blood and mayhem in the future.

Chapter 15

When Enkidu's eyes fluttered open, consciousness seizing him once more, the first thing he saw was the golden, muscular yet soft shoulder of a beautiful black-and-gold-haired woman who breathed deeply in the peace of sleeping bliss. The silk of her hair poured over his right biceps, and her back pressed against his barrel-like chest, while his left forearm rested in the saddle formed by the curve of her waist between her rib cage and one sleek, muscular hip. Nothing separated their bodies save for a thin sheen of perspiration. The only other things that touched them were the cool predawn air, the simple mattress they lay upon and a thin sheet of slick gossamer cloth.

Malesh was entwined with him, her supple form spooned against his, and Enkidu let the heaviness of his eyelids drag themselves closed. He didn't want to disentangle himself from the half-Annunaki goddess, her cheek lying on his muscle, using it as a pillow. He allowed himself a small smile, enjoying the scent of her hair, the warmth of her golden skin.

It had been a week since Humbaba had employed the power of Annunaki technology against the pair, and the jolting panic of the other's near death had stripped them of the illusion that they were not in love. This scene, this feeling, was familiar to Enkidu, trickles of visions slipping through the cracks that kept him from his lost identity. He ran his hand along his jaw, feeling the tiny cybernetic ports now hidden under his bushy beard.

Commtact pintles. Enkidu/Grant grimaced at the knowledge that came unheeded, a flood of glimpses and hints of a far future world while keeping the things that mattered in the shadows. Malesh, while healing the burns on his chest from the initial heat blast of the skimmer's guns, had gently probed his psyche, exploring the latticework of thoughts that were readily available. It wasn't some form of built-in psychic shield, nor was it a matter of technological jamming of telepathic contact. There were literally parts of his mind missing, actual matter that had been left behind a barrier that could not be penetrated by mental power.

Enkidu had told her of the slowing of time as he was shooting down the enemy skimmer, and Malesh's features soured.

"You are between times, split from yourself," Malesh had said. "The only thing that comes close is the operation of a threshold."

Malesh looked on in curiosity, as the word she had just mentioned was not strange to Enkidu, at least in terms of his vocabulary and practical knowledge. Enkidu had been also more than a little frightened as he began to speak. "The threshold is a device used by the Annunaki to travel between parallax points in a way that's a lot like making jumps with a mat-trans and the interphaser."

"I don't presume to find your technical references familiar, but simple logic suggests that humanity has found its own means of opening wormholes as a means of folding space," Malesh said.

"That's how… " Enkidu had struggled as a name on the tip of his tongue eluded him. "That's how I remember it being explained. I remember seeing a piece of paper being folded, and was told that the sheet of paper was our plane of existence. There was a grain of rice on one spot, and when the paper was unfolded, the rice had moved, but it hadn't touched any of the space in between. That's the explanation in my head for how teleportation works."

"And the threshold does the same thing," Malesh had replied. "But it could do far more."

That conversation had been days ago, and though the outlaw goddess had spoken no more of it, Enkidu could read it as a subtext in her every waking moment. The threshold was a means of returning Enkidu to his home time, and like most of the children of the gods, Humbaba had possession of one. It was how the Annunaki traveled from one court to another without exposing themselves to the eyes of man.

Enkidu knew that Malesh was fighting in the depths of her spirit, trying to reconcile her concern for him and her need to have him by her side. Malesh stirred, a gentle moan escaping her lips as wakefulness returned to her. She rolled slightly, turning her head to look at her lover, the one human ever to equal her in single combat. She ran her fingertips lovingly along his cheek, combing through his beard. Enkidu could see the subdued, wry joy on her lips as she did so, her golden cat eyes gleaming in the dark like twin gems.

"Your thoughts are brooding, love," Malesh said.

Enkidu kissed her neck, hiding himself behind her black-and-blond mane.

As if she were boneless, Malesh turned until she was eye to eye with her lover, lips meeting his, fingers tangled in the long, ashen dreadlocks hanging down the back of his neck. Enkidu knew he couldn't hide, so he chose to lose himself in the passion of her embrace. The two lovers turned to each other and abandoned themselves to lovemaking.

An hour later, their bodies glistening with perspiration, Enkidu and Malesh parted, breathing deeply. He had known her for only the past six weeks, going from a hired assassin to her compatriot in rebellion, to finally her lover. His recognition of her, his disjointed view—which allowed him to peer at the future stream of her multi-faceted life—had told him that his knowledge of this woman extended across millennia. Thousands of years from now, the owner of this time-lost body and Malesh's soul would meet and fall deeply in love, a chain that bound them so tightly that even in this journey, Enkidu was pulled to her side.

The afterglow of their coupling started to fade in Malesh's beautiful eyes, melancholy struggling to reach the surface.

"My beloved warrior," she whispered, stroking his salt-and-pepper-colored hairline. "You are needed elsewhere."

Enkidu lowered his head, kissing her along the line of her collarbone, enjoying the saltiness of her skin. "I am needed here, too, or else I wouldn't have been called to this time. It was my destiny to be here, battling at your side and sharing your bed."

Malesh's smile fought off the melancholy, golden cheeks darkening with a blush. "I cannot keep you forever."

"Then we should make the most of what we share now," Enkidu told her. "Though I believe we shall never be far from each other. Something pulled me to you, something that touched me at the first moment I had laid eyes upon you."

Malesh managed a stronger smile, but only with the added nourishment of a fresh kiss. "I never believed in destiny. Nothing is forged in this world—there is no golden rail leading from one thing to another. We make our own fortune."

"But there are threads, strings that can lead a hero through a maze and back to his princess," Enkidu said. "This is not a trail of crumbs that could be erased by the passage of hungry birds."

Malesh stroked Grant's long, tightly muscled torso. Her medicines had undone the deep scars of her claws and the heat of exploding plasma bolts. All he had were the scars that he had arrived here with, mementos of the life he had lived before dropping into her lap. There was a twinge, a jolt of something that pulsed below her navel. Her biology was changing subtly.

She looked into Grant's dark eyes, smiling. "Enkidu, you say you were destined to accompany me."

"I would follow you to the gates of Hell," Enkidu told her.

"We may well be forced through them, in that case," Malesh said.

The two lovers huddled closer, this time not for intimacy, but to plot what Malesh felt would be the journey that would return the man-bull home.

THE ELIMINATION of the remaining wounded guardians of the Cedar Garden had gone easily. Edwards had taken point, having missed the "fun" of the initial melee, utilizing a twentieth-century SPAS-12 shotgun as his preferred tool for dealing with the attackers who had survived the war of only a day ago. It was grisly work, and at the end, even Edwards's enthusiasm for extermination of the unholy abominations had abated, drowned by the greasy black blood of the slaughtered zombies that pooled around their boots.

Kane examined the massive, heavy-logged gates, seeing how well they had withstood the passage of centuries. Experimentally, he fired a round from his Sin Eater into one of the thick posts that had made up the ancient barrier. The gunshot reverberated in the Glow Stick lit chamber.

"Did we miss one?" Edwards asked.

"No," Kane answered. "Just seeing how durable this gate is."

"Let me just put some C-4 on it. I'll cut through it easy," Edwards offered.

Kane reached into a belt pouch and withdrew his multitool. He extended an Allen wrench, a slender polygonal length of steel, and sank it into the bullet hole. It had barely entered the log when he heard the click of metal striking the projectile's base.

"Less than an inch of penetration from a bullet that's been designed to go through light armor," Kane said. "An inch against a barrier which is probably a yard thick, if we're lucky."

"I'll just jump to Cerberus for some more," Edwards said.

Kane shook his head. "The kind of firepower necessary to slice through would bring down the roof of this chamber, and we're hundreds of feet underground."

"So, what?" Edwards asked.

"I'd say chainsaws, but even that would take hours to cut through. Besides, my need to look inside a mushroom garden isn't that great," Kane noted. "I just want to make sure no one breaks through from the other side."

"You think there'd be anyone else left?" Edwards mused.

"You don't put up gigantic doors to protect a cupboard," Kane said. "The cavern could go on for miles."

Edwards looked at the blasted mess of ancient corpses that had carpeted the chamber floor. "This doesn't look like miles worth of zombies."

"Take a look at the stone by the cave-in," Kane ordered. "There's a corridor farther down that way, leading under the temple. I want to see what happened to wreck this joint."

Edwards nodded.

As he trod through the battlefield's aftermath, he saw a ghost-white face accompanying him in the shadows.

"Domi, you don't have to come," Kane said.

"Gray skins all finished. Sinclair has Brigid and the other whitecoats," the albino girl answered. Her clipped, simplistic speech patterns didn't escape Kane's notice. Domi loved Grant in much the same way Kane had. The brawny ex-Magistrate had been the closest thing to a father figure that either had had in their lives. Kane's father had been stolen for genetic material. Domi had never known her parents.

To Kane, Grant had been a mentor, a teacher, the wise counsel who had guided a young man's energy and enthusiasm into a finely honed warrior. To Domi, Grant had been the first man ever to show her concern and compassion. The big man was family to both, and Kane knew that he and Domi were nearly brother and sister because of that bond. Lakesh had made it seem that Kane was the linchpin of the Cerberus warriors, but without the ethics that Grant had drummed into Kane or the protectiveness that he had given Domi, life would have been much different.

Kane knew that there was an intricate lattice of relationships between the primary three, four counting the feral outlander girl who had grown from savage to guardian in five years. The bonds of friendship were a strength that they shared, something more than romantic infatuation or accidents of genetics. The four people had chosen each other as family, and that choice was a level of strength that few could break.

It was also Grant who had been so important in the tight bonds between Cerberus and New Edo. His relationship with the samurai Shizuka was a cement that only added to the strength of the humans striving against the rebirth of the Annunaki's cruel rule.

Kane put a hand on Domi's shoulder, and a smirk cracked her pale features. "Baptiste is going to find exactly where we have to be to rescue Grant. And then we go back to Thunder Isle, hop in the time trawl and go get him."

"Make it sound easy," Domi said.

"No. I make it sound simple. After all, it's simple for someone to move a mountain one spoonful at a time," Kane answered.

"Just gonna take a lot of work," Domi concluded.

"Right," Kane said. "Then again, how many times have we saved the world?"

"Seems like every three months," Domi returned with a wink.

"We'll get this done," Kane said, giving her a hug across both of her slender shoulders. The albino girl chuckled as they left the grisly floor covering behind.

Domi broke out of Kane's embrace and trod lightly ahead. Between the two of them, the darkness was little impediment. The albino's ruby-red eyes picked up the slightest illumination and amplified it. With Kane's Glow Stick and his own sharply tuned instincts, even the slightest rustle in the shadows was a gleaming beacon.

"Smell that?" Domi asked.

"Yes," Kane answered. Though his right forearm throbbed with the presence of Grant, be it just a symbolic energy or something more, he still had the Sin Eater and its hydraulic holster wrapped around it. Grant's occupation had done nothing to slow down his fast-draw or his aim, despite the perceived weight and warmth added to his limb. Right now, all it would take would be a simple mental reflex to activate the folding machine pistol and discharge a burst of armor-piercing 9 mm rounds into a hostile target.

Kane might not have been adept at figuring out the intricacies of time travel, but if there was a problem made of flesh, blood and hostility, he was certainly equipped to deal with it.

Domi had her knife drawn, the blade a living extension of her arm, as had been proved when she'd held off the shambling horde the other day. Their extraordinary talents and skills had been a deciding factor on countless occasions, against everything from marauding bandits to gods reborn. Whatever loomed in the cavern ahead would receive the surprise of its life if it intended to attack them.

The Glow Stick started to fade, so Kane hurled it into the inky depths of the tunnel, letting it bounce to illuminate or distract any ambushers who might have made this particular hole in the ground their hunting territory. Nothing moved as the chemical light rolled down the hallway. What Kane did notice, however, was that there were deep cracks and fissures in the otherwise smooth walls.

"Quake?" Domi asked as she examined one of the rifts that ran from the floor up the wall.

"No. These seem to be radiating out from a center," Kane said. "An explosion maybe?"

"Air's stale, no movement," Domi said. "No burn smell."

"So not an explosion, unless we're looking at something that doesn't use gunpowder," Kane said. "There are plenty of bombs which wouldn't show up like that."

"Doesn't smell like stale ozone," Domi said. "What the hell?"

Kane and Domi continued on, unable to make sense of the faint scent in the air, their brains running frantically over the possibilities.

The two people rounded a corner and looked into a multistory chamber. From Kane's new chemical light, they were able to see that floors below and above had been shoved violently out of the way by an all-too-familiar column. Extending at least two hundred feet, the Annunaki scout ship had been propped up on its aft end, the nose spearing up through floors beneath the main temple. Only the strength of the marble and the shape of the craft's bow kept the floor of the temple from collapsing.

Kane smirked. "Wonder if Grant still remembered how to operate that old boat from the last time we were on one."

"Just like in Greece," Domi noticed. "Snuck in, started ship?"

"Looks like it," Kane said. He took out a high-powered flashlight and aimed it down into the depths below. "Water down there."

"Bodies, too," Domi added, her ruby-red eyes able to pick up figures amid the shimmering reflection of the torch.

"That's the smell. Waterlogged corpses?" Kane said.

"Thousands of years old," Domi said. "Funny kind of rot. Not pretty."

Kane looked down the spine of the scout ship. It had risen hard, cracking apart as it had struggled to straighten up. The craft had old scars from where it had torn through its own hull in an effort to rise. Down at the bottom, the aft end of the ship was crushed against the back of another.

"It has to be Grant," Kane said with a whistle. "He'd always wondered how much damage one of those things could cause at ramming speed."

"Doubt it was that fast," Domi returned. "But it still did good."

"I wonder how well that's wedged in," Kane mused, looking up toward the cockpit.

"Couldn't read computers even if you climbed up," Domi mentioned.

"No, but…" Kane stopped and activated his Commtact. "Baptiste, I found out what shook up the temple."

"It wouldn't happen to have been a ship from the subterranean hangar, would it?" Brigid answered.

"I'm looking at it right now," Kane said. "Let me guess, you found a map of this joint?"

"The Annunaki were nothing if not thorough with writing about their buildings," Brigid told him. "I have a layout for the entire complex."

"But no news of the day?" Kane asked.

"Some news," Brigid replied. "Apparently, around five thousand years ago, a stranger appeared out of nowhere. After a fearsome battle where the son of Enlil himself had to take a hand, he was captured and held as a prisoner. For weeks they tried to read his mind, but Enkidu the man-bull was immune to their probes. They took it as evidence that he was far too savage to be tamed."

"Weeks?" Kane focused on one bit of information. "It's going to take us weeks to figure out how to get back in time to rescue Grant?"

Brigid cleared her throat. "Kane, time travel is not linear. We've only spent a few days wondering where Grant went, but once we've managed to pinpoint where he would be, we could go right there and pick him up."

"And he was held captive in the temple?" Kane asked. "We could just pop in there and rescue him."

"If we did that, we might cause irreparable damage to the time stream," Baptiste said. "Besides, even if we did show up with all of our firepower to rescue him, this wasn't a temple. This was Humbaba's banquet hall. Given the extent of the blueprints I looked at, this was an underground palace, a self-supporting city."

"So we could just go anytime and pick Grant up. All we'd be doing is allowing him to live the history which has…more or less…been recorded," Kane said.

"There you go," Brigid announced. "Now you got it."

"Do you have an exact date?" Kane pressed.

"I'm still working on the translations. So far, all I know is that apparently Enkidu had been prisoner for four months before Humbaba showed him off to his young half brother, Ullikummis," Brigid explained.

"He was here, too?" Kane asked. "All of these fuckers like to hang out together. But four months…mindprobes?"

"And rebellion," Brigid said. "The man-bull could not be broken by whip or mental sorcery."

"So what happened to him?" Kane asked.

"Humbaba, in his great wisdom, decided to turn one unbreakable prisoner into an unstoppable weapon," Brigid said. "Through coercion, they sent Enkidu out to slay…Gi Malesh…his sister."

"Sister," Kane muttered. "So let me guess. Gi Malesh is this Gilgamesh dude…except corrupted by historical misspellings."

"None other," Brigid said. "Nothing more on this record. I'd have to look elsewhere…"

"Then how about we take a look inside the scout ship that struck the temple," Kane offered.

Brigid remained silent. Kane knew she was already musing about what kind of knowledge could be gained from the cockpit of an Annunaki scout ship.

"I'll be right down," she said.

Chapter 16

Anxious energy got the better of Shizuka. Back at the Thunder Isle facility, her body had recovered from its ordeal on the event horizon of a temporal warp, and psychologically, her nerves and spirit were once again in top condition. For the past twelve hours, she had engaged in cleansing Zen meditation and isometric exercises in order to sharpen herself in mind and body. Opening her eyes, Shizuka got out of the hospital bed, quickly discarding her gown in order to put on more appropriate clothing. There was a knock at the door, and the samurai leader knew that she wasn't going to hide her impatience.

"Enter," she said.

Daryl Morganstern entered, holding a tray of food when he was frozen in shock at the sight of a topless Shizuka glaring at his intrusion. "I...you said to come in."

Shizuka nodded abruptly. "They're breasts. I assume you've seen them bare before."

Morganstern opened his mouth, then clenched his eyes shut. "Mr. Grant's going to eat me alive for gawking at you."

Shizuka snorted. "Grant is not the jealous type. Open your eyes before you put my food all over the floor."

Morganstern did so, walking over quickly to set the tray on a table.

Shizuka slipped on a T-shirt over her head. Much to the mathematician's dismay, the stretchy fabric was body conforming, and for the braless woman, it was not much more modest than being completely topless. The leader of New Edo gave Morganstern a friendly poke in the shoulder. "Besides, I'm pretty sure Grant would be more offended if you didn't appreciate my physique so much."

Morganstern looked quickly down at himself, but Shizuka tapped his chin, bringing his eyes to her level. The samurai smiled. "I meant the bug eyes and stammering, Daryl."

"Oh, yeah," he said nervously. "You're getting dressed?"

"It's been days since I was pulled out of the trawl," Shizuka replied. "Right now, I am not weakened. The only reason I agreed to stay in that foul bed was to humor the doctors who seemed to think I was scarred by my experiences."

"I think the reason you were restricted to quarters was to keep you from getting involved in the search for Grant," Morganstern admitted.

"Those were my feelings, as well," Shizuka replied. "Lakesh means well, I know I wouldn't have one of my own samurai search for someone he's desperately worried about."

"You're desperately worried about Grant, aren't you?" Morganstern asked.

"I'm different," Shizuka answered.

"How?"

"I'm in charge. I'm also much more disciplined," she told him. "Where is everyone?"

"Currently, Kane and Brigid are back in Eridu," Morganstern told her. "They've been there for about two hours."

Shizuka nodded. "Not much I could do there."

"If I may, there is one thing I wanted to check," Morganstern said. "I believe you would be the ideal ingredient in this experiment."

Shizuka narrowed her eyes, suddenly distrustful. "What have you got in mind?"

"I'm attempting to use an alternative method of locating Mr. Grant," Morganstern explained. "If you would join me."

Shizuka nodded. After slipping her sword harness over her shoulders, she accompanied Morganstern to the temporal dilator chamber, where Waylon was currently running more diagnostics.

"Waylon!"

The slender young engineer turned off the monitor and looked at the unlikely pair as they entered. "So, this is the bewitching samurai of New Edo?"

"One of many," Shizuka said. She leaned over to the mathematician. "This is Waylon?"

Morganstern nodded. "A little information. We're from the 1980s, where ninjas and samurai were the coolest things on TV and comic books. The fact that he's meeting a real-life samurai is making his day. That you're a beautiful samurai woman…"

Shizuka sighed. "There's nothing glamorous about me."

Morganstern motioned for her to look down. Shizuka saw that the straps of her sword harness crisscrossed her chest, enhancing the tightness of her shirt and making her breasts more prominent. She looked up to Waylon, who apparently hadn't blinked for a moment.

"Forgive him," Morganstern added.

"To tell the truth, I'm flattered. I never thought of myself that way," Shizuka answered. She joined Waylon at the controls. "Daryl told me that you had an idea about how to locate Grant."

Waylon took a deep breath, then tore his gaze from Shizuka's chest. "Actually, this was inspired by some of Daryl's pontifications on the nature of space-time and how it can be biocentric."

"Space-time is what?" Shizuka asked.

"Biocentric," Morganstern repeated. "It means that apparently the laws of physics and reality conform to life as much as life is influenced by the environments created by physics."

"Mankind has produced the universe to suit its survival," Shizuka translated.

"Mankind. Perhaps other alien races that we have not encountered. Indeed, look at how easily the Annunaki remolded their hybrid forms to become the overlords," Morganstern told her. "The Annunaki, being a race far older than humanity, have been able to figure out short-cuts across the surface of the planet, which Dr. Singh has based his mat-trans design upon."

"What does this have to do with me aiding you in finding Grant?" Shizuka asked.

"Waylon and I were discussing with Clem Bryant about the ease with which Kane and Brigid found Grant, or at least the fragment of him residing in Kane's arm," Morganstern said.

"Grant was interacting with us as a shadow poised at a right angle to our universe. Entering that dimension would have given them a long and distant search, given that we were dealing with the plane through which we travel via mat trans, circumventing normal space," Waylon told her. He gave a puppy-like whimper as his eyes fell upon her again.

"Concentrate, Waylon," Morganstern said.

"Oh, I most certainly am," Waylon replied.

Shizuka leaned in closer. "I appreciate the sentiment, but if we don't find Grant, I will use you for sword practice."

Waylon's eyes widened. "But if you cut me in half, you won't get much practice."

"Rattan sword. They hurt even through armor padding," Shizuka reminded him.

Waylon cleared his throat and looked at the console. "Part of what we were discussing was that there may have been some outside force which isn't readily observable in the third dimension that steered them toward Grant and vice versa."

"Something like a personal link," Shizuka replied.

"It's not mathematically impossible," Morganstern said. "After all, it takes two dimensions of removal from our current state of being for the numbers on gravity and light to balance out."

"The math for those two don't add up?" Shizuka asked.

"So the math for something like a soul bond, either through romantic love or deep friendship, might actually be a deciding factor in which people can reach each other," Waylon said. "The emotional anchorage you have toward your loved ones could have actual tensile strength."

"How strong?" Shizuka asked.

"Grant was able to reach through the event horizon of a malfunctioning temporal displacement field, take your hand and pull you out," Morganstern said. "I'm not saying that the gravitational pull of the time field was anything approaching that of a black hole, which is so powerful that it can stretch planets into one-atom-wide chains of matter being drawn into it…"

"But it's not going to be an easy task, no matter what," Shizuka answered. "His link to me was the anchor I needed to survive. And because I was weak…"

"You weren't weak," Waylon said. "You were weakened by a trauma that your conscious mind couldn't comprehend and your biology took two days to recover from."

"It'd have been the same as blaming yourself for not rescuing Grant after a tyrannosaur chewed on you for a few minutes," Morganstern added.

Shizuka took a cleansing breath. "So what are we going to do here?"

"I'm going to set you up and we will begin matter transmission through time," Waylon told her. "You won't be going anywhere, but the machinery will be recording data regarding anything that does extend with you."

"On the off chance that my link with Grant is still extant," Shizuka noted. "All right, let's do this. If we're lucky, you two aren't talking out of your asses. And if I'm lucky, I might even slip through the cracks back to join him."

"You nearly did fall through the cracks," Morganstern noted.

Waylon lifted his head. "You were on the other side."

"Does that mean anything?" Shizuka asked.

"It means that, quite possibly, you might have already been transmitted back in time," Waylon told her. "Some part of you, akin to the tesseract of Grant embedded in Kane, went to someplace else, or more precisely, some *when* else."

"I don't feel anything missing, except for Grant," Shizuka replied.

"We are talking about her dangling in another dimension," Morganstern said. "It's likely that she could have spent more than a few minutes in the vortex."

"I couldn't tell you how long I was in there," Shizuka agreed. "I barely remember what it was like on the other side."

"Neither could Kane and Brigid," Waylon said. "Which is surprising, given her eidetic memory."

"I went traveling?" Shizuka asked.

"Not with Grant being an actual physical anchor for you," Waylon said. "However, you could have stretched out to contact someone else at the same time."

"Only if you believe in reincarnation," Shizuka replied. "I know I do."

"The conservation of energy dictates that reincarnation is also a possibility," Morganstern told her.

"Nothing ruins the magic of faith like scientific examination," Shizuka cut Morganstern off. "Now, let's see exactly what happened to me."

The samurai woman took off her sword harness, hanging it safely out of the way. If the time stream was able to rip parts of a psyche or a body away, then she didn't want to lose the *katana* that had been in her family for hundreds of years. She entered the central platform, her small, unshod feet making no sound as she turned to look at the two scientists. "Send me through."

Morganstern looked to Waylon. "I don't have to remind you that if we screw this up, Grant will probably walk through time, show up in a taxicab and open up an industrial drum of pure pain on us."

Waylon took a deep breath, giving his friend the hardest glare he could come up with. "Daryl, shut up and stand back. I am about to do science!"

Morganstern smiled as he turned to his computer monitor. The transmit sequence engaged, and the crystals at the ends of the horn atop the central pylon began to emit sparks. The platform pulsed, and Shizuka looked around her.

This time, her transition into time was controlled, and when she disappeared, projected only moments into the future, the samurai could see the void stretched out around her. A fibrous, seemingly organic tendril was rooted within her, and she looked back and forth, seeing the tether disappear in both directions, shadowy bodies connected to them.

Shizuka's first instinct was to grip the cord, but it was ethereal, and she had the impression of a fingertip trying to touch itself. The body around her was her brain's means of making sense of the discordant in-between universe. She existed, as did the other bodies on this power line, but they were information, packets of living energy reconstructed by the Chronos machinery to project her.

The ribbon of her multidimensional form had folded, turning and twisting as Shizuka could see an offshoot of herself, writhing free from the conventional line—if such a description could be applied in this alien realm. With a surge, Shizuka leaped, trying to reach the time line she was about to intersect. She found her temporal counterpart, a woman who was well over six feet tall and solidly built. She could see a man standing in the distance, even as she approached herself, a phantom out of time, finding that her spirit had resided in a goddess carved of golden muscle.

The man suddenly came into sharp clarity; it was Grant. As much as she had been drawn in by the tether between herself and the woman, she could feel his attraction, their bond such that he seemed to see her. Outside of time, she could see his brain as if it were Swiss cheese, not physically damaged, but his intellect was full of holes, missing gaps of information. She started to reach out, to touch Grant's face. His hair had grown out and was bound in thick, ash-colored dreadlocks, his mustache drooping down into a beard that was still jet-black. His body was more tightly honed than it had been before, but Shizuka could attribute that to the life of a prisoner and his struggles to free himself burning excess stores of calories.

Grant reached to touch her when the powerful pull of the time trawl and Malesh's sudden acceleration into the wood yanked her away from him. She returned to the temporal dilator, her hand clenching into a fist.

"Another second. You couldn't wait another second!" Shizuka growled.

"You found him?" Morganstern asked.

"I saw him, nearly touched him," Shizuka answered.

"We didn't know," Waylon said. "I'm sorry."

Shizuka looked at the pair. "It wasn't your fault. My counterpart moved, as well. She tore off, leaving Grant behind, separating me from him. I was yelling at myself, at her, as much as anything."

"Well, according to the data stream we received from your hop, we've actually managed to home in on Grant himself," Morganstern said. "Unfortunately, the way that time travel works might prevent any of you from going back after him."

"Right. The transmitter cannot release a living being into a time period where it already exists," Shizuka reminded him. "Don't forget, I've been protecting this island for a while, and I've been studying what it does."

"You think that because an earlier incarnation exists at the target site it would interfere with the flow of time?" Waylon asked. "I simply thought it was a case of biological resonance. Since the incarna is actually composed of different cellular structure, we can deposit Shizuka there if we need to."

"Can I go or not?" Shizuka asked.

"We can send you," Waylon confirmed. "I have the trawl ready, and we have temporal coordinates."

A radio handset on the counter beeped, and Waylon picked it up.

"Thunder Isle, Waylon speaking," the engineer said.

"You'll do," came Kane's voice, rasping over the speaker. "I'm inside the cockpit of an Annunaki scout ship beneath the court of Urudug. Currently, it's an inert lump, not a spark of energy left in it. I was wondering if you could do something for me."

"Check to see if we can access whatever memory banks the scout ship possesses?" Waylon asked. "I'm not certain I want to tangle with even a five-thousand-year-old navigation chair, not from what I heard."

"Put on your man pants, kid," Kane grunted. "No navigation chair. This thing is old, and anything biological has dried up and mummified centuries ago. However, Baptiste seems to think that we have crystals that have stored information in them."

"Crystals. Then that should be simple," Waylon returned. "All I'd have to do is properly calibrate a laser to read the data. Depending on the type of information compression, we'd get a good display."

"Dynamic," Kane said, grunting.

"You're still in the cockpit?" Morganstern asked. "Is the ship in some form of erect storage?"

"You could say that. I have a feeling that Grant decided it would look better if he stood it up. Either that, or he's worse at parking than I ever thought," Brigid said over her Commtact. "Kane, I found another panel."

"I'll be there," the Cerberus explorer replied. "Get to work on the data readers, guys."

"Kane?" Shizuka spoke up, taking the radio.

"You're better?" Kane responded.

"Yes. Waylon, Daryl and I might have something more to help narrow the scope of our search," Shizuka said. She related the tumble through time, the near hallucinogenic encounter she'd had with Grant.

"How come she remembers?" Kane asked.

Waylon pushed his glasses up his flat nose. "We sent you to a different dimension than the one that the time trawl utilizes when it's working properly. You were in a neighborhood which was either a zone of lost signal or was full of static and noise, utilizing a radio analogy."

"Or Shizuka's in a pool, while you dumped me in the sewer pipe," Kane grumbled.

"A sewer pipe where you found our friend," Brigid admonished. "We had to be thrown in the same wild trajectory as Grant had gone—otherwise we would have had no idea where he was."

"True," Kane muttered. "I wouldn't have been able to get Grant out of the sewer if I were swimming in clean water."

Brigid cleared her throat. "Shizuka, you have confirmed that Gi Malesh is a woman from your flicker in that time?"

"Yes, and I can see that Grant has lost pieces of his intellect," Shizuka said. "He seemed to be in full fighting trim, and he recognized me. He's sitting astride the time. Stretched out, blurred, at least according to how it looked from my vantage point."

"That being sitting at a right angle to the time and place Grant was," Kane concluded.

"Yes, though it was more like looking through a pond. He was mostly submerged, with just the back of his head and shoulders poking above the surface," Shizuka said.

"Which explained why he was able to see you," Brigid replied. "He was at a vantage point where he could see in time, as well as outside of it."

"Any idea of what the two of them were doing?" Kane asked.

"Like I said before, Malesh seemed to be in a hurry, and Grant was holding his sword, looking at both of us with concern on his face," Shizuka explained. "I want to come with you when it's time to pick up Grant."

"More likely we need you there," Kane returned. "According to some of the theories being thrown out by our quantum physicists, adding you to the equation would actually help us hone in on him better."

"Thank you," Shizuka replied.

"Waylon, Daryl, good job, you two," Kane said over the radio. "I owe you."

THE CERBERUS redoubt's laser laboratory was uncommonly crowded as Waylon adjusted the filter on the main emitter. One of the crystals taken from the Annunaki ship sat in a cradle a few inches from the lens.

Lakesh, Bry, Bryant, Morganstern, Shizuka, Kane, Domi and Brigid Baptiste were all in attendance, each of them wearing a pair of heavily polarized lenses as protection in case of an errant beam reflecting off an imperfection in the crystal. While the laser wasn't operating at a voltage necessary to cause injury in the form of heat burns, its candlepower was more than sufficient to destroy the rods and cones that made up the inner eye. Permanent blindness was always a consideration when it came to working with light amplification on even this scale.

Waylon stepped back, then pressed the button on a remote control. The laser hummed to life.

Kane sighed. "I don't think it's working. Where's the beam?"

"This isn't a targeting laser, Kane. Nor is it the energy weaponry you've been encountering of late," Waylon told him. "Right now, I'm working off some pretty old school technology. You've heard of laser disk and DVDs, haven't you?"

"You mean like the vids in the rec center," Kane answered. "Yes."

"This is operating on the same frequency as the vid players. It's beaming out, agitating the crystal in order to scan the information stored within," Waylon said. "Where did this crystal come from?"

"It was beneath the helm of the scout ship," Brigid explained. She repressed a smile at the knowledge that Kane had had to hang upside down to acquire it, grunting and snorting with effort. Had he not been wearing a shadow suit under his jeans, Brigid could easily see him in the role of a plumber from a twentieth-century television comedy, replete with butt cleavage.

"It was a hell of a lot of work," Kane said. "I just don't want it to be in vain."

Waylon looked up at the screen. Mathematical equations were racing across it, and he swallowed. "Daryl, it's your turn."

Morganstern stepped to a work terminal that was displaying the same scrolling data. "Thrust vectors and course indications. You found the little black box, Kane."

"Well, its Annunaki equivalent," Kane answered. "Are you reading those numbers that fast?"

"You mean you can't?" Brigid asked, standing beside Morganstern. "This is translating directly from Annunaki numeric and alphabetical symbols."

"Which is why half of this shit is gibberish," the mathematician grumbled. "Pardon my language."

"It's all right," Brigid returned. "Lakesh, could you double-check these numbers for me?"

The head scientist of the redoubt came forward as Brigid scribbled down some figures on a notepad. Lakesh's graying eyebrows inched toward each other in concentration. "The final course manipulation of the ship occurred forty-five hundred years ago, directly under the temple in Eridu. Dear Brigid has the exact coordinate necessary for the time trawl. Your math is good."

Brigid smirked. "My boyfriend's is better."

Morganstern couldn't hide the reddening of his cheeks. "It's not often a number cruncher comes in useful."

"And don't trip over yourselves thanking the engineer who built a reader of stored alien flight data," Waylon groaned.

Shizuka took Waylon's hand and drew him in close for a chaste, gentle kiss on the lips. "Don't be so whiny."

Waylon wasn't blinking again, a crooked smile on his lips. His mathematician friend shook his head and guided the smitten engineer to his chair in the corner of the lab.

"Are we done with all the homework?" Kane asked.

Lakesh nodded. "After reprogramming the interphaser, I've set it so that it can work in conjunction with the time trawl. There's also an additional module I've piggybacked onto the system."

"A way to open a time hole so we can reconstitute Grant with his components," Kane said.

"You'll have to be inside the radius so the interphaser can extract Grant from your forearm," Lakesh said. "Which is why I've designed a special carrier for it."

"A backpack?" Brigid asked, looking at it. "Kane's going to run around with a pyramid strapped between his shoulder blades."

"Would you rather wear it?" Kane countered.

"Looks stupid to me," Brigid replied.

"Only because we need to protect it for its multiple duties. Otherwise, you could just hit the recall and it would come back here," Lakesh explained.

"Why can't we reassemble Grant here?" Shizuka inquired. "God, that sounds grisly."

"Because if Grant and Malesh are going to be in Eridu, then we'll need to help him attain what he was supposed to do," Lakesh said. "And that means killing Humbaba and sealing off the Cedar Forest forever."

Kane looked at the coordinates. They were simply gibberish to him, but they were the key to hurl him to the beginning of human history in order to rescue his friend.

"Come on, people. We have some history to make!"

Chapter 17

Once more, Enkidu was thankful for Grant's knowledge and skills, if forever frustrated at the lack of identity such memories provided. He and Malesh had been swimming for a mile. Even the outlaw goddess was starting to lose her endurance as they swam to a bubbled dome in the roof of the submerged tunnel. The air from the rubber bladders they carried was life sustaining, but it certainly wasn't anything that Enkidu wanted to rely on. They'd had to submerge every so often in the underwater cave, a huge corridor that was designed to accommodate skimmers, like the one he had battled two weeks earlier.

There was also a larger class of ship that shunted under the surface to launch from the center of what would later be called the Persian Gulf, or farther out so as not to be seen by the fishermen and seafaring traders of the era. If the enormous scout ships were seen, there was little worry on the part of the Annunaki, who had encouraged superstition. Sea monsters were considered a regular sight in these lands. Indeed, out of boredom, more than a few creatures that Enkidu had assumed were pure myth had been constructed by the Annunaki.

The minotaur he'd battled on the night he first met Malesh was a prime example. Indeed, Humbaba himself was another specimen of genetic dice rolling and feature cobbling, as was the beautiful cat-eyed woman clinging to a rock for a rest. The two people hung on to the crags, proceeding in near absolute darkness.

Only near darkness, thanks to a little bit of knowledge that Enkidu had gleaned from Grant's years of working beside Brigid Baptiste. The pair had small, aerated nets that had been packed with bioluminescent shrimp. Alone, the creatures would provide very little help, but Enkidu and Malesh had fished to capture dozens. Together, the glowing creatures not only allowed the two to see each other, but also to make certain that they were on their course. The tunnel was an arduous trek, one that would have left less physically capable people limp and useless.

Enkidu knew that he wasn't sweating, that it was the waters of the Tigris that had soaked him skin and bone. Before making this swim, Enkidu had taken a sharp knife and scraped off the shaggy mass of overgrown hair. He was bald once more, his beard trimmed down to a mustache similar to the one he had when he'd first arrived. The urge had been sparked by a dream as Grant spoke to his tesseract from his place lost in time.

The lost Grant knew what his friends were planning, thanks to the presence of his other tesseract embedded in Kane's forearm. Enkidu awoke, and groomed himself for a battle that he and Malesh had calculated to be the end of Humbaba's despotic reign. Enkidu also had a debt to pay to Shamhat. The reptilian Igigi scum was a murderer and torturer, a beast who had broken spirits and turned human beings into slaves. His whip had lashed Enkidu's back, but the harshest of pain was guilt over his failure, knowing full well the consequences that Shamhat had laid before him.

"I have been almost literally dying for a chance to experience a few things that Humbaba has forbidden," Shamhat had told him, his tongue sliding over scaly lips, reminding Enkidu more of a toad than a reptilian servant of a god's son. "But once Humbaba learned of the esteem you held these hairless monkeys in, he loosed me. Please, do not come back, for the joys I will experience will be legendary."

Enkidu had recovered his breath, his strength replenished by their rest.

"What's going to be legendary is how far down his neck I can shove his fucking head," Enkidu growled as water lapped at his nearly naked jaw.

"We must be disciplined, love," Malesh admonished. "If we give in to emotion, we may get sloppy."

"I'm not in the mood for sloppy," Enkidu/Grant returned. "I'm in the mood to make a horrible mess."

Malesh's face, illuminated by the glow of her luminescent shrimp, showed a faint smile. "I will admit that I intend to leave Humbaba a gory mess, as well."

"Besides, my anger seems to give me focus. The fouler my mood, the more likely I am to ignore minor things, like achy muscles from a three-mile swim," Enkidu said.

Malesh splashed some water at Enkidu's face. "Wise lover, turning anger into something good."

Enkidu wanted to reach out to her, but this wasn't the time or the place. They were hundreds of feet below the ancient city of Eridu, in darkness and in the path of entering and exiting Annunaki spacecraft. He didn't know if the craft would notice the two swimmers, or even if they would have cared. The multiton displacement of the scout ships, however, would churn the water so violently that neither of the two outlaws could hold their breaths, even if they could quickly return to the surface and not be ground into the silt at the bottom of the channel.

"Are you rested?" Enkidu asked.

She nodded. "You?"

Enkidu didn't have to answer as he let go of the rock, slicing through the water's surface for as long as there was room and air for him.

Dread filled his stomach, as he felt he would never see his half-Annunaki goddess again.

HUMBABA SLOUCHED on his throne, the future man's coat worn about his neck as a cape, since his massive arms and shoulders couldn't fit even into that oversize garment. He liked the feel of its Kevlar weave and leather on his shoulders and back. So many of the other Annunaki "governors" had a taste in robes, if they wore any human-style clothing at all. Some spiced them with gold threads, or dyed them with fruit juices in reds, blues and purples, among other colors.

Humbaba's kilts had remained simple, sackcloth in color, but the sight of Enkidu in his ankle-length black jacket, moving at blistering speeds, had inspired a passion for the garment he used as his cloak. Black was the color of a god's messengers, the ravens and crows, birds that had been manipulated by the Annunaki and the Tuatha de Danann to have the power of speech and memory. The genetic engineering necessary for such improvements was surprisingly little. Only a few of the jet-black creatures had actually been modified, but here and there, such talented mimics had disappeared into the wild, making a bid for freedom and independence. They interacted with other corvids, breeding with them to spread the gifts bestowed upon them. Such dilution would limit the ability of later generations, but the messengers were among the few who had survived their utility to the Annunaki.

He rubbed his cloak between his thumb and forefinger, relishing the feel of the dark material draped around his neck. The black of the ravens had become a powerful symbol in Humbaba's mind. It was the color of not only cleverness, but also freedom and rebellion. He wouldn't be a lackey for Enlil, used up and discarded as a corpse. He would escape and begin a life of his own. In his loins lay the seed of the Anhur. He could revive the extinct race, under his own mastery.

The raven-black coat draped over one shoulder gave the son of Enlil a slightly more fearsome feeling. Humbaba had never been a creature to take interest in fashion, but his wardrobe had expanded. Now his kilts and sashes were dyed black like the leathery coat. It felt good, and he had developed a sense of narcissism, in so far as he dressed grimly, adorned to look like a god of death, which fit him.

Shamhat appeared at the side door behind his throne, the Igigi shuffling from foot to foot.

"Any news on my kin, slave master?" Humbaba asked.

Shamhat, still uncomfortable in his master's presence, had been glad for Enlil's intervention. The punishment he'd received filled the subterranean palace with shrieks of agony, but only for an hour. Shamhat had even regained control over his legs and sphincter the day after. "Your father's ire at the wasting of our ships has leavened. I am certain he has agents within the court of Urudug, watching to make certain you do not stray again."

Humbaba pulled a link of entrails off his long, leonine snout, flipping it at the Igigi. "You mean Father has more than you spying on me?"

Shamhat trembled at the pronouncement, plucking the rubbery intestine from his shoulder. "Sire?"

"As Enkidu would say, don't give me that bullshit," Humbaba returned. "Father distracts me from your folly, and applies even sterner scrutiny to the comings and goings here. It's so that I barely get a chance to teach you your lesson."

He turned and looked directly at the Igigi, making him flinch, grasping one of his buttocks.

Shamhat sighed. "My presence was merely to extend the war between you and your sister, for it amused him."

"It's amusing now that humans who used to be my cannon fodder are now acting against those who still are?" Humbaba asked. "Or perhaps that we don't capture prisoners anymore, thanks to their leadership? If men believe themselves to be of worth, then they will no longer pay attention to their gods. Where would we be then?"

"I…I know not," Shamhat answered.

"The battles are raging, and Malesh has finally revealed herself to them. They are blinded by her magnificence, as meager a creature as she is," Humbaba grumbled. "Have our scouts spotted her lately?"

"No, sire," Shamhat said.

"Then she must be planning something," the Anhur-Annunaki half-breed said. His golden eyes scanned the court. There was the usual assembly of Annunaki and Igigi, interspersed with representatives of other races who were simply passing through on Earth.

The walls were lined with Nephilim drones, each of them standing ramrod alert. None of the cloned soldiers would sag and laze off, grown tired and idle. As they had no imagination, no sense of self, their duty was everything. As a lark, Humbaba had one stand guard until dehydration and lack of sleep killed him. The Nephilim were perfect, and far less likely to engage in intrigue than the Igigi.

Humbaba knew that Shamhat's people were not long for the Earth. Their usefulness as thinking pawns simply meant that they could be turned into spies and double agents. Humbaba had his own moles in various other courts, even in Enlil's throne room. The novelty of intrigue was starting to wear thin, and the slippery snakes were going to have to be disposed of, replaced with something better, creatures that could actually interact with the apekin who were the secret overlords.

"If we do not have enough Nephilim, I want you to breed more in the vats," Humbaba said.

"How many would we need against a human and your partly human sister?" Shamhat asked.

Humbaba chuckled. "What you would assume to be too many, fool. How many would you align against me?"

"A thousand," Shamhat admitted.

"Then you have your number," Humbaba growled. "Do your duty for me, before informing Father of the games his children play."

Shamhat lowered his head in shame and left the stage behind the giant's throne.

Humbaba flexed his massive fist, hungry for his sister's arrival. He idly wondered what her heart would taste like.

ENKIDU RELEASED the nearly empty air bladder, bubbles escaping its neck as it sank to the bottom of the underwater spaceport. With Malesh at his side, he clung to one of the four parked scout ships floating in water. Again, terms sprung to life in Enkidu's head from Grant's experiences. This place appeared to be some form of submarine pen, small jetties between each of the big ships. On the shore, he could make out at least a dozen skimmers, their mirrorlike hulls gleaming to reflect the subdued lighting in the space dock. The massive chamber was barely lit, with only a few alert sentries standing guard at the far end of the port. Their placement was indicative of the fact that Humbaba did not consider the possibility that someone could swim for five miles down an underground river.

Both of them were exhausted and thoroughly saturated. It had been a good idea that Enkidu had shed his ash-gray mane for this swim. He didn't relish the idea of sopping wet curls slapping him in the face with each head movement.

Enkidu/Grant silently asked himself who the wise guy was who actually had suggested this back-door infiltration.

"You did," Malesh whispered as she hung on to the scout ship.

"Reading my thoughts," Enkidu grumbled.

"Surface thoughts," Malesh said. "Still no way inside."

"If it's anything like Urudug, you'd probably have to go up my ass," Enkidu told her.

"That's a beautiful mental image," Malesh said, the look on her face clearly indicating her disgust at Enkidu's grouchy response.

"I'll make it up to you," Enkidu told her.

Malesh looked down, as if peering through the surface of the water they floated in.

"What's down there?" Enkidu asked.

"Nothing that cannot wait," Malesh replied. "Thank you for everything."

"Including the beat-down I gave you?" Enkidu asked. "Come on, we're not done living yet. Don't treat me as if either of us are on a date with death."

"Even if we do triumph over Humbaba, there would be nothing to protect us from the wrath of my father," Malesh said. "He enjoys observing our fights because it keeps us from turning against him. If I succeed, then I will rise to the level of threat."

"Humbaba first, then Enlil," Enkidu promised her.

Malesh caressed his face as the two huddled together, hanging on projections of the spacecraft to recover their strength for the next leg of their invasion of the court of Urudug.

SHAMHAT WAS an Igigi whistling in the graveyard, stricken with the awareness that his life was close to forfeit. If he offended Humbaba one more time, there would be nothing to stop his revelation as a spy. Spies in the houses of the Annunaki were considered to be the greatest form of entertainment. The healing matrices would work overtime to ensure that he would return to perfect health for the next day's torture. The already cruel overlords of this backwater outpost were the kind to repay betrayal with a living hell.

Shamhat's wails of agony would be the music by which Humbaba would dine, his vocal cords manipulated by other Igigi masters of pain and suffering. The reprises in the rejuvenation chambers were an even worse form of cruelty. It would be there that Shamhat would relive his day's torture, even as his body lay in comfort, health recovering and pain suppressed.

If his entire existence had been turned into one of agony, then eventually Shamhat would grow used to it, but the rests would remind him of the life of joy he had abandoned with his exposure as a spy.

As he approached his desk, his knees gave out. He was sapped of strength out of pure terror. Shamhat had to attend to the creation of hundreds of Nephilim who would bolster the numbers of Humbaba's protectors. A thousand drones was an impressive number, equal to any ten legions of human soldiers.

With that many warriors on hand, Humbaba would never even have to lift a finger.

"There," Shamhat spoke softly, looking at the crystal he had inscribed with the program. He inserted it into a slot on his desk, where it began to glow, reading his writing and transferring the orders within to the clone vats. "There are the orders that will safeguard you, master. My life is hanging by the thread of your whim and my performance of my duties, but you are a certain thing. It would be easy to let Malesh win, but there are too many variables to ensure my survival."

The Igigi rose, frowning as he knew it was true. He had chosen the devil he knew as opposed to the mercy of Malesh and Enkidu. At least with them out of the way, Shamhat would be able to stay on his best behavior, manipulating events so that Humbaba would see his reliability.

"I am alive on my knees, while the apekin will die on his feet," he muttered with wistful melancholy. "Such is the way of the Igigi."

Shamhat left his office in darkness, returning to his master's side.

DESPITE HOW WET his hands and feet were, Enkidu was still able to find firm purchase that enabled him to climb to the back of the scout ship. Malesh followed, the two swimmers naked save for the straps by which they had secured their equipment bags to their backs. They crouched, maintaining a low profile, but so far, luck had been on their side. The Nephilim stood constant guard, keeping their eyes on the passage leading to the rest of the subterranean palace of Urudug.

He took the time to release the biochemically lit shrimp from their neck bags. They had served Malesh and him nobly, and they deserved their freedom.

Humbaba's court was secure and hidden. Who would dare to enter into the chamber through five miles of underwater tunnel? No one but us damn fools, rose the grouchy voice of Grant in his tesseract's thoughts.

As a consequence of the impossibility of intrusion, there were hatches on the back of the scout craft that lay open, allowing easy access for the drone crew and their Igigi officers. It would be a long time before the concept of scuba diving would arise in the human race, or even the undersea suits that were nothing more than an iron dome with a hose for oxygen.

Malesh set down her pack. The outlaw goddess had little need for much equipment, thanks to the nature of her otherworldly natural strength. Her fingernails were as sharp as knives, and she was swift enough to reach nearly any opponent in the space between heartbeats.

Enkidu slid his ASP around his wrist, protected from immersion by an oiled skin. He wasn't sure what would happen with exposure to salt water, and since he wanted to keep his arm, he had safeguarded it. The three cobra head–shaped emitters rested easily along the back of his hand, ready to spit out their lethal whispers of fire and death.

It was an equalizer against an enemy who outnumbered Enkidu and Malesh. The two outlaws had been unable to bring any of their liberated army on this mission; they had been the only people capable of making the underwater journey, and the plan had been one of surprise and audacity, coming on the heels of a stealthy infiltration. The two people opened their packs, and Enkidu slid on his battle uniform. His normal leather-and-cloth kilt would provide protection to his groin and upper legs, while a boiled-leather chest plate gave his torso armor. It would be nothing against the searing plasma discharge of an ASP forearm blaster, but in hand-to-hand combat against Humbaba, it might provide some wiggle room, giving him the difference between air knocked from his chest and ribs sticking through flesh. Use of cover and stealth would make up for his vulnerability to the Nephilim's energy weapons.

His other tools were much simpler than the alien blaster around his right wrist. Once more, his *kopesh* and knife, replacements for the ones lost in battle with the minotaur, would serve him when quiet was necessary. And they were going to need to be silent killers on board the Annunaki scout ship. There would be a skeleton crew on board, and they needed to be eliminated with bloody efficiency.

Right now, Malesh's forehead was wrinkled with concentration. Her presence in the court of Urudug would be detected by her psychic bond with her brother, Humbaba. Only by suppressing her own alpha waves by pure will was she able to keep him from detecting her presence. Conversely, she wouldn't be able to locate him, if necessary, not without losing their element of surprise. As such, Malesh had to rely upon more than her talons and great strength. She, too, had a knife and an ASP forearm blaster.

Enkidu could feel her lack of presence in his mind, and for the first time since he'd met her, he felt truly alone, like when he had just arrived. It was a dizzying feeling, and something that made him feel more off balance, as well. He reached out and cupped the back of her head, touching their foreheads together.

There was still no telepathic bond, but they had worked out their plan. From now on, they couldn't communicate across more than a whisper's distance, and it was a wound that ached in Enkidu's chest.

"I'm sorry for leaving you alone," Malesh whispered in his ear.

"I'm sorry that you're alone again, too," Enkidu replied.

If there was any truth, then it was that Malesh, in her exile, stripped of the luxuries of Annunaki culture and technology, save for her knowledge of the alien race's medicine, was punished by the simple fact that she was a stranger in an alien world. She had been reduced to scrounging off the land to survive, living in a hole in the ground, without a soul to communicate with. For a natural-born telepath like Malesh, the solitude was unbearable.

Enkidu's arrival had been a salve on that. Returning to that world of silence left her feeling as an agoraphobe in an open field, or a claustrophobe in a coffin.

"We have poured the wine," Malesh told him, her voice regaining some of the iron it had previously held. "We should drink it."

Enkidu smiled, all the while cursing himself. Such a jolt of pride and love mere moments before the butcher's work that needed to be done was a bitter concoction.

They were in the den of their enemies, and they had to act.

And the wine they would be drinking, they hoped, would be Humbaba's spilled blood.

Chapter 18

Grant's strength, once more, was a gift to the shadow known as Enkidu. He pulled back on the Nephilim's head, hand clamped over the drone's mouth to stifle anything that would resemble a cry for help. The point of his bronze knife, hammered home by all the weight and muscle he possessed, had proved far more efficient at penetrating the finely woven smart metal than simply the cutting edge. The blade twisted in the creature's kidney, throwing it into renal shock and stilling it forever.

Enkidu lowered the corpse to the floor, pushing it into the space beneath its duty station to keep it out of sight. The ship had a skeleton crew, but even that was a formidable group, according to Malesh. She said that there were easily two dozen of the creatures on the two-hundred-foot-long craft. By knife and surprise, the two of them had to eliminate the crew of the craft, so they had to separate the chores of killing the semimindless drones.

So far, it had been a quiet infiltration, but Enkidu knew that a mistake would imperil all of their efforts. While it was unlikely that they would be inundated by a swarm of Nephilim at this stage, there were three other ships surrounding them, each of them with the same size crew, and the same capacity to do what they were planning. The guns of the other scout ships could rip apart their ride easily.

Enkidu had just finished with his seventh target. He was over half done with the bloody work on this ship, but the end of the line was the bridge. There, four Nephilim and an Igigi officer of the watch remained on station, ready to activate the craft's mighty engines. They would either wait for the rest of their crew to arrive, or they would launch immediately, should the situation warrant it. The scout was designed for a crew of close to one hundred, but with its off-shift staff, it could still operate and utilize the guns or sensors of the ship to accomplish any of its jobs.

He padded along the hallway to the control room, seeing that the door was open. Odd humming harmonics filled the air, rather than the electronic beeps and drones he'd expected. The ship was a semiliving creature, a lesser version of its "mother," the enormous *Tiamat.* Like the Nephilim, it was not truly sentient, and was augmented by more conventional technology, but the scout ship was still mostly organic with inlays and cybernetics to allow for interface and control. It was unsettling, though again not unfamiliar. It wasn't a process of Malesh's imprinting the layout of the craft in his mind. He'd been on a craft like this at least two times before.

His familiarity was irrelevant now. The Igigi and his bridge crew stood between him and control of the scout ship. With it, he'd have a well-armed ship with more than sufficient durability and thrust to make the court of Urudug regret its war with Malesh.

Enkidu slid his knife back into its sheath and drew his *kopesh.* He'd need the powerful cutting edge to dispatch the last of the crew on his side of the ship swiftly, but without alerting the crews of the other scouts floating in the underground bay. The stretched time scale he experienced would be the edge he'd need to deal with them handily.

With a step, he was through the door, *kopesh*'s curved and hooked blade naked and hungry for blood. The Igigi captain hadn't heard his tread, and the Nephilim were focused on their duty stations, operating with cold, almost mechanical efficiency. With his second's gaze into the future, he knew that none of his opponents were going to react to his assault and he strode to the Nephilim operating the communications and sensor console.

He was thankful for Malesh and her knowledge of the alien craft, especially the layout of the bridge. In one stride, he was on the Nephilim, *kopesh* whisking easily through the head of the alien drone, skull parting and slurping off the top of the body. It hit the floor like a half of a coconut, spewing out the clump of brain matter that had filled its dome.

Even as his sword connected, the world crashed into Enkidu. His senses were overwhelmed by a torrent of pain that froze him where he stood. The inside of his own head seemed to swell, and he wanted to vomit from the experience. When the moment passed, he was standing on the bridge. He had struck so swiftly that none of the Nephilim had noticed him, but as he looked at the *kopesh*'s blade, he saw the drops of blood coming off its edge.

They fell in normal time, and the Doppler effect he experienced was no longer there. Time had snapped to normal with that bolt of sudden pain.

Just my luck, Enkidu thought. He didn't have the time to figure out why he had lost his unusual perspective on time, just that he was now a third as fast as he used to be.

The Igigi officer had heard the grunt of disappointment that inadvertently escaped from the time-lost warrior. It turned, cold reptilian eyes locking on the massive shape of a half-naked Grant wielding a bloody sword on its bridge. Lips parted with surprise, eyes widening as it tried to make out what this intruder was and why it was here. Enkidu still had a fraction of a moment to act, and he lunged, slashing down at the Igigi's neck.

The officer spun quickly, turning out of the path of the blade just enough that its smart metal armor deflected the force of the blow. Instead of having its torso sliced from neck to sternum, the Igigi was tossed to the floor, letting out a stunned grunt. Enkidu cursed as he saw two of the remaining Nephilim turn and look at him. The Igigi had sent out its telepathic orders to the drone creatures, alerting them to the presence of an intruder on the bridge.

Enkidu sidestepped and kicked the alien in the jaw, listening to its mandible shatter against the hard, tough leather of his boot's sole. The Igigi was out cold, but he wasn't sure how much of a message the creature had gotten out. It wasn't as if Shamhat had communicated with Enkidu at any distance other than normal speaking range, so perhaps there was hope that there wasn't an alarm raised throughout Humbaba's stronghold.

There were still three Nephilim present, and the drones rushed him, their armor-clad, muscular bodies slamming him to the ground in a coordinated tackle. Snarled in a mass of limbs, Enkidu found himself once more without his sword and unable to reach the knife in his belt. His right fist was pressed against the chest of one of the alien grapplers, while a second had immobilized his head to prevent a head butt. He didn't know what would happen if he fired the ASP he wore at contact range, especially up against the flexible woven-metal armor of his enemies.

Right now, there was no other choice, and the longer he delayed, the closer he got to discovery and a surge of alarms. The ASP's cobra heads responded to the reflexive forearm muscle twitch. They released their powerful charge, and Enkidu winced as Grant's hand roasted under the backwash of the bolt that ripped through the chest of one of his Nephilim opponents. The creature gurgled painfully as it died, but its fingers were still locked around his arm in a death grip.

Enkidu's left arm was pinned against his side as another of the Nephilim caught him in a bear hug. He needed leverage to get loose, so he stamped his feet against the floor and pushed himself up and off his back. The alien with the bear hug slid, still hanging on, but now Enkidu could bend his arm. With a shrug, he freed himself almost to the shoulder, then ripped the knife from its sheath. The Nephilim loosened his grasp to clutch at Enkidu's knife hand, but the blade was a feint.

Rather than attempt to deal with an alert opponent and lose what effectiveness the bronze knife had against the smart metal, Enkidu rammed his elbow hard into the alien's sternum. Ribs flexed, and even if they didn't break, they caused the drone enough pain that it rolled away from Enkidu.

That left the hands holding him in a headlock, a knee jammed against his spine. The Nephilim noticed that its partner was knocked away, and pulled harder on Enkidu's neck, threatening to break it. He twisted his arm around to stab at the man, but he didn't have the freedom to strike at the drone. Trapped, off balance,

Enkidu grimaced, realizing that his fight was over before he'd even had a chance to begin. He cursed the gods for taking away his enhanced time sense. His tripled reflexive response would have made this bridge attack nothing less than a one-sided slaughter.

Now Malesh was going to be alone against Humbaba and his unyielding soldiers.

The grasp on his face loosened, the Nephilim releasing a spray of arterial blood that rained down over Enkidu's head. The murderous drone fell off his back, and Enkidu folded forward, free from the pressure cranking mercilessly on his spine. He gasped for breath, and spoke, knowing he'd been rescued by Malesh.

"Love?" Enkidu asked.

"No. She is," came the curt, simple reply.

Enkidu looked to see a tiny white-as-alabaster woman with ruby-red eyes holding a wicked knife that she wiped on the shoulder of the dead Nephilim. "Who?"

Out of the corner of his eye, he saw a blur in action. For a moment, he thought that it was Malesh, but as he turned and focused, he saw a black-haired woman wielding a ribbon of mirror-polished silver. The Igigi he'd kicked in the jaw had gotten to his feet, but both of his arms were now spurting stumps, the ASP-clad limb dropped in front of him. The stunned Nephilim turned to aim his blaster at the Japanese swordswoman, and Enkidu lunged, clawing at the drone's leg.

Shizuka saw the flurry of activity out of the corner of her eye as she ended the Igigi captain's suffering with a quick stab through the heart. She turned in time to see the three cobra heads of his ASP glow. Enkidu/Grant slammed into the Nephilim and knocked him sprawling to the floor. Domi scooped up the fallen *kopesh* and lopped off the alien's head with a swift movement.

"Grant?" Shizuka spoke.

Enkidu looked at the face, the familiar image from before, when he'd first laid eyes upon Malesh. She called him a name, but that didn't register in his mind. He had hoped that the moment he'd been addressed by his true identity, he'd recover all of his memories, but nothing came magically to him.

A sickly twinge rolled through his chest. "I don't remember you."

THE RECONSTRUCTION of the derelict scout ship's final minutes, thanks to the computer records and the remains of skeletons on the bridge, showed that things had grown hectic. Brigid's keen observational skills and eidetic memory helped her to reconstruct the scene, even with the deck tilted violently.

It was a simple matter of cross-referencing the bridge that she'd discovered in Mongolia against the one they'd been aboard. Her ability to access every single detail she'd ever seen was phenomenally useful in retelling the final moments on board. That was how Kane made the decision to send Domi and Shizuka to the bridge in order to assist Grant while he and Brigid Baptiste were heading toward the engine room.

Kane knew from Shizuka's description that the tall goddess known as Gi Malesh was a part of her history, much like Cuchulain was part of him. If something befell her, there was no telling what kind of damage could befall Shizuka. It was known that the past was immutable, at least from their vantage point in time, but Brigid knew that Kane and the rest had been in the ship at this moment. It had been a message that the archivist had programmed into the navigation crystal to herself in a mathematical code that was based on chess moves. The past, and their future, had literally been written in stone by Brigid Baptiste.

Now Kane and Brigid were tearing down a hallway to the engine room, weapons drawn and ready. Kane didn't have to ask Brigid if what she had read was correct. The woman's mental abilities seemed almost magical at times, so if she was certain that they had arrived on the scene just before a tragic tactical error on both Malesh's and Grant's parts, then Kane knew he and Brigid had to be on hand for trouble in the engine room.

Brigid's message from this time period, which was still in their future, was left vague, except to point out that there was damage in the engine room of the scout ship, damage indicative of a massive battle between two powerful forces. Even as Kane reached the last hallway to the boiler room, the craft shuddered, a distant boom muffled by the heavy doors of the chamber. He glanced back to Brigid.

"Keep going!" she answered. "We should be right on time. Just go with your instincts!"

Kane nodded, lowered his head and leaned into his run, charging toward the door, which was actually a circular aperture, reminding him of a living valve. He took aim at the controls with his Sin Eater, pumping a heavy 240-grain round into the crystal lattice embedded in the living panel. Sparks flew as the stones shattered, and the aperture flicked open, its multiple layers folding back to reveal one of the most beautiful women he'd ever seen, her hands locked with the massive paws of a large, shaggy creature. The beast's face was twisted in exertion against the goddess, pushing her down, but its eyes were blank, the back of its neck adorned with a knob that had no other means of attachment than what must have been subdermal anchors wrapped around its spine.

It looked up to see Kane and Brigid in the entrance to the engine room, black, soulless eyes registering the two newcomers as a threat. The distraction was enough for Malesh to get her feet beneath her and apply enough force to push back.

"Jakko?" Kane muttered, snapping the Sin Eater up and firing two quick shots at it. The beast shuddered under the armor-piercing impacts, but its only reaction was to upend Malesh and hurl her at them like a human missile. Kane swung his gun aside and lunged, catching the woman across his body to cushion her fall. As he was bowled over, instinct urged him to scramble away with Malesh, moving them back from the doorway even as a searing bolt of energy lashed across the threshold.

Even as Malesh was airborne, Brigid brought up her weapon, a Copperhead rifle, and ripped off half of a magazine into the anthropoid. Her SMG's tiny 4.85 mm bullets peppered the beast, driving it back but not drawing any blood. The creature leaped into the depths of the engine room, out of sight. She scanned the entrance, then ducked back out of the door, barely avoiding being struck by an ASP bolt. "That wasn't Jakko, but definitely the same species. Most likely, these creatures were servitors at this time, assigned to heavy lifting in the engine room."

"How did you know?" Malesh asked, telepathically translating as she recovered from her sudden tumble.

"There were only two dead Nephilim," Brigid said. "I know that this is insufficient crew for this area, especially for off shift."

Kane paused and shrugged out of the backpack containing the interphaser. His tumble hadn't affected the device in its armored carry shell, proving Lakesh's skill at constructing the device. Even so, it was a heavy load that would only slow him down if he were to engage with a massive opponent like the beast who'd tossed Malesh like a rag doll.

"Two more, and the Austro," Malesh said. Kane was surprised when she employed the Annunaki's ethnic slur for this particular slave creature.

Kane whipped around the door, moving with his usual swiftness. As the Sin Eater was literally a part of him, a limb unto itself, he only needed to line up the gun between his eyes and his targets to hit his target with deadly precision. The Nephilim who'd taken a shot at Brigid released a painful grunt as a heavy-caliber slug tore through its heart, splitting the heavy cardiac muscle in half. The creature was dead on its feet as its spine was snapped by the same bullet bursting out of its back.

The last of the armed engine room shift blazed away at Kane, but the human moved too swiftly. Its drone mind, not programmed to deal with humans utilizing automatic weapons, didn't aim to track Kane, simply firing where the man had been brief milliseconds before. The hairbreadth of time provided enough distance for Kane to be a few feet out of the way of the writhing tendril of pulsing energy. His Sin Eater spoke again, a line of bloody blossoms sprouting along the Nephilim's centerline as the machine pistol burped out its lethal message. The creature toppled backward, pelvis, spine and ribs reduced to splinters by the passage of five high-penetration rounds.

The last of the reptilian drones was dead, but that didn't mean much. Kane knew there was an eight-foot-tall creature with arms as thick as tree trunks stalking through the chamber, and who knew what kind of weapon it was seeking out to even the odds against its human opponents. His keen senses and his preternatural point man's instinct all alerted him that trouble was coming at them.

Kane whirled even before his conscious mind registered the sound of machinery ripped from a wall. His arms swung out, hooking Brigid and Malesh around their waists, and his momentum carried all three people out of the path of an arcing interface terminal. Resin and crystal shattered as it crashed into the floor, cracking the heavy chitin of the scout craft, showing off the Austro's power.

"I think he's still angry," Brigid said breathlessly as she looked at the scars knocked in the floor.

"I hadn't taken an Austro into account," Malesh admitted, looking battered. She set her jaw and concentrated. Her face and posture straightened, her strength returning to her visage. "He's strong, chosen for the ability to lift two tons of equipment, ore and crystals."

"Two tons," Kane said with a whistle. "No wonder he shook off all of our bullets."

"The Australopithicus was physically impressive, according to the fossil records, but I never…" Brigid began.

Malesh locked the archivist with a hard glare. Brigid nodded with renewed knowledge.

"They are not invulnerable. No master makes a slave immune to harm," Malesh explained to Kane. "The trouble is, the Austro's masters are Annunaki. Full-blooded Annunaki."

Kane sized up the tall golden-skinned goddess with the cat's eyes and the leonine mane of black and gold. "You held your own. I would bet that your father's Enlil."

She nodded. "And Humbaba's my brother."

"Introductions later," Kane muttered, catching the heavy tread of the ape-man's step. "Company's coming."

"What do we do?" Brigid asked. "We can't use grenades in here, not with the stored energy modules. The destruction would be catastrophic."

Kane sighed. "And I do so love catastrophic destruction."

With that, he raced into the open, giving a war whoop to draw the eight-foot beast's attention. The Austro's black, glaring eyes locked on to the human warrior, and its lip curled up in a snarl. With three long, loping strides, it was close enough to swing its massive fist like a wrecking ball. Only Kane's swift reactions and agility protected him from a blow that would have torn his head from his shoulders. The Cerberus warrior brought up his combat knife, lashing it across the hairy giant's belly, but the creature's thick, shaggy hair and leathery skin were just too much for even the cutting edge and every ounce of force that Kane could muster. The Austro lashed out again, its powerful forearm grazing his shoulder. Even with the glancing blow and the rapid stiffening of the shadow suit's polymers, Kane felt as if a boulder had landed on his arm. The knife dropped from his numbed fingers.

"Now," Kane said aloud, even though he probably didn't need to.

Malesh had sensed what he was doing, even without opening herself up and baring her consciousness. With the Austro distracted, however, she was able to leap on its back, her talons flashing on either side of the beast's neck. The thick hair on its neck stopped what would have been a mauling grasp, but the ape-man bellowed in pain as Kane opened up on its belly with the Sin Eater.

The Austro clutched Malesh's wrist with one powerful paw, and swatted Kane with the other, pain slicing through the numbness induced by the nodule installed on the nape of its neck. Its brain cleared momentarily; its reflexes had improved enough to land its attacks. Kane grimaced as he flew through the air, cartwheeling toward the bulkhead.

Kane tucked his knees to his chest, slapping the floor with both hands to deflect his momentum. He didn't want to test the shadow suit's resistance to impacts. The handspring launched him upward, sucking the energy from his sideways spin. He pushed out with both feet, kicking the wall, but letting his legs flex, bleeding off more of his speed. It was jarring, but at least he wasn't squirted out of the neck hole of his skintight uniform.

The Austro grunted in pain, struggling with Malesh, who was engaged with a tug-of-war over the monster's shoulder. As the ape-creature turned, Kane could see the sharp nails on Malesh's feet dig into its back. The power of her legs was more than enough to penetrate the heavy fur and leathery skin, blood soaking it. It caused pain, but the Austro wasn't going to bleed to death from a few small bullet holes and toe scratches. Kane had to act before the eight-foot-tall beast whipped her against the floor with enough force to splinter her skeleton.

Kane took aim at the Austro's groin with his machine pistol, pumping out a 6-round burst. It was a low, cheap shot, but the odds were too great against them. The more Malesh fought, the more her concentration was strained.

Once that broke, Humbaba would know she was here, and the whole of the palace guard would swarm into the port. Even protected by the heavy skirt of thick fur, the creature's genitals were hammered mercilessly. The Austro bent over, agonized, and Malesh wrapped one of her corded, golden arms around its throat. She stabbed her other fist into its chest, and only then did Kane see the ASP blaster wrapped around her forearm.

While a stray beam of plasma energy would have been risky in the engine room given the charged energy modules, at contact range, there was no chance the goddess could miss. She unleashed the searing thunderbolt, drilling a charred hole through the Austro's rib cage. The stench of cooked meat filled Kane's nostrils, and the battle for the engine room was over.

Malesh rose, panting from the dead beast's corpse. "Damn."

"We encountered another like this," Kane said numbly. "It, too, had been turned into a pawn by a madman who thought he was a god. What a damn waste."

Malesh looked up. "It is the Annunaki's way, Kane of Cerberus."

"You know me?" Kane asked.

"You may have said to wait for introductions, but Grant didn't," Malesh said, looking at Kane's forearm. "You've come to take my Enkidu away from me."

Kane wrapped his fingers around his forearm, feeling the pained pulse throbbing through his bones. "I'm sorry, Malesh."

The goddess extended a hand to Kane. "But I know you won't leave me alone, with Enkidu's destiny unfinished. For that, I thank you."

Chapter 19

Humbaba slid his index talon down the material of Grant's armored trench coat. He loved the feel and sound of the hard nail on the weave of Kevlar and leather as it vibrated up his finger. He wondered where its owner was at this moment, what the creature he called Enkidu was plotting alongside his sister. With the court of Urudug sprawled in front of him, he grimaced at the failure of his warrior cadre to bring in his sister, Gi Malesh.

Two people had given his human thralls and even his Nephilim warriors a hard time, hitting hard and running for cover, freeing more people from his command, building a small, ragtag community in the woods where Humbaba had gotten the magnificent cedar logs for the gate to his garden. Only in the past week had the pair allowed small, agile squads of their followers to harry his forces.

With that increase in activity, Malesh and Enkidu had seemingly disappeared from the field. For seven days, none of his few surviving agents in the field had reported anyone resembling either the tall, dark bronze man-bull or the even taller golden goddess attacking them.

For two months straight, neither his sister nor his former cat's paw had spent more than two days off from their constant raids, freeing slaves and stealing tributes and treasures for his court. An entire supply route had been cut off by their efforts, a state of constant warfare that had reduced a fifteen-thousand-man army of Eridu by two thousand men. No Annunaki governorship had lost two thousand soldiers in such a short time. The skirmishes between Humbaba and his rival city states had never resulted in losses of more than a dozen soldiers in a month.

There were just two of them, and they had succeeded in decimating his army. What was even more infuriating was that Malesh had somehow convinced most of those lost troops to defect. Humbaba had been a benevolent ruler. The fighting humans he commanded were treated well in their victories, and reminded of the price of failure in no uncertain terms. What could his sister, with only pilfered gold and a few sundries for day-to-day survival, offer to cause those men to defect to her side?

For a brief moment, Humbaba considered the possibility of his sister whoring herself out, buying a change of loyalty with her sexual favors. The master of Urudug didn't consider it beneath his interests to take human slaves as lovers. For him it was more of an instance of one dalliance; the poor, fragile things were hardly capable of withstanding his appetites, his vast strength and his inhuman size. With Malesh, she could more easily allow her pawns to survive and continue to battle for her sake after lovemaking.

Humbaba frowned.

The turncoats would be dealt with, put to the sword as they were captured by the rest of his legions. Once he located his sister and her bestial consort, the traitors would be easy to dispose of.

There was a tickle at the back of his mind, something that made Humbaba sit up and take notice. A psychic tingle ran up his spine, sparking at the base of his neck.

At his sudden rise to alertness, his Nephilim thralls all turned, taking notice of their master's distress. He glared at the reptilian drones.

"Battle stations," he growled under his breath, commanding the armored warriors.

They moved with precision, herding slaves to the corridor leading to their holding cells. The members of his court who were not trained or meant for combat knew their place as the leonine giant's mind reached out to them. Visitors were escorted by the Igigi and other hangers-on to a safe place.

Humbaba rose, Grant's trench coat rustling on his shoulder as he did so.

"Sister!" he bellowed, both for the cathartic feel of the words rumbling through his massive chest and to focus himself to broadcast like a beacon of rage. "I can feel you!"

The tingle turned from a thread of psychic static to a full-blown clear signal. There was amusement in his sister's heart, though she shielded her thoughts so that Humbaba could not locate her.

"Gi Malesh! Tell me where you are, so I may greet you with open arms," Humbaba called out.

"I'm just downstairs," came her response. "Let me pop up to see you."

With a snort, Humbaba whirled. Already his Nephilim horde was moving as one, battle pikes and ASP wrist blasters at the ready. They surged toward the foyer leading down into the depths of his underground palace.

A powerful wind suddenly whipped up, a hurricane of pressure that picked up the drones and hurled them throughout Humbaba's great hall. The half-Annunaki titan dug his hind claws into the marble floor, and he could feel himself being pushed back by the torrent of heated air. Nephilim spiraled through the air, forcing Humbaba to swat them aside, his powerful forearms shattering their ribs and spines as he deflected them.

They were disposable pawns, of no major import. Shamhat was already on the job to brew more of the soulless constructs. This gale would only batter and unbalance most of his protectors. It would be of no great matter; the mighty Humbaba could deal with his little sister and the even smaller Enkidu, no matter what trickery they were using.

That's when the palace shook around him. The floor tilted suddenly, his great hall thrown askew as a mighty force slammed into the ground beneath him. The shattering impact under his feet hurled the leonine godling to his hands and knees.

Humbaba rose, his eyes red with fury. Never before had he been driven to his knees, and this foul trickery only added to that insult.

ENKIDU LOOKED at Kane, who bore two burdens. Though he had been told the man's name, he was a complete stranger to him, a memory far from a tantalizing hint.

The first of the burdens was a pyramidal backpack, well armored, but Kane carried it, clenching the shoulder straps in his left hand. Enkidu knew the name for the device, knew the name of the skintight body armor that Kane wore, even the name of the pistol sheathed in his hydraulic forearm holster. Anything relating to his own identity, or his history with Kane, or the three women who accompanied the man, was completely cut off.

The other burden was a pulsing presence, infused with Kane's flesh. It was visible, audible, but it was a distracting, painful pressure inside of his brain. It felt like a puzzle piece being jammed through one of his eye sockets, but Enkidu endured.

"Why isn't he remembering?" Kane asked Brigid Baptiste.

Enkidu looked to the flame-haired beauty, also clad in body-hugging black polymers. The woman's bright green eyes flashed brightly as she examined the situation.

"We have two pieces of a three-part organism, Kane," Brigid said. "This is why we brought the interphaser and kept it with us. There is one other part that we have to summon."

"Grant himself," Kane said. "Except his body is right here, and I've got his brain in my damn arm."

"Not his brain. Just his ego," Brigid answered. "Grant's sense of self. These two have been cast as shadows from a higher dimension, and as such, they are not aligned properly."

"This is going to hurt, isn't it?" Kane asked.

Enkidu rubbed his throbbing brow. "It's no picnic for me, either."

"Sounds like Grant, too," Kane mentioned.

"Practical biochemical information stored in his brain cells," Brigid posited.

Shizuka, one of the two women who had come to Enkidu's rescue, spoke softly. "It merely sounds like Grant, but it is not him."

"So where is Grant?" Enkidu asked. "And what's going to happen to me once we put all the pieces together?"

"Like Kane said, it'll probably hurt," Brigid said. "But if you're inquiring about the personality you developed here, I don't know. This is a metaphysical conundrum that I hadn't anticipated."

"Smaller words for us in the dumb section," Kane grumbled.

"Enkidu is Enkidu. He might have aspects of Grant's personality, or he may be Grant. Or he has developed as an entity in his own right," Brigid said. "We recombine everything, we could end up killing a sentient being."

Enkidu and Kane looked at each other, then at the four women with them.

"You keep saying I'm just a shadow, but I feel real," Enkidu said. He glanced at Malesh, her beautiful features cast into a frown. "Can a shadow be in love?"

"Talking too much," Domi interrupted. "Time's wasting."

Enkidu sized up the tiny albino creature, then set his jaw firmly. "She's right. The more time we waste, the harder it becomes for Malesh to hide her presence."

Malesh and Shizuka both reached out to him at the same time, poised to deliver a comforting caress, then they stopped, regarding each other.

"Not a hint of jealousy," Kane muttered under his breath.

"They are the same," Enkidu said. "Back when I wasn't living a second at a time like normal people, I saw their bond."

Domi cleared her throat. "What do we do?"

"We came here to destroy Humbaba and free his slaves," Enkidu said. "This Grant you're talking about, he knows how to work well with you people."

Malesh swallowed. "My love…"

Enkidu reached out and cupped her cheek. "I have to do what must be done. I'm sorry for leaving you alone, my goddess."

Enkidu then turned, extending his hand to the four travelers from another era. "But I am merely a shadow. A tesseract, you called it?"

Brigid nodded, chewing her upper lip.

"Kane, it is time to open the door," Enkidu said. "My destiny is cast."

Outside the small antechamber off to the side of the great cedar gates, on the other side of the concrete hatch, the roar of the scout ship's engines rose, the powerful thrust blowing past through the corridors of the palace's central spiral ramps. Having programmed the craft, the time travelers had reached the end of their knowledge of this period. All they had was a vague bit of knowledge that the Cedar Garden was sealed, and there had been no sign of their corpses.

Kane grimaced as he powered up the interphaser. "If it's worth anything, Grant would have bitched a lot more but come to the same decision."

Enkidu managed a smile. "That is worth something."

The interphaser hummed to life. Its recall signal, configured to travel across a temporal channel monitored by the Operation Chronos machinery instead of the central mat-trans network, pulsed outward, providing an anchor for the wormhole cast not in three-dimensional space, but along the directions of time and antitime.

Even as the signal turned into an aperture in reality, Enkidu felt himself being twisted apart. He could see Kane writhing as the ghostly Grant identity burned through his forearm, turning into a wispy ghost. Two golden, throbbing beams erupted from their cores, spiraling up into the ether of time, rising until they met in the far distance.

"I knew this was going to suck," Kane said, holding his agonized limb. His knees were rubbery beneath him, but he still fought to stand.

Enkidu looked at his ethereal counterpart, who returned the gaze. Both of them were frozen, unable to speak as they were impaled with pain. Above them, a burning ember was pulled down, dragged like a balloon on powerful tethers. Enkidu felt himself stretched out, pulled into a thick rope of protean unbeing.

His throbbing head was no longer in pain, nor was it actually a head anymore. Here, existing in a pocket at the horizon between universes, he was an entity without form or mass, facing a blazing core that pulled in him and the ghostly ego.

The crash of existences flowed into Grant, and nausea swept through him as apparently he once more owned a digestive system to feel the effects of its disruption. The pain of his shadows flowed into him, and Grant fought, knowing that he had to fit his lost segments back together. It was a struggle that even his mighty sinews could not aid him with, only the force of his will as he struggled to make himself whole.

Enkidu felt himself once again. Knowledge poured in to fill the gaps in his mind. It was a moot point, he told himself. Once he reintegrated with Grant, his existence was over. Those memories were like a sugar coating atop a lump of poison. Still, Enkidu could not resist supping upon the dish he ate, greedily reveling in a lifetime of experiences and emotions, enjoying their rush.

Grant gripped the Enkidu identity as they tumbled through interdimensional space.

"Enkidu goes on," Grant rasped. "I've been watching from up here."

"But you?" Enkidu asked.

"I go on, too," Grant promised. "Hang on to me."

"Do I have a choice?" Enkidu posed, knowing no answer was needed.

Then, from their vantage point, Enkidu saw the Earth cast before him, time and space rendered as flat as a scrawl on a sheet of paper. Below, Kane, Shizuka, Brigid, Domi and Malesh were frozen, a snapshot taken of an instant that they hovered above.

"But you needed me. I was your tether," Enkidu said. "Your body. I'll be just a ghost. Are you going to do to me what Kane did?"

"It took me a bit to see what was going on myself," Grant answered. "But looking from this perspective is easy if you know how. I don't have time to teach you, but I don't have to."

Enkidu turned to Grant. "What?"

Suddenly, Enkidu felt himself picked up and hurled, sailed like a dart through the gaps in reality until he came to a landing.

When Enkidu's eyes opened, it was to the cracking of the shell of liquid nutrients that his body floated within. The thunderous force of the scout ship's engines was a storm inside his skull as he crashed to the floor of Shamhat's laboratory.

GRANT OPENED his eyes. His reintegration was complete. He wore the clothing that he'd donned, save for the trench coat, back in New Edo.

Malesh looked on in horror at the totality of the change from her Enkidu to the man he used to be, but even as her eyes rested on him, a calmness passed over her features. Grant could only smile. Keeping secrets from the golden goddess was next to impossible, especially with the bond he shared with her.

He crumpled down to one knee as an overwhelming surge rushed through his brain, a violent reorientation that took some knowledge from him, but not everything. He remembered the events of his time as Enkidu, but only in the form of a vid that he'd watched, not actual experiences. The tesseract that existed here had gone through physical changes that his core identity hadn't. He still felt a slight paunch over his otherwise muscular frame's midsection.

"Zombies heard us," Domi said from the end of the tunnel looking over the alien fungal garden. "Coming to look."

"Are you all right?" Brigid asked him.

"Just move," Grant ordered them. "We don't have time right now."

"When will we have it?" Kane asked as he threw open the access hatch.

"When we don't have a few thousand damn zombies crawling up our asses," Grant growled. "Go!"

The groans of gray-skinned, fungus-animated drone creatures filled the narrow tunnel. Kane stooped only to retrieve the interphaser, and the group of people exited the corridor, slamming the concrete wedge shut.

"Think the door will hold?" Grant asked, heaving his big shoulder against it to keep it shut.

"It won't break for another forty-five hundred years," Brigid returned. "Trust me."

Grant nodded, straightening up. "I might just do that."

"Humbaba is not pleased," Malesh said. "We should go to recover the newly born."

Brigid Baptiste's right eyebrow rose in puzzlement, but a knowing smile crossed her lips. "Where do I go, Grant?"

"You can handle it, Brigid?" Grant asked.

"What did you just tell me that you were going to do?" the archivist returned.

"My mistake," Grant said. He turned to look at Shizuka, wondering if he had to say anything to the samurai warrior who held his heart. Her silent nod of assent was answer enough for him.

"Welcome back," she told him. She drew her sword. "We have business to attend to."

Grant gave her cheek a caress. "I know."

Kane lobbed a Sin Eater and its holster to Grant. "Everyone else gets a cheerful hello. Me, I get the growl."

Grant quickly slipped into the forearm rig for his machine pistol. "How else were you going to believe it was me?"

Kane sighed. "I should have known when the pain moved from my forearm right to my ass."

The Cerberus leader's attention was drawn by the distant rumble of dozens of booted feet up the ramp, his sharp ears picking them up even before Domi's acute hearing. "Company's on the way. Hum-daddy's recovered from the knock he took."

Grant slipped into a spare armored trench coat, shutting the chest clasps to wrap his torso for maximum protection. He'd have preferred his old Magistrate armor, but that and the shadow suits would have taken too long to put on. It didn't matter; the coat was comfortable and he moved with fluid grace in it. The Sin Eater snapped into his grasp, and he looked to Kane, giving him a one-percent salute before he and his partners once more took on a horde of enemies in the thrall of an angry god. Despite the approaching threat, a smile crossed his lips as he settled into the familiar after too long in a nightmare he could barely remember, let alone comprehend.

"It's good to be back."

SHAMHAT STRUGGLED to his feet in the wake of the scout ship's preprogrammed attempted launch. The breeding vats for the Nephilim were nearly all destroyed, their green, egglike cocoons splashed down the side of the craft's hull. The Igigi slave master had escaped being sucked out of the control laboratory and down into the huge chasm ripped through the palace by the two-hundred-foot space ship. He looked at the floor where several of the birthing matrices had been maneuvered for evaluation.

"I almost had you all ready," Shamhat said, looking at the Nephilim bodies sprawled across the ground. They were all still, save for one who didn't seem quite formed. Instead of shimmering scales adorning his flesh, the dermis was smooth, stretched taut over powerfully sculpted muscles. As nutrient gel sloughed off his shoulders and head, thick ropes of hair began to descend, shielding the creature's face as it struggled to its feet.

Shamhat's throat constricted with panicked realization as the creature rose to its full six-foot-eight-inch height. A shaggy mane of hair spilled over shoulders the size of melons, and from under a heavy brow, dark eyes smoldered with untapped rage. The Igigi's telepathic abilities lay bare a mind that had been mostly closed to him before, surface thoughts echoing a deep-down spite for he who had tamed the bestial figure before him.

"I curse you, Shamhat," Enkidu grumbled, his voice deep yet soft. "I curse you for the methods by which you 'civilized' me to your ends."

"Halt!" Shamhat cried out, stepping away from the naked, dripping titan before him.

"You have no orders for me anymore. The leash you wound around my neck snapped," Enkidu said, taking one stride closer to him.

"I didn't waste any slaves, not for Humbaba," Shamhat said. "Either way, I was working in yours and Malesh's favor! Enlil entreated me to make the odds equal between his twins."

"You didn't punish the people you waved before me as a price of failure?" Enkidu asked. "You, who took delight in abusing them on the flimsiest of excuses?"

"Why do you think that the Nephilim sent after you were so ineffective?" Shamhat returned. "Enlil…"

Enkidu's arm shot out, powerful fingers wrapping around the Igigi's throat. Long fingers squeezed, cutting off his words. "Enlil was bored, not benevolent, and you don't care about me, either. I'm a tool. A toy."

"Mercy," Shamhat croaked.

The door to the laboratory opened, and Enkidu recognized Brigid Baptiste as she entered, Copperhead SMG held pointed at the floor. He greeted her with a nod. "Brigid."

"Enkidu," Brigid replied. She scanned the room, taking note of the cloning facilities on hand. "Happy birthday."

"I'll be with you in a moment," Enkidu said. "I have to make good on a promise I made to myself."

"Please," Shamhat gurgled. "I'm the inhuman one. Your compassion must extend to an unarmed, helpless foe."

"Normally it would," Enkidu told him. With a violent twist, he crushed the Igigi's vertebrae against one another, fingers collapsing Shamhat's windpipe with the same exertion of muscle. Yellow, terrified eyes bulged as his scaled lips worked noiselessly, mouthing words. He knew he only had a few moments left. "The trouble is, I've seen enough of your handiwork that you've sold off any right to mercy other than a broken neck."

Enkidu released the Igigi slave master, his form collapsing to the floor. The only things still moving were his lips and eyes, his spinal cord severed by crushed, jagged pieces of neck bone. Shamhat blinked two more times before death claimed him. Shamhat's reptilian features took on a serene calm that had been denied to his countless victims, and in a way, Enkidu was glad for the brevity of any suffering. As much as he hated the Igigi for his crimes, cruelty was not a part of his being.

Enkidu knew that now without a doubt. He and Grant were not different in the slightest, except for the era they existed. Even the women they were devoted to were the same soul that had been bound by love to them.

Brigid and he looked down at the corpse, then at each other.

"A fitting end for his kind," the archivist said.

Enkidu sighed, his somber, saddened visage belying the flippancy of his words. Even the murder of an alien monster was no reason for joy, just relief at riddance. "Best birthday present ever."

With that, the two people exited the cloning laboratory, hurrying to rejoin their comrades.

Chapter 20

The two men crouched behind the cover of a corner, their Copperhead submachine guns more than a match as they pumped out precision bursts into the Nephilim soldiers trying to advance from Humbaba's great hall. For each of them, it was as if they had been completed.

For Kane, it was figurative. While on his own, the wolf-lean warrior was a formidable warrior, but he still preferred to have his friend at his side, watching out for him. It was a simple case of two fighters having formed into a well-oiled machine, able to read each other and the battlefield so completely that it was as if they were telepathic, a single combatant that was more than the sum of their firepower and fighting skills. Kane had been away from his friend for more than half of a week, but it had felt like months.

For Grant, it was both figurative and literal. He had been an ethereal spirit, existing on a plane of reality that he couldn't remember except for snatches of sensations and the impression of time immemorial passing as he floated in the null space. As it was, he was as cleanly shaven as he had been the night he'd crawled into Shizuka's bed, and since he didn't remember using a razor on his scalp and his jaw, time had stood absolutely still for him. What he did remember were the experiences of his disparate halves, although he knew of them only as an observer, not a participant. Enkidu and the ghost that had haunted Operation Chronos were merely shadows, windows that he peered through in order to keep his sanity anchored as he floated in the null space that a human body was not meant to inhabit and a human mind barely had the faculties to experience. As it was, Kane back at his side made him feel as if he had both of his arms.

"Who did you send Baptiste after?" Kane asked as he drilled a Nephilim through the head.

Grant unhooked a grenade from the harness that Domi had brought for him. "Enkidu."

"So putting him together would have killed someone real," Kane said.

Grant whipped the gren with all of his strength, bouncing it off a far wall up the ramp. As it rebounded, it landed in a group of Nephilim who had taken cover around a corner, trying to get an angle on the two humans. The detonation of the implode grenade rumbled down to them as severed limbs rained down the ramp. "It would have if someone weren't already creating a bunch of bodies without a brain in their heads."

"The scaly bastards we're hosing down?" Kane asked. He trotted across the base of the ramp, taking advantage of the distraction of their enemy.

"Yeah. Seems like my little time worm is a weird thing," Grant answered, feeding a fresh magazine into his SMG. "That's the one thing I remember from being lost. I could see myself as a worm."

Kane nodded. "I kind of remembered that, too. Sort of like a blur or smear of your image."

Kane's marksmanship dropped another of the alien drones.

"Mine did this crazy loop back on itself before it split in two," Grant told him. He motioned for Kane to cover him as he trotted up toward the landing where the enemy were huddled. The Nephilim didn't dare look out, knowing that the moment any of them exposed themselves to look, they'd catch a bullet. The hand signals meant that their conversation was ended for now. Business was at hand, and the two Cerberus warriors were the tip of the spear.

Even as the two men occupied the horde of Humbaba's reptilian soldiers, Malesh, Domi and Shizuka were scaling the spine of the scout ship, using it as a means to get behind the Nephilim cadre. The mess of fallen drones and dismembered body parts were testimony of the aggressive nature of the palace's guard and the immovable object that they had slammed into.

A Nephilim warrior snaked his arm around the corner as Grant padded up to the top. The alien had an ASP energy blaster on his wrist, and he appeared to be trying to blindly fire down on Kane and Grant's former position. Kane motioned that the drone's arm belonged to Grant, and the big ex-Magistrate nodded in assent.

His powerful fingers locked around the Nephilim's wrist, clamping down with all the force he could muster. Grant pivoted, using his considerable mass and superior leverage to haul the would-be sniper out into the open like a rag doll. The drone barely had the sentience to squeal as it was whipped face-first into the corridor's wall. The thing's face caved in, splinters of skull whipping its brain to a froth, even as neck bones popped out of alignment. Instantly dead, the Nephilim bounced off the wall and skidded down the ramp on its back.

Two Nephilim reacted to the sudden disappearance of their friend by stepping into the open to deal with Grant. Kane's Copperhead snarled out a salvo of bullets that cut off the creatures' attempt to avenge their comrade. The whipsaw of automatic fire carved the life from them and they toppled back onto the landing.

Grant rolled another gren around the corner as Kane covered him. The big man pressed his back to the wall as the miniature bomb detonated twenty feet up the ramp. The corner of the ramp deflected shrapnel, and the wide-open landing with its high-vaulted ceiling meant the shock wave was little more than a tooth-rattling annoyance to Grant. Wounded drones staggered into the open, where the two former Magistrates made short work of them with their submachine guns.

Grant didn't think that the blank-eyed creatures had enough brain power to actually suffer, but he couldn't put away his concern for the humanoids as they flailed about with mortal and crippling injuries. There was also the knowledge that Enkidu…his other half? His son? Whatever Enkidu was, he now resided in a biological envelope that wasn't much more than one of these beings.

His Commtact hissed to life with Domi's whisper.

"In position," the feral girl said.

Kane jogged up to join Grant. "Do it."

The sound of a single automatic weapon was accompanied by the hissing shriek of plasma bolts discharging from an ASP. Grant knew that Shizuka's contribution to the assault wasn't going to be audible, as her *kumi* made little more than a twang as it launched its arrows with enough force to pierce multiple bodies. Neither he nor Kane had to see the effects of Shizuka's mastery as a pair of Nephilim crashed to the landing, pinned together by a single, bloody-tailed goose-feather shaft.

Kane whistled at the sight even as he maneuvered into position, at a right angle to the rain of death unleashed by Domi, Malesh and Shizuka, catching Nephilim who retreated from the sudden onslaught. Energy beams seared into the wall, bullets sparking chips of stone from the floor, burned, riddled or transfixed corpses tumbling to the ground in a flood. Living opponents were few and far between, a grisly testimony to the efficiency of their allies.

Finally, the shriek of energy weapons and autofire died out. Grant and Kane called out to alert their friends that they were stepping into the open. The flanking attack had only lasted a minute and, combined with the slaughter inflicted by the Magistrates' grenades and marksmanship, created a carpet of corpses sprawled on the incline, blood flowing like a river around the men's boots.

"Malesh, does this look like everything Humbaba has?" Grant asked the tall goddess.

Her catlike eyes swept the scene, taking an inventory of the bloody aftermath. "We've halved their numbers. My brother is too keen to have thrown all of his forces into action against us."

"What about the guards who would have been in the part of the palace that we crashed the scout ship through?" Kane asked.

"I took them into account. We can expect thirty more Nephilim on hand, plus some of his Igigi officers," Malesh admitted.

Kane turned to Grant. "Igigi?"

"A different breed of scaly servant. These can think, but they're not quite as good a set of soldiers as…" Grant paused, toeing the corpse of one of the drones. "Igigi can be scared as well as they scare others."

"You speak from experience," Shizuka observed, trading her *kumi* for her *katana*. Any hope of recovering her arrows was out of the question, and the few shafts remaining in her quiver were not going to be useful once they staged their assault on the main hall.

"One of them, Shamhat, did some bad shit to me… Enkidu," Grant explained.

"He's received his reward, Grant," a deep baritone called from just down the ramp. The assembled Cerberus warriors and Malesh turned to see Brigid Baptiste and a man who was naked save for an improvised kilt wrapped around his waist and the coiled metal of an ASP around his wrist.

Enkidu was easily as tall as Grant, though his body was more finely honed and developed. Faint whip scars, formed by the doppelganger's memories of his brief life in Urudug, adorned his broad shoulders and back. They were easily recognizable as variations of each other, but Enkidu's skin was more of a dark olive than the deep brown of Grant's African-American heritage. The man-bull's long locks were also of Mediterranean origin, contrasting with Grant's bald pate.

"Was this your doing or mine?" Enkidu asked, looking himself over. "Not that I'm complaining."

"I couldn't tell to save my life," Grant said. "But at least it saved yours."

Malesh nodded, stepping closer to Enkidu, pausing only to look at Grant's face. "So much like mine…but not."

Grant nodded. "I belong to someone else."

Shizuka was soundlessly at his side, her slender arm around his waist.

"So how come there are two of you now?" Domi asked.

Brigid cupped her chin for a moment, then began to speak. "In the simplest of terms, Enkidu was destined to exist."

"It must be a day for miracles—Baptiste explained something in only five words," Kane muttered.

Brigid wrinkled her nose. "Humbaba is still active, and the tales that filtered down through to our time say that Gilgamesh and Enkidu slew him, incurring the wrath of the gods."

"And that means there's still the chance he gets killed," Kane said, pointing to Grant's counterpart.

"Not killed," Malesh said. "Taken away."

"This isn't written yet," Shizuka said. "And there was no mention of our presence here."

"Besides, story says she's a he," Domi added. "Can't go believing everything you read, Brigid."

"No, you cannot, apekin." A thought ripped through all of their minds. As one, the group looked up the ramp to see Humbaba standing, his fists on his hips. His muzzle was adorned with blood and intestines, and his eyes were alight with malice.

"Humbaba," Malesh said, wincing at the telepathic intrusion.

The half-Annunaki giant nodded. "You came to see me. I would be a poor host if I didn't entertain my guests."

In a heartbeat, the Cerberus explorers exploded into action. Kane's and Grant's Sin Eaters snapped from their holsters with lightning speed, followed by Domi drawing her pistol and Shizuka breaking into a charge. Enkidu was hot on her heels, his *kopesh* singing the same song of a blade being drawn as he followed her. Brigid Baptiste was the slowest to react, but even her reflexes had been only a tenth of a second slower than her comrades as she whipped her Copperhead to aim at Humbaba.

Humbaba stopped them cold, unleashing a bellow that was only slightly softer in volume than the most powerful explosions that the assembled Cerberus warriors had ever heard, the roar stabbing through their ears at a volume that was more painful than the high-power blasts of Kane and Grant's grenades. Even as their ears were spiked with pain, a wave of mental static slashed across their brains, the telepathic equivalent of the lion's roar.

The assembled humans dropped to their knees in pain as one, weapons tumbling from numbed hands. Even Malesh had stepped back, equally stunned but still standing as Humbaba chuckled at how he had taken down most of his enemies.

"I am the son of Enlil," the half-Annunaki giant proclaimed, looking down upon his foes. "And the rumors spread by you little apes have no bearing on the true history of this pitiful rock."

Grant and Enkidu looked up as one, recovering from the telepathic shout first. Both men struggled to their feet, Grant's Sin Eater having retracted when the half-Annunaki governor hit them with the psychic and sonic waves. Enkidu picked up his hook sword from where it had fallen. Both sets of eyes locked on Humbaba.

"We're not working at the same speed we did when we first met this bastard," Grant said.

Enkidu nodded, a grim smile on his lips. "No. But we're still relatively fresh. And we're ready for him this time."

The Sin Eater clacked into place once more. That was all the answer Enkidu needed to inform him that the two men weren't going to back down.

Humbaba's leonine head rolled back as he released a stentorian laugh. "Aren't you monkeys cute? Come. Let us play."

"Your war is with me!" Malesh snarled, her powerful legs launching her across the twenty-foot gap between them. Her talons flashed through the air, and Humbaba was ready for her. The pair tumbled backward in a flurry of lashing claws and earsplitting roars.

Without pause, Grant and Enkidu charged to her aid, even as a pair of pike-wielding Nephilim rushed into view. ASP and Sin Eater erupted in the same instant, Enkidu and Grant drilling their opponents so quickly that the long pikes discharged into the air over their head.

"The big sticks shoot," Enkidu noted, stooping for one fallen weapon. "A nice upgrade from the ASP."

"Let's see what they do to the big pussy," Grant answered, grabbing up the other pike.

As the two men swung the sharp-ended lances around, more of the Nephilim appeared wielding their own pikes.

Grant's forward momentum was halted as three of the enemy had lurched into his path, the four spear-shaped blasters snarled against each other. He dug his feet in as the Nephilim pushed against him. With a twist, he managed to entwine his pole arm with theirs. One of the warrior drones caught the shaft of his own pike in the face, the powerful blow splitting his scaly skin and exposing a cheekbone. A second twist pushed the points of the other two weapons toward the floor, their tips glowing hot enough to raise gouts of smoke on the ground. Grant jerked his pike back half around for one more swing, listening to the crunch of jawbones as the two Nephilim caught the full force of his handle.

On the other side, Enkidu was faced with a pair of the cloned cannon fodder. He stabbed one in the chest with the point of his confiscated weapon. On contact with the smart-metal wrapped around its torso, the point flared with enough heat to make the finely woven armor's "threads" pop. In another moment, the charged spear was clear through his opponent, the Nephilim toppling backward and wresting it from his hands. The other fighter tried to inflict the same wound on Enkidu, but he stepped in tight, his left shoulder striking the shaft of the pike and deflecting it. He aimed his fist at the drone's belly and cut loose with the ASP coils wrapped around his forearm. A hot ball of energy curled the hairs on Enkidu's chest and forearm. The heat on the receiving end of the bolt did far more damage to its target than its shooter. The Nephilim whose face Grant had opened with the handle of his weapon staggered toward Enkidu, who met him with his left elbow right in the throat.

Seven bodies lay at the feet of the twin warriors, and two dozen more formed a living wall between Grant, Enkidu and their destination—Malesh's side.

"Fuck me," Grant and Enkidu said in unison.

"There'll be time for that later," came a feminine voice attached to a blur that shot past them. The thousand-folded steel of Shizuka's *katana* rang out as it lashed at the armored bodies of the Nephilim. Kane and Domi appeared, bracketing the two men, their guns barking together, bullets hammering at the metal-clad drones. Sin Eater and Detonics .45 punched through the flexible weave of their armor, shattering ribs, bowling over soldiers that hadn't felt the slicing edge of Shizuka's sword.

Brigid was a heartbeat behind Kane and Domi, her rifle batting mop-up for wounded Nephilim who had staggered away from the slaughter ground where their comrades had fallen. She targeted the ones shaking off their stunned status, bringing up their ASP energy blasters to avenge their injuries and their comrades. Short bursts ripped into the wounded but still-viable opponents as they took aim. Brigid hit those still standing, nailing them down for the rest of eternity.

Domi brought her attention to a floored enemy who was still in the fight, despite his entrails slinking across the floor from his opened belly. Her .45 bullet smashed in the space between the Nephilim's eyes as Shizuka brought down her sword to lop off its ASP-adorned arm.

"That was a mess," Kane said, treading through pooling blood. "Where are Humbaba and Malesh?"

The bellows of combat that would have directed Kane's keen senses toward the conflict between the scions of Enlil were now blurred by echoes off the high vaulted ceiling of Humbaba's great hall. The leonine godling had plunged the large chamber into darkness, only a few cracks in the ceiling filtering down weak streams of sunlight.

"The corner," Brigid said.

Remembering the section of the buried temple that they had entered, Kane made a beeline toward the fight, the others following in hot pursuit. The six people reloaded on the run, Shizuka having sheathed her sword and exchanged it for one of the Nephilim's power pikes, joining Grant and Enkidu in their appropriation of Annunaki technology to deal with the massive Humbaba.

Grant looked at his lover as she held the energy-spitting spear in one hand. As good as the woman was with the sword and the bow, she was a woman samurai first of all, and the first weapon a young girl trained with was the double-headed blend of ax and spear known as the *naginata*. The concept behind both the Nephilim pike and the *naginata* were essentially the same, especially considering how the superheated point had sliced through the torso of a drone as if it were butter.

Not that they could do anything with their ranged weapons. Malesh and Humbaba were in close combat, rolling atop each other, trading swipes of their razor-sharp claws. As they got closer, the humans were stopped by the oppressive mental pressure of the psychic runoff from their telepathic battle. Fighting body and mind, the two half-gods were in the center of a maelstrom of chaos and rage, a field that humans entered only if they wanted to have synapses fried by the crossfire of two superhuman wills.

Backing up, Enkidu glowered at the snarling Humbaba as he backhanded his sister, pinning her beneath him. Grant echoed the spite burning in Enkidu's eyes, clutching his power pike in a white-knuckled grip. The two men opened fire with their energy lances, but Humbaba was gone, leaping off Malesh with blinding speed and agility. He'd moved even before the temporal counterparts had triggered their weapons, betraying an ace in the hole that had not been revealed before.

"That's how he was able to hit us when we thought we could see him coming," Grant said.

Enkidu nodded. "He adjusted for our precognition with his own."

Humbaba landed in a crouch, his bloody face now bereft of the intestines of human prey, this time replaced with claw wounds caused by his sister's talons. For all the slashes on his big body, he was still spry and quick. Malesh, on the other hand, needed to lean against the wall to stand up. It had been a simple matter of pure size canceling out any advantage in skill or speed the smaller godling had. When Humbaba hit, it was with the force of one thousand pounds of muscle behind it. She was covered in cuts, and one eye was swollen, clenched nearly shut. Blood dribbled from the corner of her mouth, and her knees wobbled. Malesh was recovering, as her stance grew stronger, but the battle had still taken a toll on her.

"If I could dominate my sister so completely, what hope do two mere humans have?" Humbaba asked. "Without your enhanced speed, you are simply victims suffering from delusions of adequacy."

"I think his mouth just wrote a check his ass can't cash," Brigid said, her voice cutting through the chamber. "We've dealt with worse than an overgrown tabby like you, Humbaba. We've faced your father and his brothers!"

Cat's eyes glared at the flame-haired archivist. "I forgot about you other mewling monkeys. Come, do your worst!"

Bullets and plasma bolts erupted, spraying the spot where Humbaba had taunted them, but nine feet of solid muscle moved much faster than they could adjust for. The only thing the Cerberus group had to show for their united volley of firepower was a scorched patch of wall. Humbaba was a blur rocketing over their heads, launched by leg muscles that carried his thousand-pound frame with ease and grace for the years of his life. Like a crashing meteor, he landed in the middle of their group, hitting the ground hard enough to crack the stone and make it shake.

Fortunately, Kane and his companions had good reflexes of their own, scattering before Humbaba's great bulk smashed one of their number to paste.

A grim chuckle escaped the half-breed's throat. "This is going to be fun."

Chapter 21

Shizuka hadn't allowed the last syllable of Humbaba's proclamation to pass before she whipped around, three feet of forged steel honed to a fine edge lashing out at the leonine godling's back. Humbaba reacted to the deadly chop at the last moment, turning what would have been a spine-severing stroke into a deep, long gash on his shoulder. He spun away from the Tiger of Heaven's arch, even as she lunged outward with her power pike, its burning tip raising a dark scar on his abdominals.

Humbaba wove, trying to escape the whirlwind attacking him, bounding over the small Japanese woman at a height where he avoided her singing *katana* as it whistled through the air. The nine-foot-tall, thousand-pound hybrid of Annunaki and lion-man genetics landed with a ground-shaking thud, immediately coming under fire as Domi cut loose with her Detonics Combat Master, its .45-caliber slugs impacting on tough hide and unyielding muscle underneath. Humbaba took six slugs to his abdomen, all of them feeling like sharp punches, but the powerful handgun hadn't penetrated his skin, despite the pain. With a feral snarl, Domi whipped her combat knife around in an arc, and Humbaba sidestepped barely enough to keep her foot-long blade from spearing into a vital organ in his exposed belly.

With a pivot, Humbaba whirled, Grant's cloak flashing in the albino woman's face, the heavy bands of polymer and Kevlar slapping her hard enough to knock her back. He whipped his fist out to catch Domi, but she had been knocked out of the path of his massive hand. The talons on his mighty paw only glanced off her shadow suit, one claw catching her above her pert breast and opening the skin and the polymer-blended uniform from just above her left breast to her shoulder.

Domi scrambled backward, grimacing at the flesh wound as it bled profusely.

Brigid Baptiste stepped up, her Copperhead blazing and pelting Humbaba with 4.85 mm rounds. The small, lightning-fast bullets fared only slightly better than Domi's big, booming .45 auto. The high-velocity projectiles appeared as glimmering studs in his skin, only barely penetrating Humbaba's fur and thick dermis. The hybrid son of Enlil snarled with grim fury, forgetting the feral little albino in favor of this new foe, who inconvenienced him more. The fifty-round magazine of the compact submachine gun didn't run dry because Brigid was disciplined on the trigger, firing short bursts, relying on the half-Annunaki's hubris at his bulletproof nature.

"Neat little toys. I might just allow my soldiers to invent them so they can conquer the world," Humbaba grumbled with a smirk. He started to lash out at the flame-haired archivist, then paused and leaped up, rocketing away over their heads.

Grant lowered his power pike, his intent to stab the godling between his shoulder blades blatantly telegraphed. He winked to Baptiste, who nodded in assent.

As Shizuka and Domi were occupying Humbaba's time, Grant and Enkidu informed Kane and Brigid that the alien's telepathy had given him the advantage of reading his enemy's attacks on him.

The reason that the samurai woman and the feral girl had been able to touch Humbaba was because they operated on instinct, not conscious thought. Shizuka, in battle, existed in a state of Zen consciousness that didn't think or focus on any single part of the world about her, but took in everything in her presence. In this manner, the Tiger of Heaven was not distracted from the subtle cues of threats around her, but it had also left her mind clear and uncluttered, able to move without hesitation. Domi, on the other hand, didn't fold into a disciplined mental state, but entered a bestial rage, one that she could focus and restrain with the accuracy of a surgeon's scalpel. Such instinctual and primal mentality also cleared her conscious mind of strategy and tactics, clearing any hesitation and making her reaction and action instant.

"He reads our minds to dodge us," Grant had said.

"He can't read Shizuka or Domi," Enkidu added.

Brigid Baptiste's intellect was such that she was able to subsume this knowledge, hiding it from Humbaba as she rushed to Domi's rescue, covering those thoughts with other mental gibberish.

The three women had been able to hide their tactics so that they could get the drop on Humbaba, but Brigid wondered about the men, who had neither a wild, bestial side nor mental or martial discipline to mask their intentions.

That's when Grant had displayed his stratagem, letting Humbaba read his intent loud and clear to flush him into the middle of another attack.

Operating on pure reflex, Kane and Enkidu reacted to Humbaba as the powerful form launched himself into the air, a leap that couldn't be steered, even if the half-Annunaki foe could read their instincts. Sin Eater and power pike erupted in unison, and Humbaba let out a growl of pain as an armor-piercing 9 mm slug and a charged plasma beam sliced through him. The shots landed in nonvital areas. He was hurt, but his massive physique and alien physiology would allow him to survive those injuries.

Distracted, the giant cat-man didn't land on all fours. He crashed head and shoulders first into the ground, leaving him open for Grant and Brigid to lunge at him together. Grant's energy lance cut a nasty furrow along Humbaba's chest muscle while Brigid's TP-9 cracked out a peppering volley of gunshots that tore out clumps of his mane and carved small 9 mm divots in his muzzle.

Enraged, Humbaba snapped his long legs straight, kicking both Grant and Brigid in the chest and hurling them across the great hall's floor. Only the protective qualities of her shadow suit and Grant's physical conditioning and Kevlar trench coat kept the two people from serious injury as they landed and rolled on the thick stone floor. As it was, they were launched nearly forty feet, and neither was standing up quickly.

Kane opened up with his Sin Eater on full automatic, emptying his 20-round magazine in the floored, sprawled hybrid when he had no leverage or footing to roll out of the way. It was ruthless, and counter to his normal strategy of not killing an enemy who was down, but Humbaba was the living exemplar of an opponent too dangerous to give an even break. Humbaba couldn't stand up or vault out of the path of Kane's bullets. That didn't make the giant vulnerable to the heavyweight, armor-smashing rounds. Humbaba twisted, facing his back to the full-auto salvo. Grant's trench coat, combined with the thick, heavy muscle and bone protecting the back, were more than enough to blunt the wounding power of Kane's machine pistol.

Enkidu leaped, snarling with spite at the bestial master who had oppressed him for so long. The power pike burned hotly and he put all his weight into the stab. Humbaba snatched the shaft of the weapon behind its glowing point, and while he wasn't able to stop the forward momentum of the deadly energy spear, he redirected it into the stone floor, melting it into the ground over his shoulder.

Humbaba still jerked his head aside, his mane igniting from the plasma aura of the flaming spear point. Hair flared into a bright flower of agony that flashed across his face. Blind, pain-induced reaction took shape in the form of a telepathic spasm, sharing his misery with the humans present. A reflexive reaction turned into a swat that knocked Enkidu aside like a rag doll, crashing him to the floor.

Only the searing telepathic pain produced by Humbaba had given Enkidu enough limpness to turn what would have been a bone-breaking fall into a bruising tumble. Still, Enkidu rolled, clutching his ribs in an effort to catch his breath.

Kane, feeling Humbaba's agony from the flash fire of his mane, stiffened, his eyes clenching shut in an effort to protect them from a burning that only Humbaba had experienced. Even blinded, the ex-Magistrate drew his combat knife and lunged toward the twisting beast on the floor.

The hybrid was blinded and totally off guard, unable to read Kane's mind. Unfortunately, beating at the fires of his mane, his forearms protected his face from the stabbing point of the knife. Instead of piercing an eye socket or spearing through a throat, Kane had opened up Humbaba's right forearm, catching the saw-backed blade between the ulna and radial bones. Arterial blood gushed from the injury, catching the human in the face, further compounding the telepathically shared blindness with hot, salty liquid stinging his eyes. Once more, Humbaba's powerful limbs lashed out, but Kane twisted, still holding on to the knife's handle. Steel snapped as Kane proved to be a nearly immovable object and the half-Annunaki's arm was an irresistible force.

Once more, the telepathic half-breed broadcast his pain throughout the chamber, halting Kane in his tracks long enough for Humbaba to swat him with a powerful backhand. The shadow suit hardened in response to the hammer blow, forming a sheath that kept those massive knuckles from breaking his ribs like a stack of twigs. Kane, however, had nothing left over to brace himself, sprawling to the floor, the broken handle of his knife bouncing from his numbed fingers. Kane rolled out of the way as the agonized, vengeful godling swatted at him.

The fires in his mane had died down, but his eyes had been dried out and were shut, trying to deal with the acrid smoke and ash that burned him. Half-blind now, brain reeling from the distractions of multiple injuries, Humbaba's punch landed on empty floor, knocking a crater in it.

"You damn little monkeys!" Humbaba roared. "I'll kill you all!"

Shizuka shook off the effects of the hybrid's telepathically broadcast pain at that moment, clearing her mind of the phantom sensations in her eyes and face. She'd discarded the power pike and drew her *kumi,* nocking an arrow in one smooth, swift movement. The leonine giant sat up groggily, snarling in naked rage, covered in burns and cuts. The taut, nonstretching string built up enormous potential energy as she bent the composite bow back.

"No human has ever dared to make an Annunaki bleed!" Humbaba roared.

Shizuka opened her fingers, releasing the bowstring. "I dare."

The shaft sank its full length into the godling's chest and he clutched at the feathered nub sticking through his deltoid muscle. Where small-arms bullets didn't have the mass or kinetic energy to pierce the alien hybrid's thick skin, muscle and bone, the razor-tipped arrows had all of that in abundance. She drew another arrow, slipping it onto the string, and was taking aim for a second lightning-fast shot when Humbaba lunged at her.

Her martial-arts-honed reflexes saved her from the bulk of the half-breed's charge, but one thousand pounds of rampaging force was a significant impact even as a glancing blow. *Kumi* and arrow tumbled from her hands and she spun, crashing into Domi, who had hurled herself to break the samurai's fall. Humbaba skidded to a halt, glaring at the two small women who had been the first to draw his blood. As he half turned, claws extended to rip the female humans to shreds for their sins against an Annunaki overlord's chosen prince, a golden form rocketed into his back, spearing him against a three-foot-thick support pillar.

Bones crunched under the force of Malesh's tackle, and the son of Enlil let out another grunt of pain. Malesh raked her talons on either side of her brother's neck even as he bucked against her, knocking her back.

"Finally decided to join the party, little sister?" Humbaba growled, blood flowing down his chest. Deep pants brought frothing blood to his nostrils as he glared at his kin. "I thought a weakling such as you would let the humans finish your work."

Malesh rose from the floor, sneering back at her brother. "Like you tried to do with me? The trouble is, enslaved men have nothing on free people fighting for what they believe in. The destruction of our father's tyranny is their goal in their time. You are simply a symptom of the disease Enlil has spread across this world!"

Humbaba snorted, despite the spurt of crimson escaping his nostrils. "I'm not dead yet."

"Neither are we!" Grant spit. He'd picked up Shizuka's fallen bow and its razor-tipped shaft. Even as Humbaba reacted, the arrow pierced the hybrid's shoulder. Once more injured, his leonine head rolled back to release a roar of pain.

In the same moment that Humbaba's jaws opened, Enkidu threw a fist-size object at him. Though winded and rasping agonized breaths, he'd managed to pluck a grenade off Grant's harness and hurl it with all the might in his good right arm. The miniature bomb struck Humbaba hard enough in the mouth to break off one of his canines as it barreled to the back of the godling's throat.

Humbaba reached for his neck, gagging at the sudden intrusion. Off balance from the attacks made by both aspects of Grant, he was easy prey for Malesh to seize him by the arm. The seven-foot-tall warrior goddess whirled, whipping her brother with all of her might into the corner of the great hall where the floor had been pushed up to almost touch the ceiling. Stone collapsed around Humbaba for a moment, pinning him and keeping him from spitting out the grenade.

A heartbeat later, a thunderbolt crack resounded, Humbaba's legs twitching as they lost contact with a brain that now was permeating the stone around what used to be a skull. Dust rained from the ceiling, burying half of the son of Enlil's corpse, his long limbs dangling along with the tails of what used to be Grant's trench coat.

Grant panted, holding up his counterpart, Enkidu. Malesh helped Shizuka and Domi to their feet.

"That's obviously where we'd left him," Kane said.

Brigid nodded. "Exactly the proper position. History is right where it's supposed to be."

They looked at the two couples, Grant and Shizuka and Enkidu and Malesh, embracing each other, eyes closed as they reveled in the contact with lovers and family.

Kane smirked. "We traveled through time, killed off a god, and Grant is back together with his woman. My work here is done."

"But not theirs," Brigid noted as Domi joined them.

"Tough times for them?" the albino girl asked, looking at the couples from different eras. With a nod, she indicated that she was talking about Enkidu and Malesh.

"The gods are going to separate them," Brigid said. "And Malesh will quest to reunite with him."

"She'll find him, just like Shizuka found Grant," Domi said.

"It'll be without our help," Kane added. "We have our own battles to fight."

"Perhaps," Brigid countered. "The story of Gilgamesh ends as he, er, she enters a deep sleep beside an unnamed river."

"Sort of an anticlimactic ending," Kane muttered.

"Or the beginning of a centuries-long journey in suspended animation," Brigid surmised. "Gilgamesh's tale ended on Earth. Perhaps it concludes back on Nibiru. A happier denouement than the one written for mankind."

Domi smiled. "It'd be the only way either of them would let it end. Explains why Enlil still has a head in our time, too."

"Should we tell them what might happen?" Kane asked.

Brigid shook her head. "Malesh has closed off her mind, and hasn't touched mine to get any information. She's going to face her destiny one day at a time."

"Grant," Kane said reluctantly. "It's time for us to go home."

Grant looked over his shoulder, then nodded. "A minute more." He turned to Enkidu. "Good luck in your future."

Enkidu shrugged. "I'll take my knocks when they come. You do the same for yourself, and Shizuka, too."

The samurai woman cupped Enkidu's bearded cheek, smiling at him. "Do not forget that your goddess needs you, and you need her."

Grant embraced Malesh, taking a deep breath. "Thanks for keeping Enkidu alive. Remember that I owe you a few favors."

"Friends do not owe each other favors," Malesh answered him. "Perhaps someday, in the streams of time and space, our paths will cross again."

Grant winced as he felt every inch of battery and bruising he'd taken. "If so, I'll have to stock up on painkillers."

Malesh's laugh was just as beautiful as Shizuka's. Of course it was, Grant thought. They share the same soul, same as Enkidu and me.

Grant took Shizuka's tiny hand in his and the lovers walked to join Kane, Brigid Baptiste and Domi. Baptiste was in the process of programming the interphaser's recall code so that the time trawl could be directed to them.

Enkidu watched as the figures faded. "See you around, old friend," he whispered to the space where they had been.

"His soul is as old as yours, my love," Malesh said. "Who is to say that you will not find him here?"

Enkidu managed a smile. "Kane, Brigid…hell, maybe even Domi and Lakesh are bouncing around. We sure could use the help."

Enkidu took his lover's hand as Grant had taken Shizuka's. "But as long as we have each other, I don't fear any destiny."

The goddess and her consort walked through the darkened hall, together and unafraid.

Epilogue

Thousands of light-years from the Earth, a relatively small interstellar ship hurtled through deep space. It had been on its journey for as long as Ullikummis's prison. They had even passed within thousands of miles of each other, but the memory of a brief psychic contact between scions of Enlil was far stronger for Gi Malesh than for her half brother.

Ullikummis had been consumed by a hatred for Enlil, the mental anchor that helped the stone-skinned god maintain his sanity. Malesh shared that anger at her Annunaki father, but it was nowhere near as intense as Ullikummis's.

What carried the sleeping goddess, resting in a coffin-like suspended-animation chamber, through her centuries of travel was not rage but love.

Among the stars, at the end of the interstellar journey, Enkidu waited, sharing the same millennia-long slumber that she did.

Her vengeful father had taken action in the one way that he could best torture her, keeping Enkidu in an eternal sleep that was neither death nor life.

Enkidu, however, had lived up to his promise never to leave Malesh alone.

Resting in the chamber next to Malesh's was their daughter, Domigi, conceived the night before their swim into the palace of Urudug. She was named for the woman that Grant had loved as if she were his own child, and she had grown tall, strong and brave.

Together, they would write the end of a tale that Brigid Baptiste had only guessed at.

And perhaps they would reunite with the heroes of Cerberus someday.

For now, Malesh and her daughter crossed the gulf between stars, rushing to Enkidu's rescue.

WHEN GRANT'S EYES fluttered open, consciousness seizing him once more, the first thing he saw was the tanned, soft shoulder of a beautiful, black-haired woman who breathed deeply in the peace of sleeping bliss. His dreams had been troubled with glimpses of the space between times, leftovers from his imprisonment in the time stream.

But he thought of his family back at Cerberus. He'd spent a few days recovering from his adventure at the beginning of human history, and drinking in the joy of Shizuka's companionship.

He hated the thought of leaving her side, but he also missed the people who were the brother, the sister, the daughter he'd never had. Grant kissed Shizuka's shoulder.

He would find his way back to New Edo easily.

But for now, he rested his cheek against the back of Shizuka's head.

Cerberus, the Annunaki, the Millennial Consortium and all the rest of the inhabitants of the crazed world called Earth, they could all wait as Grant took his fill of the comfort of Shizuka's embrace.

* * * * *

The Don Pendleton's Executioner®
FINAL COUP

A deadly political rivalry threatens Cameroon's democracy

With the current president on the run for war crimes, an emergency election is called in Cameroon. But will the two candidates live long enough to see election day? Assigned to protection duty, Mack Bolan soon learns the politicians aren't the only ones in danger... there's a traitor in their midst who won't stop until Bolan and his team are dead.

Available March wherever books are sold.

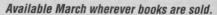

GOLD EAGLE®

www.readgoldeagle.blogspot.com

GEX388

AleX Archer
FALSE HORIZON

The road to paradise is dark and deadly…

Archaeologist Annja Creed is in Katmandu, awash in its
scents and liveliness. But this is no sightseeing trip.
An old friend has a map
that leads to a place that
lies outside our world.
But another vicious man
wants the map—and
he has Annja and her
companions right where
he wants them. Will
Annja's journey end with
only triumph…or tragedy?

*Available March
wherever books are sold.*

GOLD
EAGLE®

www.readgoldeagle.blogspot.com

GRA29